spies

ALSO BY MARCEL BEYER

The Karnau Tapes

MARCEL   BEYER

spies

Translated from the German
by Breon Mitchell

Harcourt, Inc.

Orlando   Austin   New York   San Diego   Toronto   London

FIC
Beyer

© 2000 DuMontBuchverlag, Köln
English translation copyright © 2005 by Breon Mitchell

All rights reserved. No part of this publication may be reproduced
or transmitted in any form or by any means, electronic or mechanical,
including photocopy, recording, or any information storage and retrieval
system, without permission in writing from the publisher.

Requests for permission to make copies of any part of the work should be
mailed to the following address: Permissions Department, Harcourt, Inc.,
6277 Sea Harbor Drive, Orlando, Florida 32887-6777.

This is a work of fiction. Names, characters, places, organizations,
and events are the products of the author's imagination or are used
fictitiously, and any resemblance to actual persons, living or dead,
events, or locales is entirely coincidental.

www.HarcourtBooks.com

This is a translation of *Spione*

Library of Congress Cataloging-in-Publication Data
Beyer, Marcel, 1965–
[Spione. English]
Spies/ Marcel Beyer; translated from the German by Breon Mitchell.
p. cm.
I. Mitchell, Breon.   II. Title.
PT2662.E94S6513 2005
833'.914—dc22   2005003038
ISBN-13: 978-0-15-100859-9   ISBN-10: 0-15-100859-0
ISBN: 0-15-100859-0

Text set in MrsEavesRoman
Designed by April Ward

Printed in the United States of America

First U.S. edition
A C E G I K J H F D B

Children always want to see me.
But at night, when I come, they are sleeping.
They're always dreaming of me,
but when they awake, I'm already gone.

—Astrid Lindgren, Harald Wiberg: *Tomte Tummetott*

spies

SOMETIMES I STAND FOR A WHILE SPYING THROUGH THE peephole into the hall, even when I know I won't see a single person. I stand at the peephole and wait. No, I'm not waiting, I'm just watching; the door is closed. I stood that way as a child, first on a stool, then on a box, finally on tiptoe. And I'm standing like that now. I hear breathing.

At home or in a strange apartment, in a new housing block with low ceilings, carpet tiles, double locks on the doors. Visiting friends, or some place that smells funny, where there are no toys for me. Voices in the background, my parents and strangers in the living room, or simply a wall clock, the hum of a refrigerator, nothing.

I'm not allowed to touch the glass. The stairwell is just a step away, blocked only by the door. But the image comes from a great distance. If I watch steadily, the objects slowly draw nearer, as do the shadows on the perimeter. The most inconspicuous details outside strike the polished glass as if attempting to directly penetrate my retina.

Through the peephole everything seems near and yet untouchable. Flight is impossible. Flight is ruled out, but the path for flight lies before my eyes.

This is how I am standing. I don't see anyone. I'll stand here for a while.

• spores •

HE REMEMBERED HER at once. He'd spotted her name completely by chance on a poster on a kiosk. The opera was visiting his hometown. They'd been neighbors and playmates—just the two of them usually, because the neighborhood kids teased the girl. Because of her eyes, of the way she looked. First they made fun of her, then of him. But he'd always liked her Italian eyes. She was the only one in her family who had them. Her parents' and siblings' eyes were a different color, as far as he could recall. More than ten years ago.

When he saw her name that morning in the city, it seemed at once as if he'd always been searching for those eyes. It was a warm morning in early spring, and it didn't take him long to decide. He stepped into the nearest flower shop and ordered a bouquet without even knowing whether he could get a ticket.

He'll surprise her in the dressing room after the performance. The flowers will be standing there when he enters.

He's in search of her eyes. By evening he will have found them.

A year ago he would not have tried. As an unemployed or part-time worker, he would not have gone to the opera. Not the down-at-the-heels traveling salesman, moving from farm to farm with his case of samples. Not the hawker standing outside the department store, praising miraculous cleaning agents and potato peelers, newfangled rollers for home permanents. He would not even have appeared before his childhood friend as a journeyman electrician who had spent six months wiring a new housing development on the other side of the redoubt, near the rifle range.

That smell, the fresh plaster, the cable ducts. The farther he advances, the more slowly he works: only five houses to go, then three, and still no idea how to support himself afterward. Only the top floor remains, the outlets and switches in the bedroom, then he's out of work again. After he's clamped the final cable and gathered his tools he has a thought: he could join the army. Someone who knows wiring should have a future there; he could easily learn to lay communication lines.

They took him immediately. In exchange for the run-down shoes that shamed him, he received a pair of leather boots. His skills as an electrician were indeed useful. And his excellent eyesight. What helped him most, however, were his stories about flying. At the age of sixteen he'd been drawn to gliding, and at twenty-five he'd lost none of his enthusiasm; drifting gently, often even unnoticed, above the countryside attracted him as much as ever. And in the cockpit, a silence no airstream could disturb, no matter its strength or speed.

———

HE OBSERVES the soldiers in the stalls below, the officers in the boxes. He wishes he were in uniform. But although it seems strange even to him, they mustn't know he's one of them. He can't breathe a word about the air force, not the slightest hint: seventeen years after the Great War Germany still can't have an air force.

He had barely joined the army when, in January, he was ordered to report to the company commander along with a handful of his comrades, all of them technicians, although he alone had flight experience. They were informed that a new air force was being created and that they had been selected to help establish it. The German minister of aviation no longer intended to submit to the victors' dictates, but for the time being it would be best to work in secret. On February 1 they officially resigned from the German army and had to give up their uniforms. Since that time he's been wearing civilian clothes, and he's still unaccustomed to them.

He hears his company commander saying, Patience, just have patience: the switch from incognito to official recognition will happen soon enough. He was among the first to learn about the new air force. The company commander and the minister of aviation can count on his silence. No comrade, no unknown officer, not one person will have the slightest suspicion.

What sort of a man can't keep a secret? A person who can't keep a secret is weak in every way. Anyone who betrays a confidence, who is unworthy of a secret, loses both his own self-respect and that of his comrades. You have to be able to face yourself in the mirror. A secret is a secret.

Since early spring they've flown loops over the city, formal, unsuspicious loops. They've learned to glide, to fly in formation, to break formation, to pursue. People look up as the planes circle: a white script appears. A dive creates the first letter, followed by curves, dots, and loops; then the advertising slogan is underlined with a low pass. The civilians know nothing.

His childhood friend may be looking up with her fellow cast members. She shades her Italian eyes against the sun, traces the calligraphy with her finger. Her friends are still guessing, but she's figured it out:

"Today he's writing 'Persil.'"

You look carefully, you don't have long, it's only vapor. It loses shape, breaks apart in the air, dissolves into slender tendrils. And soon it will be gone. She doesn't know her childhood friend is up in that plane. She has no idea he's become a pilot. By the time he started flying gliders they had lost touch with one another.

HE IS MAKING a good salary, he has a new suit and a clean shirt, he can go to the opera. And he has something most people in the audience do not: a secret.

The officers in the boxes. Sitting, talking, scanning the audience before the lights go down. The airs they put on, their dismissive attitude toward civilians. Patience. The stiff collars, the polished buttons. Just have patience. Before long he'll appear in uniform too, one that hasn't been seen for a long time. And it won't be gray, that same old gray, but blue as the sky, dark as the air force secret.

A bell rings. He opens his program. Again the bell rings. He's found a picture, clearly his childhood friend. The bell rings a final time, the lights are lowered, he takes his opera glasses from their case. He knows classical music well, both from records and from the radio; he knows every note of this evening's opera, although he's never been in an opera house before. Nevertheless he feels immediately at home. The opera glasses feel familiar, even though binoculars are larger and heavier.

During the overture he waits to search for her Italian eyes, although he doesn't expect to find them. The people in front of him clear their throats. He adjusts the focus, wipes the lenses again. The people next to him are glancing at him openly. They don't know who he is. He'll soon settle in, learn to be inconspicuous, quiet. The curtain rises. A woman appears. It must be her.

HE DOESN'T KNOW the way to the dressing room. He shouldn't have stayed in his seat during the intermission, he should have looked around. He stands on the steps between the tiers, while the officers pass by. They would know how to get backstage; or—he could ask them the way to the dressing room.

He sees the officers disappear through a side door in the foyer. He should speak to them, but how? An insecure civilian wants to pay his compliments to a famous soprano after the performance. Whatever he might say would sound ridiculous to these officers.

Now, he knows, they are standing in the hall outside the dressing room, smoking, waiting for the soprano to finish removing her makeup and change so that she can receive visitors. She's no longer the girl next door. No one, no officer, would dare make a disparaging remark about her Italian eyes.

He had wanted to surprise her, but perhaps she wouldn't even have recognized him. He crosses the square in front of the opera. It had not occurred to him that she might be meeting someone. He heads for the tram. Then he remembers the bouquet standing in her dressing room. And she doesn't know who sent it.

—

TOWARD EVENING the hill turns quiet. The sun sets on the factory smokestacks in the valley, and only a few children call, as if their own noise might frighten them at the end of the day. No yelling or fighting, no more loud names, no replies to the scattered calls, which die away. Soon only the crested larks and the blackbirds remain, and the footsteps on the gravel and in the grass.

Evening falls, and the children from the hill gather together. Some have been in the fields, trampling down the young corn, others descended into the valley or even passed on to the next hill. But they all take the same path home, whether they get along or not. Some go in groups, ambling, their heads close, others return for supper alone, without looking around.

As the children march along the temporary road, the ground gleams around them. Glass splinters in the gravel reflect the red sun, and parts of the meadow shine, too. Motor oil, mirrors crushed to pieces that morning, the green of bottles.

Around this time the spores appear. We call them spores because that is what they must be: spores of mold, since they aren't mosquitoes or moths, nor are they seeds or cobwebs. It must be mold falling on the hill, in the form of bright, weightless flakes that dissolve to nothing when we catch them in our hands to observe them more closely. To nothing but a tough, somewhat coarse, sticky film. No one knows if the spores appear only at sundown or if they have been in the air all day but only become visible in the evening light.

We've never heard that the spores have reached the other hills, or the valley. At first they are only single, milky dots, but by the time the sun has touched the last factory chimney, the telegraph poles on the slope are enveloped by them. They creep toward us along the fallow field like ground fog, across the farm machinery and the pasture fence, and at times the cloudy, opaque tendrils suddenly become so thick that we can hardly tell the other children apart.

Lights appear in the houses. The days are getting longer, and soon the sun won't even strike the chimney stacks at this hour. We button our jackets, stick our hands in our pockets. We stay out longer than the others, they're already at supper. We wait.

Some evenings, as the spores gradually disperse, a sweetish smell arises. It drifts after them across the fields, but we have never learned its source. Not a warm, disagreeable sweetness, lingering vaguely between stench and fragrance, but somehow comforting in the cool of the evening, as if the smell were meant to offer us relief from the excitement and heat of the day just passed, before we head home. We say nothing about it to the neighborhood kids. I like that about the others: they, too, keep secrets. Not a soul other than the four of us has sensed this fragrance that comes from far across the fields, inexplicable and raw.

THE PICTURE SHOWS our grandparents when they were young. Our grandmother has been dead a long time, she died before we four were born. Our grandfather is still alive, but up to now we've known him only through photographs, all black-and-white, as opposed to the ones in color, where we can be seen.

From films we know that young men and women looked

older in the thirties than they do today. Forty years ago men shaved their necks and wore shirts and ties, with stubble showing above their collars. No one would have gone to the opera in a turtleneck. We've never been to an opera, and neither my parents nor those of Paulina, Carl, and Nora listen to operas at home.

In this picture, our grandfather is holding a program on his knees, his head is down, staring, and he stares into the darkness without the slightest movement. Perhaps the program is opened to a double-page spread with photos: the entire cast, photographed individually after a rehearsal, with costumes, makeup, decor, but no singing.

He's looking for something. He raises his opera glasses to look down at the stage, adjusts the focus, then lowers the glasses again. He scrutinizes the rehearsal photos a second time, squinting as if he were nearsighted. He lifts his opera glasses once more: he knows the role, the costume, the makeup, yet he doesn't recognize the young woman up there. He can't call to the stage:

"Is that you?"

He has to keep still. If there were a cast change, it would be noted on a slip in the program. Perhaps they've printed the wrong photographs. It must be her. He'll surprise her in her dressing room after the performance. Maybe it's the lights, the eye shadow, or a reflection, but he doesn't recognize her eyes.

Now he's calm. For a moment he turns his attention from the stage; he knows this passage note for note, and now the singer's words seem aimed directly at him. Perhaps his Italian isn't so good—he's not sure he understands her. A long, drawn-out phrase, as if she'd been trying to catch his attention for some time. The words unnaturally accented, as if she were losing patience because he doesn't know her.

"Try to remember me."

For one long moment it seems as if the singer is turned only to him, as if she's focused on this single figure in the audience, the young man staring through his opera glasses and holding a program on his knees.

WE DISCOVER the fondant factory purely by accident. We even watch the women at the conveyor belts sorting Moors' heads into boxes. They wear aprons and plastic caps, semi-transparent, the strands of hair, shadows on foreheads. In their rubber work gloves their fingers look artificial some-how, and watery; even the skin of their faces seems to blur, and their eyes, fixed on the conveyor belt, are dull and lusterless.

Now and then the production line gets out of sync, and the Moors' heads approach in batches. The pale hands flut-ter, but the woman can't keep up with the packing. The belt continues its steady calm movement, a Moor's head passes by; it's met the quality-control standards, but it's about to fall off the end of the belt. When we see it fall to the floor and break open, we can almost imagine the dull crunch.

No one speaks except the factory foreman. He leads us through the hall and barks at the women from time to time for no obvious reason. He talks to us, but he's mainly con-cerned that we not come too near the conveyor belt, the glaze tank, or the dispenser. The production alternates weekly between Moors' heads and sugar waffles. In one case, they use cocoa powder, in the other, food coloring, and the round waffle punches are exchanged for rectangular ones. We don't pay much attention to the foreman, we're more interested in the flecks of chocolate on his white smock.

Evidently the mixture of sugar water, air, and egg white has to be forced into a chocolate shell. If it weren't cut off from the air supply, it would continue to expand. The white mass pushes its way through the tiniest crack, as evidenced by the spoiled Moors' heads gathered on a tray off to one side.

The women wade through Moor's-head paste in their rubber boots. In the morning there are only a few stubborn stains on the tiles; by late afternoon, the entire floor of the hall will be smeared with egg froth, bits of waffle, and splinters of dark glaze. The foreman points to machines and follows the falling Moors' heads out of the corner of his eye. He avoids our gaze, turning his head away from us so as not to look at us directly, and that seems to require a major effort on his part. It is as if he were at our mercy.

WE ALL HAVE the same eyes. Even when we were babies, people must have talked about our eyes. They couldn't help remarking on them when we started school.

"You all have the same eyes."

The black pupil, the brown iris, the white. As if we were Spaniards. They couldn't stop staring. We wanted to look away, but we couldn't—we had to look back.

Others said, "More like Italians."

The three of them and I all have those Italian eyes, they come from my mother and their father, who are siblings. When the others go into town with their mother, or I with my father, people probably think we're adopted. Our parents are neither Spanish nor Italian. So where do our Italian eyes come from?

People steal glances at us, but no one looks us directly in the eyes anymore—neither foremen nor teachers nor salesgirls. As if they were afraid that in the presence of eyes like ours they might have to watch everything, and each one of us. As if we might steal something the moment their backs were turned. As if we might come after someone. As if we weren't to be trusted.

Perhaps we're drawn to abandoned farmyards and fondant factories simply because we can explore them without being bothered. On these outings across the fields our eyes are simply for seeing: we don't have to be afraid that someone will come along and corner us. In empty fields there simply isn't anyone who would be tempted to tease us because of our eyes.

When the neighborhood kids yell phrases they've picked up on vacation in Italy, when they want to tease me, there's no escape.

"What are you looking at?"

I can't just shut my eyes: I must watch for trouble. I've taken a good look at the neighborhood kids and even stored up a few choice phrases concerning their jug ears and flushed cheeks and the pimples on their ringleader's forehead. I tell myself the ringleader will go to some other school soon, maybe he won't be around that much. I tell myself the neighborhood kids don't know any better. My parents say they repeat silly things they pick up from their parents. If the grown-ups would just keep quiet, so would the children.

No one can silence them. These kids never tire of their taunts, and they're everywhere. Their ringleader has to repeat a grade, so everything stays the same for another year.

But if I'm with Nora, Carl, and Paulina, things look different. There's no anger, no fear, and no averted glances. When we look at each other, we look into each other's eyes, and they're the same eyes we see in the mirror. Otherwise, the four of us don't look much alike. The difference in our faces is particularly clear when we lose control: then our eyes differ, take on another look.

When Carl is angry his eyes narrow as if he were taking aim at something or someone meant to destroy that thing or person with his look. Afterward, he starts yelling and flailing about in all directions, and then his eyes widen until the lids practically vanish.

I've never seen Paulina do that. Her eyes stop, she doesn't blink, her lids are motionless. Not a twitch; that's when I know she's upset. I've noted this carefully: the muscles at the corners of her eyes and at the base of her nose become paralyzed, and her lashes form dark frames, as if she had withdrawn from her own gaze. As if she and I were not practically the same age, as if she were not the youngest of the three.

I haven't yet deciphered Nora's eyes, and that intrigues me, because in four years it may well happen that, for some unknown reason, I come to have that same look, and Carl and Paulina may, too, when they turn sixteen.

With Nora it's not so much anger as a sudden deep disappointment. There's even a hint of bitterness in her eyes when she's annoyed. It seems to me the sort of look you can have only when you've searched all your life for something and haven't found it.

NOW WE KNOW the origin of the sweetish smell that follows the spores in the evening. We always felt that it didn't float up from the valley, didn't spread from the stream or the main road, but approached the hill from behind, from the plain. But we didn't know about the distant factory beyond the fields.

And yet it wasn't the smell that led us to the factory, the smell wasn't even in the air at that time of day. The combination of cold nights and warm spring days brought out distinct odors: in the morning there was the fragrance of grass and dew and then, toward noon, flowers and an occasional whiff of gasoline, but the sweet, raw smell never arrived till evening.

We left earlier than usual that morning, with a picnic basket and the pocket money that got us into the factory at noon. We set out on three bicycles and a borrowed moped. We were supposed to take turns riding the moped, but the others wouldn't let me have it, and for a long time I trundled along behind on the worst of the bicycles. Only when I became angry and stopped dead in the middle of the farm lane did Paulina finally switch with me.

Angry, I sped off on it, away from the others. I wanted to get out of sight, I didn't want them to see me, I was almost in tears. I kept the accelerator at full throttle: I didn't care what it did to the machine. The plain ahead of me, the dust, the stones flew past, as I headed straight for the goal of our previous outings. And in doing so, I crossed an invisible border.

I didn't look back. From behind, my ride may have seemed like flight—just a cloud of dust trailing across the field. I wanted to flee, yet the last thing in the world I wanted to do was go back home. Vacation had just begun. It was our first extended stay together, and I knew before I arrived that these three weeks would outshine any other vacation I'd ever had.

Deep down, I was slightly happy when the motor finally began to sputter and the engine failed as it ran out of gas. Perhaps I'd just needed a little time to myself. The three of them were used to having siblings around, but I wasn't;

I was an only child. Now I could sit at the edge of the path with my dusty face and dusty hair and wait for them. Their three heads were barely discernible among the fields: my cousins, two girls and one boy, fallen far behind. Soon they would be with me.

In our search for a gas station we proceeded farther into unknown territory, and that's how we found the fondant factory.

At the end of our tour we buy paper bags filled with Moors' heads and sugar waffles for less than they cost in the stores; these are damaged, with dark brown, nearly black shells and white whipped filling. When we leave the factory, we hide the moped in the bushes near the main building, since we've already spent all of our money.

The factory is not our first discovery, perhaps not even our most important. We plan to come back tomorrow to get the moped, and maybe we'll buy more broken chocolate in the days to come, but at some point we'll forget the factory. New discoveries will eclipse earlier ones. We may return someday by chance and wonder why it's so long since we've been here.

Certain discoveries inspire us right from the start, and we want to share their enjoyment at once. Others we don't know what to make of. We explore an abandoned farmhouse, isolated, far out in the fields. We break open padlocks and find waxed tablecloths, still littered with bread crumbs, and the smell of old people. We see nothing of interest, even though four pairs of eyes are at work. Still, we decide to keep this farmhouse in mind, for we sense that it might prove useful someday.

There are discoveries that we discuss at length each evening before we go to sleep, and others that we don't

know how to discuss and so don't discuss at all, treating
them almost like secrets.

—

SOMETIMES WE GO to the redoubt, an open area in our district that's officially called the Old Redoubt. Now it's a
meadow in the midst of a birch grove, with a wild growth of
shrubs along its borders. We enjoy coming here because we
can hide and watch the entire area. We can entrench ourselves against the neighborhood kids more securely here
than anywhere else.

The name itself goes back to a time when the redoubt
served as a training ground for army marksmen. But it's
hard to imagine that shots were ever fired here. It might
well have been dangerous: there's a settlement of single-
family homes at the far end that grew up before the Second
World War, and the other end opens out over a valley where
a munitions factory for heavy artillery and tanks has always
stood. Our parents even worked at this factory once, not
long after our grandmother died—sometime in the early
sixties, perhaps, before we were born. We've never asked
them much about it.

Besides, there are no indications that there was ever a
rifle range here—there are no concrete butts in the bushes,
and the old shell cases must have long since rusted away,
fallen to bits over the course of forty years. When we do find
shell cases, they're more recent ones—blanks and tear-gas
canisters. Someone around here must be taking target practice, he may even have a real gun. We'd like to see him
sometime, but it seems he comes out mostly on rainy days,
for the shell cases we find are often embedded in dry clay.

The moment it begins to rain, our rubber boots sink
into the mud of the redoubt, and later, when the ground is

solid again, you can see our prints everywhere: deep holes with blurred outlines where puddles once were, and clear impressions, showing every groove in our soles, where we finally made it to solid footing.

Who comes secretly to the redoubt for rifle practice when it rains, and what is he shooting at? We search the area, we keep our eyes on the ground, we gather mud-caked shell cases without having any real idea what we want to do with them. We're drawn to an unknown marksman.

An old man, perhaps, who practiced here in the thirties and still comes today, unable to forget the past. He shoots at birches, he fires into the air when no one is around. He doesn't want to be seen, because there's something slightly ludicrous about his target practice. He loads his gun, aims, and pulls the trigger, as if he really wanted to do away with someone or defend himself against a dangerous enemy, as if it were a matter of life and death. But no one has ever seen this still-unvanquished foe. He is invisible, and leaves no footprints, even after a rain.

But why we care, why we think there's a mystery here, we can't say. Perhaps it's just a few older boys who want to show off for a few of their friends with a stolen tear-gas gun. I've never been particularly interested in guns, and I don't play with toy soldiers anymore. I did when I was little, but those days are gone. I walk past shooting galleries at the fair—I would jerk my head when the gun went off and miss anyway.

What discovery could possibly await us here in the redoubt, where the sound of the siren comes up from the valley every day at noon, when the workers at the munitions factory take their lunch break?

Not so long ago, when other mysteries meant more to us, the oddity of this unknown marksman would not have seemed so fascinating—we might not have even noticed it. Last year—if I had been here on holiday then—the discovery of the fondant factory would have occupied us entirely. We would have wondered if the chocolate flecks on the foreman's smock hinted at some mystery. The traces of Moors' heads on the hall floor would have occupied a central position in our meditations for days on end. And we would have made a great secret of the fact that we ate broken chocolate after brushing our teeth, when it hardly mattered if our parents found out at all.

Last year, we would not have rummaged through the trash cans on the redoubt, nor would we have felt much interest in the torn-out pages that we are now smoothing out, our hands both eager and reluctant to touch the paper. We piece the two-page spreads together, although the individual scraps of paper are revealing enough: color photos, close-ups, not much text.

We look, holding our breath, flipping hastily through the pages of half a booklet, the four of us sitting side by side on a bench, not laughing, not speaking, looking quickly. At most, we move our lips silently when we come across an unknown phrase. Most of the text is just balloons that say, "Go on," "Harder," "Yes, yes, oh yes," and "We're coming," or else men and women speaking some foreign language.

We have no idea who looks at such booklets besides us. Men with baggy pockets, red-faced perhaps, pretending to be joggers, out of breath from the unaccustomed running, coming to the redoubt in their tracksuits for no other reason than to leaf through their little booklets in peace. You can never tell from the pictures how long the story has been going on—a few minutes or an hour—nor can you ever know when the next jogger will arrive, whether it will be tomorrow or a week from now that the next crumpled pages will be found, always distributed among several trash cans.

In these pages, someone is always there, standing out of sight. You think he's somewhere in the background, then realize with a shock that he's actually in the foreground, outside the photograph, standing in the exact spot from which the scene is observed. When we look at the booklets, we're beside an invisible man who has forced his way into the lovers' apartment and caught them by surprise with his camera.

The most important mystery at the moment, however, is our eyes, and we won't rest until we know what's behind them. Everything else has to wait: we won't come back to strange old soldiers and their target practice until we've got the neighborhood kids off our backs.

THE FIRST TIME I see the other kids on the hill lying in wait for us, I'm afraid. It's not the same fear I feel at home, I'm not just afraid of fights and torn clothes, there's something else too, an unfamiliar feeling in my stomach. As if the fight were already under way, as if I had already received the decisive blow in the belly that would drop me to the ground the next moment.

"We've already told you a thousand times where we got our eyes."

It turns out everyone knows but me. Not only Carl, Nora, and Paulina, but all of the neighborhood kids, too—everyone here in our district. Nora berates the ringleader: he's just too dumb to get it. We got our eyes from our grandmother, an opera singer who now lives in Rome. He claims we haven't come up with any proof of that yet and that we never will, because we've made the whole thing up.

But Nora sticks to it: our grandmother is so famous that everyone knows her except stupid neighborhood kids.

It will be dark soon, and it's a long way from the redoubt to the hill, so everyone slowly starts heading home. After the ringleader signals to our foes to break off, he turns around; he has to have the last word.

"Be sure to let us know the next time your granny appears on television."

We head on back, too. I hadn't known we had a grandmother living in Italy. I'd thought our grandmother died long ago.

"Of course our grandmother's not still alive, we just made that up."

So it's true what my parents said: our grandmother died when both of her own children were young. My mother was still going to school then, and my uncle finished his apprenticeship and left home soon afterward. I'm not sure what to believe—I'd been afraid that things might be totally different.

"And she was an opera singer? I didn't know that."

Yes, she was an opera singer. Nora stops. The area of single-family homes is behind us now, we've reached the supermarket. Soon it will be all uphill, all gravel road and no sidewalk. I don't know whether I should continue.

"And Italian?"

No, they just said that so the neighborhood kids would leave us alone. I can't see Nora's face clearly anymore—our eyes seem to disappear as the sun sets. Nora almost bursts out laughing.

"We told them you live with our grandma in Italy, that you're going to boarding school in Rome. I think they fell for it. They must really be surprised at how good your German is."

Carl doesn't think it's funny, because now we have to explain why I haven't brought any proof with me from Italy—records, or an opera program with our grandmother's name in it. Rehearsal photos would have done, too. A single picture of our grandmother in costume. Of her eyes.

Ahead of us we see the silhouettes of the neighborhood kids, the houses on the hill. Most of them, except for ours, are almost shacks: maybe that's why the neighborhood kids abuse us. At one time there were only gardens on the hill, with little summerhouses and toolsheds, which were only later added to bit by bit. Yet almost no one had a permit, and eventually some of them might have to be torn down.

"But only our grandmother died, right?"

Yes, our grandfather is still alive, and he lives not far from us, near the redoubt.

"Is that why we go there so often?"

A shrug is the only answer I get. Could it be that we walked past his house on the way home?

"No."

Carl looks at me, and I glance quickly ahead again along the road. The gravel crunches. Before the others can think I'm an idiot, I stop asking questions.

I've never been to Rome, or anywhere in Italy. And I wouldn't want to go to a boarding school either. The story they've made up about our grandmother isn't bad, it's the sort of story only a group could invent. I've always tried to make up stories to tell the neighborhood kids at home myself. Once I even claimed that I wasn't an only child, that in fact I had a little brother. Of course they wanted to see him, wanted to know if he had the same eyes. He's in the bathtub right now, being given a bath, and no one can go in. They were almost ready to believe me, but then they noticed there was no light coming through the crack beneath the bath-room door. My story had stood up for only a few minutes, and then I was alone again, the others making fun of me. What sort of a brother takes a bath in the dark?

But now I have to make sure I'm always with my three cousins, that I never let them out of my sight. What if the neighborhood kids catch me sometime and ask me about Italy? I shouldn't have taken off from the others on the moped. What if our foes had appeared in the field, and me with no idea at all about our grandmother?

Why hadn't my cousins told me right away? The neighborhood kids would have made short work of me, any help from the others would have arrived too late. But the neighborhood kids know nothing about our trips across the fields, or the fondant factory. And I don't want to argue with Nora, Carl, and Paulina—they told me the story soon enough.

I've always known that our grandmother died long ago. I've always known that our grandfather is still alive. I can't remember if I've ever heard before that our grandmother was an opera singer. There are still a lot of things unclear about that.

"But the part about the eyes is true? Did our grandma have brown eyes like ours?"

Our grandmother must have had Italian eyes. When she was still young, our grandfather looked for them onstage through his opera glasses. It's possible that as a child she even went through the same thing we did.

"Where did she get those dark eyes?"

It's not far to the house now, we'll soon catch up with the neighborhood kids. Now the spores, too, will slowly arrive. To tell the truth, I don't much like the smell that comes across the fields with the spores. In fact, I wish the smell that arrives with the setting sun would disappear, it's so sweet and thick you feel as if you can barely breathe.

⁓

ONE SUNNY AFTERNOON when we are home alone, we find something no one else has seen, at least not for a very long time. Nora was looking through the bookcase for the telephone book but instead pulls out a photo album hidden in the back.

It's not the typical square volume with padded synthetic covers and self-adhesive pages where photos are held behind transparent glassine sheets. This is a rectangular album bound in black cardboard, with black card-stock pages. We find no pictures of ourselves, no vacation photos taken by parents, no snapshots of us in postures we don't recognize, with faces scarcely our own.

We don't like having our pictures taken, but we're often caught from behind, or don't turn our heads aside in time; our hands are lifted too late, or we stand there paralyzed. From baby and childhood pictures on, the photos are all pretty much the same. The four of us, blurred, with runny noses and open anoraks, entering the house from the street, hands behind our backs so no one will see the arms of our coats, torn in a fight with the neighborhood kids. Dust or soot clings to our faces, we're not smiling, our eyes are wide open, pupils red from the flash.

Paulina and I, still in grade school, sitting in a parked car, looking as if we've been caught at something. Perhaps we already sensed someone approaching with a camera. Nora and Carl by a campfire—probably from the brief period they were in the scouts—with open, twisted mouths, being forced to sing. You can tell they'll be leaving the youth group as soon as possible. If these pictures weren't in our photo albums, no one would connect them with us.

Even though the light would be better out on the back terrace, we withdraw to the corner of the couch to examine the unknown photographs. We sit bunched up, and Nora holds the open album on her knees—she's the one who found it. The photos are protected by a parchment paper with a spiderweb pattern imprinted in it, so that we see them first as if dulled by a patina, blurred by a veil, until we lift the protective leaf and the contours and contrasts stand out sharply. The pictures are as old as the album, with serrated white edges, and there are captions that even Nora finds hard to decipher.

At first the pictures don't mean much to us, they show scenes usually found in family albums. One figure stands out immediately, however: a young man we don't know, who appears in several photos, with different backgrounds in various parts of the world, but always in uniform.

Apparently on leave, his face out of focus, the man is standing on a sandy path. Behind him bushes and a picket fence—where could that be? A few pages further on, a snow-filled pine forest, probably taken on an outing, Nora isn't sure. I discover parallel lines in the snow and, at the outer edge, in the distance, a ski patrol. Carl points out insignias on the snowsuits: this can't be an outing.

Other soldiers are in the same frame with the young man. A series of photos from Nürburgring shows, in addition to a line of cars, the entire troop, pressed together for the picture. Then the Maria Laach fur farm, Deutsches Eck, Eighth Company. Nora deciphers them, letter by letter, and we slowly realize that they even spent their leave in uniform.

A barracks square, soldiers lined up on both sides for roll call, and in the middle five men: four standing at ease and one saluting, clicking his heels. Even though we see him only from a distance, we know he's the same man we've seen in the other photos. Whose idea was it to photograph a scene like this? The man in the uniform must have requested it himself, as a souvenir.

Over the years the number of decorations and medals on his chest increases. If the pictures got mixed up, we could put them back in the right order on the basis of the decorations alone, the polished base metal reflecting the sun and the magnesium flash.

Then, after a portrait in a steel helmet appears for the first time, followed by several empty pages with corner mounts still sticking to them, the album ends.

THE YOUNG MAN, we estimate, must have reached the approximate age of the old people living here on the hill by now. One neighbor in particular occurs to us: we call him the Pigeon Man, because his house has a pigeon loft in the attic. He doesn't speak to anyone, perhaps he talks only to his pigeons, when he gathers them every few weeks to take them to a carrier pigeon show. Otherwise, he stands silently at his garden fence, once in a while cradling a gun in his arm, as if we were after his birds.

The man in the photo album is not carrying a weapon in any of the pictures. He's someone we've never seen before, and yet we know at once that it must be our grandfather.

His face is hard to recognize. We can't make out any particular features—at most a repressed smile, perhaps only a squint, a twitch at the corner of his mouth, with the light in his eyes. In several of the pictures the brim of his cap casts a shadow over them, and yet for all the uncertainty it's clear that this young officer does not have Italian eyes. Which means we must have inherited ours from our grandmother.

AFTER THE STEEL helmet portrait, a few scattered and un-sorted photos have been inserted in the album, as if they were going to be pasted in at some later date. Further on in the black cardboard volume, the parchment paper with the spiderweb pattern lies over blank pages, a time for pasting the pictures in having never arrived.

In these loosely inserted photos, nothing remains of our grandfather as a young man, not even the shadow of his upper body extends into the picture. The man we have been looking at is himself the photographer, and now we see with his eyes, gaze with him through the viewfinder.

And now you can tell that he always carries his own camera, conscientiously recording every subject of possible importance, in whatever situation. He even takes the camera into the air-raid shelter at night when the alarm sounds. The moment the sun rises again, he looks for a good shot: in the center a smashed-in double door, gaping windows on both sides, and behind them a pile of rubble fallen from the upper floors.

The young man stands in the street and we sit huddled on the couch, and yet we're looking with him. The light isn't good—it's still early in the day, or maybe there's the dust of debris in the air. The picture looks a little fuzzy, a further indication of dust. On the back of the photo, a note: "22/23 October, after a bombing raid," and next to this, in a different pencil, "Left side of the ground floor: our apartment."

Perhaps he hadn't held still when he took the picture.

The night table on which the camera always stood ready for use lies buried beneath the rubble. But when everything has been destroyed, what makes a person want to take a photo of it? Above all, Paulina wonders, how can you stand in front of your own house the morning after an air raid and take a snapshot of what's left? That's not the way we look at things, we don't look with those eyes.

In one photo, it's unclear what the subject is supposed to be. The year is 1944, and the caption reads "Friends visit," but there are no people to be seen. Just the sitting area in the empty living room: a dagger hanging on the wall—an ornament, perhaps—and the patterned shade of the floor lamp, from which a model airplane dangles on a string. We can't decide if the photographer is interested in the general atmosphere of the living room, the ornamental dagger, or just the model.

We know this type of airplane from the toy shop. We may have even had this model ourselves once—we could check, the things are still in the basement. We used to spend entire winter afternoons gluing parts together in the right order. Mornings, before we'd even had breakfast, we would paint the plastic pieces with finely pointed brushes, as if we had a lifetime to spend on them. As if we would always find this interesting. The next day it was over, a distant past that no one was ever to know about. We gathered up the half-finished models, along with the paint, and the glue and put them in boxes so we could forget them as soon as possible.

A kid's toy. But we don't see a kid in a single picture. The photographer must have assembled this model himself: for weeks he must have sat enthusiastically over the kit, and every free evening after dark he would draw the curtains and take up the work again, tinkering with nail files and tweezers under a small lamp until he could finally hang the finished model airplane in his living room.

In the midst of the air war, this bomber steadily circles the sitting area, the salt and pepper shakers, and the crocheted tablecloth. The house is unharmed: everyone sits together at the table, and whenever anyone looks up they see what they might be facing that night. The house, the crocheted tablecloth, and the model airplane may all be gone tomorrow.

Perhaps we might have got to the bottom of this picture if we could have looked at it a little longer, but when we hear footsteps on the back terrace, we stick it between the black pages and slip the album back into the bookcase just in time, into the spot where the telephone book should be.

—

WE DIDN'T FIND the eyes anywhere in the album: our grandmother is faceless. We would have needed just one picture of our grandmother, in costume, with our Italian eyes, but it's not there. Nor is there any photo in the album that shows her alone, a portrait photo. She smiles like the others in group photos, but she's faceless—they're all together, in the living room or in the countryside, holding hands or keeping a short distance between them, so small that no one notices.

Nowhere are her eyes like ours, either the light is bad or she squints, or she turns aside just as we do. Our Italian eyes are hard to see in photos, too—not dark brown, just the red from the flash.

That's not her face, and those aren't her eyes, neither in the group photos nor in the pictures with her fiancé or, later, with her husband, our grandfather in his uniform. The two of them on an airstrip: they've just landed, she's still sitting in the open cockpit, and he's standing on the wing, bending down to her, but they're not looking at each other, they're looking at the camera.

In every picture, our grandmother knows she's being looked at. Not only by the photographer, but by other people, too—later, when they look at the photo. People our grandmother has never seen. Like us.

Perhaps she didn't want to stare at a stranger with her Italian eyes, and that's why there's no portrait. But that can't be it: as an opera singer, she knew that she had to look strangers in the eye, and that her eyes would be sought in the dark by others.

Didn't our grandfather ever take a picture of her alone? On an outing, just the two of them, posing her in front of lush greenery to bring out the color of her eyes? On that airstrip, just after they landed, her eyes bright after flying with him across the broad countryside. Our grandfather in that air force uniform surely took his camera out then—her husband, who is always taking photographs and who never misses a chance to have his own picture taken.

Our grandmother may have been coy, avoiding the camera. A young woman, a young man: he would have talked her into it, tricked her, perhaps, saying there was no film in the camera anyway. He would have got her in front of the camera, she could forget about him for a moment, and he'd press the shutter.

If our grandfather managed to assemble all the guests at a family party for a group photo, even though some were deep in conversation beneath the trees and others would rather have remained at the table eating pastries—if all those long-since-scattered guests gathered once more, late that afternoon, because our grandfather called and waved and urged them onto the lawn with just the right turn of phrase—then he was surely capable of talking our grandmother into taking a moment after the group photo to pose for him.

He knows how to take pictures, he knows how to line subjects up in front of his lens. He's a pilot, he knows about the cameras in the tail of every airplane, he knows how to fly so that aerial photographs turn out right, he knows the rhythm of the automatic shutter and from the cockpit he can count the pictures along with it.

OR MAYBE OUR grandmother disappeared from the photo album later, and the gaps, the empty pages, and the loose pictures involve her.

Perhaps someone removed all the photographs in which she was herself, in which she did more than twitch her mouth in a polite smile, and her eyes were not in shadow. All the pictures in which one could see her Italian eyes. Perhaps the direct gaze of our grandmother disturbed someone viewing the pictures just as much as our gaze seems to disturb people.

Our long-dead grandmother in a garden, young, with friends. Our grandmother at the same party, with her future husband. A series of souvenir photos of her performances— the flowers, blown kisses, admirers. Our grandmother in fantastic costumes, totally different from the same old uniform—robes, jewelry, wigs—at times our grandmother openmouthed, singing. And always those eyes.

It may be that someone couldn't stand that. Perhaps he started by trying to cut the figure out of the group photos with nail scissors, slowly, his lips pressed tight. Or even with nail clippers, that would be difficult. Someone has removed the figure from a garden shot, only a few pansies remain, the tree in the background outside the bedroom no longer has a trunk, and the other people in the picture are complete strangers.

Another figure is cut out that has nothing to do with her—another portion, the shadow and the melancholy gaze, so that in the end only clouds remain, or not even that.

Yet somewhere a hand is left behind: a singer's unmistakable hand lies on the forearm of a man's dark suit. Or the falling fold of a lavish costume, if left on for the opening-night party. A cut-off shoe in the grass or, at the edge of the sky, a few fine lines, barely visible to the naked eye and perhaps nothing more than specks of dust on the lens, but they could just as easily be eyelashes from a missing face, extending a few millimeters into the landscape.

You can use a magnifying glass, but it doesn't help; you can never be sure that the figure has been removed. No trace of the opera singer. The photo is empty, yet something still remains: that disturbing gaze just can't be shaken off. It can be seen in everything, it has touched the shadows and the tree, it still rests, long after the Italian eyes are gone, on the viewer.

Not even rehearsal photos, of the sort we wished to find cut out of an old theater program and pasted in as souvenirs, are in the album. Our grandmother has disappeared. Everything about her has been removed from the family album. We have nothing to show the neighborhood kids. No proof of an opera singer, no matter how faded and hard to make out, no matter how dubious. Even more important, we don't have a single picture of our grandmother for ourselves.

As far as we can tell, our grandfather started the album. All the captions are written in the same hand. In the beginning, these are neatly penned comments, perhaps set down in spring sunshine, in leisurely recollection. On the first warm afternoon our grandfather sits in the garden: the long winter has passed, no more tinkering with the model plane by fading light, he'll have to wait for that until next fall. The corner mounts for the photos are carefully pasted onto the black card stock, a picture is inserted, bright rectangles on dark double-page spreads, and then the pen glides along beside the images: it must have been guided with firm confidence, otherwise not much would be seen of those white strokes, loops, and underlinings.

Toward the end of the album, the handwriting becomes rushed and lighter, almost a scrawl—even a slip now and then. White is difficult to erase, too. The individual pictures no longer have carefully phrased captions, just the place, date, and occasion noted on the back. Our grandfather had barely taken each picture and held the print in his hand before he inserted it somewhere between the pages. He'd have to wait until after the war to look at them more carefully.

It's inconceivable that our grandfather removed all his wife's pictures from the family album at some later date. We can't believe that. That's not how it was. He was drawn to our grandmother's eyes, they held him fast, and he realized that, if he hadn't already, the moment he saw the name of his childhood friend on a poster. It was her eyes alone he sought through the opera glasses.

· calls ·

HE DID NOT RECOGNIZE the eyes, could not make them out onstage. Through the opera glasses he saw an unfamiliar figure, yet it had to be the woman he protected from the neighborhood kids so many years ago. With all the courage he could muster. With no thought of danger, nor of the malicious and superior strength he faced. Without a moment's hesitation, in spite of his own weakness. With open eyes, he would have foreseen his own defeat: his scratched face, his torn trousers, his mother's scolding afterward, his ears boxed that evening by his father.

Through the opera glasses he followed the figure as she captured the scene with her first note. The birch grove became her grove, the lane had always been her lane. From the start her male foil was hers alone: the tenor would never dare fall for another woman as she had fallen for him. But he has deceived his beloved from the very start, has hidden from her what the audience witnessed the moment she left the stage.

She should have sensed it. She has been blind. A cry from the audience could not have brought her to her senses.

He could have allied himself with the neighborhood kids. His Sunday suit could have been saved. It would have been easy to be on the winning side. But he had not hesitated to throw reason to the wind and defend the Italian eyes of this young girl.

Through the opera glasses he saw her fall into despair. She stood in tears, drained, leaning against a tree, betrayed and abandoned by her lover. And yet she could not forget him: in every note, in every word there was the same longing as before. In every cobblestone, in every leaf, in every cloud she sensed his step, his touch, his gaze. That was her downfall, and she knew it. The entire audience knew it.

He watched as the singer covered her face with her hands in the final act, so she would no longer have to see earth, tree, or cloud. Even as a child, he knew her tear-stained eyes. Through the opera glasses he followed her as she lifted her hands to the heavens because she could not free herself from the image of her beloved, even at the end.

Perhaps he remembered her hands then, a girl's hands, as they took a stroll together on the street, on a spring day like this, and for once there were no neighborhood kids around. He was spared that day, did not have to ball his own hands into fists. But he did not want to put them into his pockets either, and he glanced over at her hands, hands that seemed out of place playing in a sandpile or climbing a tree. He wanted to mention her slender hands, her long fingers, but he said nothing, and neither of them knew enough to hold hands as they walked.

THEY SAY YOU can judge artistic talent by looking at a person's little finger. Nora claims you can tell by its length. Nora and Paulina's little fingers reach almost to the nail of their ring fingers. That means both girls are above average in talent.

Carl and I have little fingers that end below the third joint of our ring fingers. Perhaps our little fingers are too short for art of any kind. Carl doesn't care, but it bothers me, and my little fingers aren't going to grow any longer. They'll just get crooked in the coming years, making them seem even shorter than they are.

We can be recognized by our eyes but not by our hands. Our hands are different. For instance, Carl has warts on his fingers and the backs of his hands that grow back. That's why I don't like to touch his hands, but sometimes it can't be helped, like when he lifts me into the hayloft because I can't make it up the last part of the ladder.

Carl has farmer's hands. You can see he tends horses, bales hay, and works in the fields. In the fall he helps dig potatoes, and he always looks forward to riding out on the tractor at the break of dawn with the farm kids, even when it's raining and the ground is muddy. During the fall holidays he's hardly ever at home, because he's so tired that he stays overnight at the farm.

Paulina's hands are smaller, of course, and fortunately she doesn't have warts. She spends a lot of time with horses, too, and she has to keep putting lotion on her hands—perhaps the straw or horsehair dries out her skin. Her slender hands don't seem up to this work. Paulina has to watch her fingernails too, they tear easily, just like mine.

Nora probably has the nicest hands of all. Not only does

she have long little fingers, but she also has fine skin, and she moves her hands elegantly. When she sits on the corner couch and reads, she holds the book so that all you can see are her fingers. At the table, writing to her pen pal, holding the pen in her thumb and forefinger, she seems older than she is. Of the four of us, Nora is the one whose hands are most like those we imagine for our grandmother.

Our grandmother's hands have not aged. The skin is not old enough to be wrinkled or even loose, the veins do not stand out, it's far too early for age spots.

Those hands on the white cover, when our grandmother can no longer rise from the bed, when illness has already altered her face. Perhaps the bright Italian eyes are barely recognizable now, but her hands are still young. They lie there as if they are about to move at any moment, to seize the cover, shake it and hang it out the window to air.

But it is our grandfather who shakes out his wife's feather bed and arranges it, the two children who help change the sheets. They open the window at an angle, reach for her juice, her pills, pour tea into the cup on the nightstand and lift it to our grandmother's lips.

Then the three of them sit quietly by the bed, waiting to be of help again. Or waiting for the doctor, who has been coming daily around six for some weeks now. Just not the hospital, she's been to the hospital too often. The children will open the door for the doctor and help with the examination, they've watched him often enough. They will fetch warm water and a cloth, turn back the cover, and lift their mother forward while they put pillows behind her back.

Afterward, they will stay with the sick woman, close the curtains, and make a hollow in the duvet so the young hands can rest more comfortably while their father sees the doctor out. He will accompany him as far as the door, and the two will exchange a few words: the same things they've been saying for weeks.

"A double dose before bed?"

"Yes."

"See you tomorrow, then."

"Good night."

"If there's a problem, even in the middle of the night, you know how to reach me."

It has been some time since anyone said, "Get well."

Then the doctor will disappear, and the children will hear their father walk slowly into the kitchen to fix supper.

Until then—it is only four-thirty now—they watch the weak, young hands, the hands on the white coverlet. The father and the children watch tensely to see if the hands will move, whether the forefinger stirs, tries to grasp at something.

They would feel better if even one muscle moved, between her left thumb and forefinger.

It would be a salvation just to see the moons beneath her fingernails stand out a little more clearly.

OVER TWENTY YEARS ago, he trained his opera glasses on her hands for the first time. He wasn't yet wearing his uniform. In retrospect, he realized that she might not have glanced at him if he had been: she never liked to see him in it later, either.

She liked costumes. She always admired the fancy dresses for her roles, and every evening she made sure that nothing was missing and everything fit. She never left those things up to her wardrobe mistress. Uniforms were another matter. She merely glanced at them, they were all the same to her. There was little hope that she would look with favor on either the gray uniforms of the army officers who gathered outside her dressing-room door in the order of their rank to grace her hand with damp kisses, or the dark blue one in which he appeared so proudly one evening before her.

⌒

THEY ARE OFF the farm lane now. The green boughs descend to eye level, and they are isolated from the rest of the world. The song of the lark, the cries of the farmers, even the lowing of the cattle reach their ears only distantly.

They have taken their leave of the garden party to stroll through the fields, arm in arm, from the heights down to the plain—like the view from the redoubt, seen through a slight haze. The light envelops the earth and every object: the gentle hills along the river, last year's foliage, dusty fields. They see a flock of chickens behind chicken wire; the sandy soil is furrowed, barren, rough, like a military training ground.

They are not far from the pond now, close to the forest's edge, where the country youth may come for nightly outings; they have left behind the coffee tray, the honey and almond cake, real coffee, cheesecake, even fondant pastries. Behind them, now, the conversation beneath the trees, and with it the polite distance that normally characterizes such Sunday visits.

No, none of that matters anymore as they press closer together on the narrow beaten path to keep from slipping on the grassy stubble, preferring not to walk single file.

The two have left their relatives behind; they're still sitting in the garden, both sets of parents and her aunt and uncle, who own the local dairy. By now the aunt may well have launched into an interrogation of the parents about the relationship between their children. Everyone will think that they have secretly arranged this meeting.

A long-planned country outing for the parents, who are old friends, and suddenly the daughter decides to come, since she's not singing in Frankfurt or Munich that particular summer day. By chance the other family's son returns early from one of his training sessions, pulls up at the dairy, and steps out of his new car. Everyone will think they've been meeting on a regular basis, at her operas, or wherever he happens to be in flight-training. No one will convince them it's just a coincidence. Even they can scarcely comprehend how near they had come to losing sight of one another forever. Later that afternoon, the aunt is sure, they can count on an announcement.

They speak more softly now, after he has told her, at the edge of the meadow, about his first glider flight. He spoke then in a loud, firm voice, even weaving the sounds of flight into his story—the wind flowing over the cockpit and wings—as he spread his arms wide.

But now his voice trembles; they stand, he strokes her bare neck, their mouths meet in a kiss that lasts longer than any kiss before, that moves farther, along cheeks, forehead, and throat.

Yes, now everything has changed: the rumpled Sunday suit, freshly ironed that morning, no longer matters, the grass stains on their knees and backs don't matter, the touch of makeup, so precisely applied that noon and now lightly streaking her cheeks, and the smeared lipstick flecking his face no longer matters, nor the mascara as he kisses her eyes, nor her pinned-up hair, now loosening, falling in waves among the crumpled blossoms.

No, it's all different from elsewhere, where certain phrases are no more the expression of mutual desire than the caresses and kisses that accompany them, where such words simply signal a tacit agreement, an accordance with convention, and it never occurs to those involved that the words and sounds might truly be addressed to the other person. So intimate, eyes closed, the sighs, the soft cries into the pillow, the deep breaths, but it's merely polite conversation beneath the trees.

Yes, everything is different here: the whispered words learned from films and novels spur the two on still more strongly, and even an ordinary "no" or "yes" acquires special meaning now. No matter that they are clichés, it never occurs to either one how often these same words and sounds must have issued from the mouths of how many others before now.

She, the soprano with opera engagements on various stages, and he, the officer's candidate and eager pilot, are like two children now, taking off their shoes without looking, digging their stocking feet into the sandy soil.

She, here in the tall grass, her dress soon hitched high, her panties visible, and he, still struggling with his shirtsleeves, then with his arms bare to the elbows, the gleaming cuff links lying somewhere, perhaps between the dry, hard clumps of clay.

The lost hairpins no longer matter, nor the scratches on their legs from sharp blades of grass, nor the rough-edged pebbles; the complicated unbuttoning doesn't matter, the button strip, the turned-up collar of her blouse gone awry, nor the laboriously unhooked bra, the cups clamped under her armpits. Now the trembling hands again, the half-opened mouths and the tongues; the clumsy movements don't matter, the unlacing and turning up, nor the extrication from sleeves nor the perspiration.

And wrists, bending arms, shoulders and hairy chest, hairy stomach and navel, two thighs with dark curls, two

thighs with fine blond hair—barely visible, merely perceptible—and stomach and breast and throat and navel.

No more damp grass, no clods, no crunching sand, no
more insects, no leaf blades. No more cattle lowing, no
chickens clucking, no children's cries, distant, in the forest, by the pond. No clothing chafes now, or scratches, now
there is merely hair, matted together, and eyelashes flick-
ing, merely breath.

It seems it has always been like this: the breath is in the
grass, in both mouths. As it has always been, from the very
beginning.

Only gradually do they begin to hear again: the rustling
of the leaves, the birds singing once more, faintly at first,
then more and more loudly. The distant trees draw nearer,
and in the skies a dot, a lark arrives above them, and its song
has such sharp clarity that they realize they haven't heard
anything around them for some time now, not even the cattle
driven past their hiding place, or the farmer shouting and
prodding.

It seems that they've spent hours here in the field, and
they are as exhausted as if they had worked from dawn to
dusk, helping with the harvest; they are tired and withdrawn, yet refreshed and alert as their bodies now glide into
rest, a rest without resistance.

Perhaps it is raining now, a warm drizzle, already soaking
them for who knows how long. It is probably still hot; the sun
is lower now, and the cornstalks cast shadows on their faces.

THEY BLINK. The sun will soon be setting. They'll be
missed; they only meant to go for a short stroll. Yet none
of that matters, or it no longer matters. It seems to them
things have always been like this.

Navels, breasts, sweat, hairy areas are still there, and the bra, the crumpled dress, the suit, and the grass-stained shirt. His cuff links, heirlooms, have disappeared. Each hears the other's breath, they have heard this breath throughout, as if they've always heard it. They don't speak.

They dress. The bra is hooked, and the shirtsleeves stay rolled up—no one will notice anything, it's summer after all, and they'll buy new cuff links. They head back in silence, slightly embarrassed. Perhaps now, after their sojourn in the meadow among the rustling leaves, something has dawned on them, but they can't express it yet. She buttons her blouse a second time as she walks, and she doesn't notice that she's done it up wrong again. Perhaps she's still immersed in the wordless whispers, moans, and sighs, perhaps she is concentrating so fixedly on the problem of piecing the sounds together into words that she doesn't see the row of buttons.

He stumbles and nearly falls on the beaten path, he wasn't watching his step. Perhaps he's thinking of what to say to the others, how to formulate the declarations the two of them exchanged, for their words up to now have been spoken and heard far from the outside world, almost mutely. She reaches for his arm, and he regains his footing. Then she supports him while he shakes a pebble from his shoe. She sees that his leather soles are still new, just as his suit, his tie, and even his underwear, as she now knows, look brand-new. No man dresses that well on Sunday just for family. Was he truly unaware that she was coming to her uncle's place in the country? After all, he has admitted that he never stopped looking for her, never stopped seeking her eyes.

He watches his step now: perhaps he's trying to divert his thoughts from the image of the nonplussed garden party by imagining military night marches, in full battle gear, two days without sleep, staring, plodding on step after step, seeing nothing.

After auditions, in canteens, and at opening-night parties, she has seen things that her parents—and perhaps even he, who has taken her hand again—would never have thought possible. But the picture the two of them will offer, standing before their parents in less than a quarter of an hour, won't be too bad, either, if ever she chooses to tell her colleagues about it.

He hopes that no one will still be sitting in the garden, that everyone will have withdrawn into the room with the fireplace as the cool of evening approached, so that the two of them can slip unnoticed through the back door and go upstairs to wash up, neaten their clothes, and comb their hair again before they have to face anyone.

But when they arrive, the leftover pastry has not yet been cleared away. Only the coffee has disappeared, replaced in the meantime by cold cuts, brandy, and other liqueur. His mother's hand lies on her aunt's arm, the aunt stares, her father's jaw hangs open, as if he has put something too hot in his mouth, and her uncle peers down at nothing in the grass. They sense that the table talk has broken off in the middle of a question.

They stand like children returning from play; they're no longer holding hands, but neither are they children anymore. They're both in their mid-twenties, and that makes it so much the worse, their tousled hair and clothes, her blouse still buttoned crookedly, his tie bulging in his pocket.

They stand side by side before the assembled family, trying to pull themselves together. They've been laughing all the way back, imagining this impossible situation, and now he steps forward, under control—he doesn't want to grin as he delivers the phrase they've settled on—and steps up to the table, even leans on it, making the liqueur glasses rattle, and looks his parents directly in the eye.

"We've talked things over."

His aunt nods. One mother frowns, the face of the other mother brightens. One father closes his mouth, the other grins. The uncle is still examining the grass in his meadow.

She looks at him from the side: his shoulders are thrown back, his knees are locked, and his arms, too, form a straight line, although he is leaning forward among the bottles and plates of cold cuts. He seems completely oblivious of his unkempt hair for the moment, completely unaware of the hay clinging to his left ear. She hears him refer to a decision, she hears the words "finally say it," hears "secret," and "totally frank," and "We hope you'll understand."

They haven't talked things over—they didn't get that far on their walk—they simply debated at what point in the lane they might first be seen from the garden through the trees.

She looks at him, she listens to him, she feels surprised. It's not his words that surprise her but her own reaction. In any other situation, she would object at once to anyone who spoke for her—to a colleague who said "we" when he should have said "I," to a friend telling lies in her presence to someone else without batting an eye. But here, now, none of this disturbs her, she realizes she even likes the way he's handling the talk with their parents.

Her aunt says: "I was right. They're engaged."

THEY DON'T WASH up or change their clothes, they just wipe the mud from their hands with a handkerchief and carefully remove the specks of grass and flowers from each other's faces before driving back to the city without their parents.

She's still a little surprised at herself. She still hasn't contradicted him. But they've both been laughing about the scene in the garden: her aunt was right, they had all enjoyed a toast, and then the two of them had departed.

Now the sun is setting, and the meadows are imbued with a rosy glow. There are no hay wains, no cattle, they are alone on the broad country road. She's still holding the dirty handkerchief in her hand. She lets it flutter out the open window.

"Did you know your future mother-in-law always does that?"

He is looking at her, and can hardly keep from laughing, almost loses control of the car, and no, of course she didn't know that waving a handkerchief is something his family does, that all the women's handkerchiefs flutter good-bye when someone leaves: Till next time.

His laughter is infectious, and now she exaggerates the farewell gesture. The handkerchief slips from her hand. They see it in the rearview mirror, a white fleck whipped along the road by the wind from their car. But to what are they bidding farewell, after their bed upon the meadow, the rustling leaves, the exuberance, and now traveling at high speed along a country road as darkness slowly falls in the mild air? Is it Till next time, or Forever?

— •—

NOW HE KNOWS who she is. When he gazes down at the stage through his opera glasses it doesn't bother him that he can't see her Italian eyes when she sings into the darkness to a house full of strangers.

"Try to remember me."

He holds the opera glasses more calmly this evening, and his neighbors don't glance over at him, yet he keeps whispering to himself throughout the performance.

"I know it's you."

And afterward he'll see her eyes up close again. When the performance is over he won't go out the front entrance again like the rest of the audience, but, by the shortest route possible, to her dressing room. Just this afternoon she told him where the hidden door was, he just has to be careful not to lose his way.

If she has been at all unclear, if she has not been precise enough on the phone, he will simply stick with the officers, follow them at a certain distance. He will find the dressing room.

The officers are still in their boxes. Their blasé gaze sweeps the crowd as if the seats were empty. They don't realize that this look will be wiped from their faces when he strides past them down the corridor, goes straight to the dressing room, knocks, and is immediately admitted, while they are left standing outside. They will extinguish their cigarettes butts on the floor with a twist of their boots and mutter behind his back, but he won't hear them: the door will have closed behind him, and the singer will fall into his arms.

Who does he think he is, they'll think, this civilian who writes daily ads in the sky with vapor trails? He doesn't know whether these officers, who will continue to outrank him for some time, can hurt him in any way, by a passing remark to those running the opera or, if they found out about it, to his flight school. A little envy is all it takes: being shown up, offended, even losing face is something these men will not stand for, any more than he would. And an officer never gives up, he pursues his rival to the bitter end, he won't rest until his opponent is beaten into the ground once and for all.

Patience, just a little patience, his company commander told him at the start of the year. Now winter is approaching, and he longs for nothing more eagerly than his dark blue uniform. And then, his commander added, we will once more be the most highly respected branch in the service.

AFTER TWENTY YEARS nothing remains of all this. Our grandfather, who took part in the secret buildup of the air force and was allowed to don its uniform publicly for the first time in the spring of 1936, lost all interest when forced to remove his decorations at the end of the war. The air force was dissolved, but the uniform would have lasted much longer. Our grandfather gave up flying at the same time. He might look up at the sky from time to time, but he stays away from airfields.

When there is talk of rearmament, he notes it only from afar, he follows the discussions on the radio and in the newspapers; people are talking about it, and yet he has nothing to say. There is nothing secret about building up an air force this time.

Perhaps he could have rejoined the military as an instructor, but he never bothered to try. The first recruits were sworn in, but he didn't even take the cigar box from his desk to glance at the medals he'd saved. Perhaps he knew one or two names among the new officers, and former comrades quickly formed new groups, back in top shape again. But he just let the time pass.

Just recently, it seemed, the war had been over for a decade, and now a new army has been in place for two years. Our grandfather would gladly have made time stand still if he could, but he can only let it pass. He looks into his wife's eyes, their sparkle is gone, there was never a way to save them.

She left the stage before the war ended, but who knows, maybe she was thinking of taking up her career again, maybe there was always a distant desire. But with the onset of her illness a few years ago, the most distant hope has turned to dust. She no longer has the strength to sing even at home— she can barely whisper.

Our grandfather sits with both children by her bed, and although no one says anything, all four know: the voice of this opera singer will soon be silent.

At first some people said they were mismatched, the soprano and her pilot. For a long time he didn't know what his fiancée's colleagues said about him when he went with them to the inn after a performance. Then he stopped going along—his courses, the lack of sleep. Then she, too, stopped going. Perhaps he hadn't struck them as ridiculous at all, perhaps he simply seemed mysterious.

He won't ask our grandmother about that now. It's been quiet in the house for a long time: hardly a word is spoken, not in the kitchen, not in the living room, not before the children go to their bedroom, and certainly not in the sickroom. The parents have never told the children how serious their mother's situation is, that there is only one way for this illness to end.

One day in February, when the entire country lies deep in snow and the rivers are frozen, she loses consciousness. By early evening—the day has never brightened—the two young hands on the white bedcover move no longer.

WE DON'T KNOW if, at the end or ever, our grandmother's hands looked the way we imagine them.

The four of us sit together at the kitchen table and place our hands one atop the other, just as our grandfather sat in the kitchen with his two children after our grandmother died, his hands on the wood tabletop in the dull light, the rest of the room in darkness. They sat there, their hands together, looked each other in the eye, and swore that none of them would ever abandon the others.

Unlike our grandfather, we will remember this oath. He, who is so attached to secrets, will keep secret all his life why, scarcely nine months later, he married a second time. His second wife will also be a secret. Why he allowed this woman to drive his children from their home will be a secret. We will never learn why he didn't object when, shortly after their marriage, she forbade him any further contact with his children. Why he agreed to the ban she placed on any memory of his family.

We will never know what our grandmother's hands actually looked like.

———

AS HE ENTERS the dressing room in uniform one evening, he doesn't wait to be announced, perhaps he doesn't even knock. He wears the dark blue air force uniform, one year after his unsuccessful surprise visit. She can still recall the bouquet, the greeting card with the illegible, smudged script, the flower water. She could not make out her admirer's name, but she knew at once who they were from.

Now he stands before her, looks at her, and he's changed. It must have been in the newspaper, that the German air force is now official, but she hasn't had time to read a paper today. She can tell when she sees him that he won't spend another day in civilian clothes.

Before, he always came to congratulate her on her performance, which he always followed closely through the evening, singling out some aria or duet for special praise. But today it is the wardrobe mistress who steps up and congratulates him. She casts an expert eye on his uniform, praises the seams and the material, the excellent cut, and his boots in particular—he must have spent all afternoon polishing them.

His fiancée congratulates him, too, of course, gives him a kiss, feels his collar and fingers his tie, and the wardrobe mistress withdraws, although they're nowhere near finished removing her makeup and changing her clothes. He sits down, settling slowly onto a free stool. He's hardly said a word, perhaps the uniform isn't as comfortable as he had expected; one or two seams may need adjusting.

Perhaps he's exhausted, now that the tension of the wait has dissolved. It's not the exhaustion he feels when he leaves the classroom drained, nor hers after she's sung, when she slumps onto a stool after a performance, too weak to remove her own costume.

He looks doubtful, almost confused, sitting before her and staring into the corner where the costumes are hanging, the dresses, hats, stoles, and masks. He seems surprised that the dressing room isn't teeming with officers, now envious in that same old gray. He behaves as if someone must have hidden among the costumes and watched him from the moment he entered.

He turns and looks toward the mirror, sees the jars of makeup, cotton balls, and face cream as if he were seeing them for the first time.

YET OVER THE past year he's grown accustomed to this world, familiarized himself with her life. Behind the wings and with her colleagues he moves freely and naturally, like an old hand. He listens carefully, understands their slightest woes, gives advice as if he were in the theater himself: not simply a member of the audience but an opera singer, a lighting technician, a stagehand, or a director.

And he takes setbacks calmly. She remembers well the time they looked backstage together and destroyed the childlike ideas he had of opera scenery. He may have accepted the spotlights and the backdrop, they may have reminded him of his flights, of the searchlights and the cloud banks at certain altitudes.

The sets and stage props disturbed him more. He had to touch the crepe paper and the papier-mâché to be certain the whole thing was artificial, the lane and the birch grove. He realized it was all worthless when it wasn't in use— a garden table beside a weeping willow, off to one side, invisible from the auditorium, dumped there seemingly at random, meaningless. He hadn't understood that she sang each evening in the midst of all this, in this large, gloomy space. As if it were a matter of life and death.

They didn't talk about it onstage, but she sensed his deep disappointment. He fell silent and regained his form only when they had gone out to eat, and then he asked for more details. He wanted to know how hot the spotlight was, it must be sweltering onstage right from the start.

Yes, that was true, and even more so with heavy costumes, wigs, and makeup. He asked how bright the lights were, whether she could see anything at all in the auditorium. No. Did she ever make out an individual face in the crowd?

No. Nothing exists beyond the apron of the stage, only darkness. And if she seems to be looking some listener in the eyes, it's pure chance, an illusion.

PERHAPS HE FEELS a little out of place in his uniform, too, in a dressing room filled with costumes, where a costume in itself means nothing. Perhaps he realizes for the first time that a singer could just as well appear onstage in ordinary clothes and still captivate an audience.

Even words play no special role when she sings. She has to deliver the most banal, silly, improbable lyrics so that the listener gets goose bumps. Evening after evening she devotes her entire energy to the audience, no matter who they are, to strangers who have arrived for the sole purpose of being moved by her voice.

Perhaps he slowly senses that his dark blue cloth has not the slightest meaning in itself, just as her declarations of love mean nothing in and of themselves, or her vows of silence and secrecy, sung aloud for all to hear.

If he hadn't been so disappointed the first time they went backstage, she would have let him in on yet another secret. He might even have discovered this secret himself, since he was always drawn to them—since whenever a secret was in the offing, he seemed to turn up.

It's not true that she has no idea about the faces in the audience during a performance. When she steps onto the stage, the lights are indeed too bright, and even if they were lowered everything would still be a blur, since she concentrates so single-mindedly on her singing.

But there is a peephole. Before the lights are lowered in the auditorium, as the audience take their seats and the instruments are being tuned in the orchestra pit, amid the whispering and coughing, when the stage still hardly exists, the singers can peer out at the audience through a hole in the closed curtain.

She spies him almost every time: excited, fiddling with his program and opera glasses, his gaze trained on the officers, his restlessness decreasing somewhat from performance to performance. Before the lights go down and the applause begins and everyone is waved away from the curtain, she can see him clearly every evening through the peephole, just for a moment. But that moment is enough.

For over six months now, she has recognized him by his uniform alone. She knows he always sits in the first circle, on the right, in the second row. Then one evening no dark blue appears in the accustomed spot. Nor is anyone else sitting there. The seat is empty. Her fiancé has disappeared.

· silences ·

THE DARKNESS BEYOND the peephole after the light has
gone out in the hall might well brighten again if someone
pushes the switch, but the original scene will have vanished:
nothing remains of the lovers on the stairs, whose brief kiss
gave promise of merging into a true embrace just as the
light went out. Merely an empty stairwell, a roughly plas-
tered wall. Nothing remains when I close my eyes but the
picture I invented in that darkened interval.

What I can't see I must invent. I must fill in the pictures
myself if I want to see something. There is no other possibility. Every adult knows this, having learned that we need
the images we invent. Perhaps we recognize an adult by just
this characteristic insight. When one is a child or even an
adolescent, one's own inventions appear to be possibilities
behind which reality lies hidden, and we believe that reality
will appear someday, causing the invented images to gradually recede into darkness.

Today, at the peephole, I am no longer a child. I used

to want to discover something out there, and I was impatient if I watched for a long time and nothing happened—like someone waiting by a phone that never rings. I wanted to knock on the door, to lure the neighbors into the hall with the muffled sounds.

This impatience lessened over time, and I slowly came to understand that the pictures and stories I witnessed differed in no way, in the final analysis, from those that had no witnesses. I was unable to see this as a child, and at twenty I would have denied it: I had to turn thirty before I realized what it meant to be an adult, although I was still far from being one myself. For even today, sometimes I want to poke my finger through the peephole like a child, and touch what lies beyond it.

At the same time, looking back, I see that there is a sense in which I began to grow up when I first discovered the peephole. In a desperate attempt to touch the reality before my eyes, my fingertips encountered for the first time the cool, smooth lens. No matter how often I breathed on the glass and tried to wipe it clean, the fingerprints remained. Trying to remove that dull film, I fought against an intuition that develops into a certainty for every grown-up: I had long since begun to fill in the blurred blind spots with my own imagination.

I HAVE NO family album. It would not occur to me to photograph anything now. I no longer stand around uneasily, not knowing what to do when there's no chance for real pictures. In this way the old photo album we pulled from the bookcase one spring afternoon twenty years ago might be thought of as having been our school—even if our first feeling on looking through it was one of disappointment, almost pain, because we couldn't find any pictures of our grandmother and her Italian eyes.

We longed for a picture. We always hoped to see our grandmother's eyes someday, even by accident, when we no longer expected to: sometime in the future, with a mixture of gentle shock and unconditional trust, we would look into those eyes.

My cousins' parents don't listen to opera, but we still rummage through their records. We hadn't expected the photo album either, so perhaps we will find its counterpart now, a recording of our grandmother, spotted and dusty, unplayed since her death. For the first time, we take a closer look at the record covers: a man with his coat collar turned up, raindrops glistening in his hair; another man, in sunglasses, a gold chain on his bare chest. We see several men with pistols, and they all have Italian eyes, but we never find a woman who bears even the slightest resemblance to our grandmother.

At the record shop we ask for the classical section. The salesman reacts doubtfully when we mention our grandmother's name. He doesn't seem very well informed: he's sorry, but none of her records are currently available. We refuse to be put off. We scrutinize performers, directors, performance dates; the records are much too new, but we're still certain that by the time we've reached the last opera album she'll be looking out at us.

Not one single picture, not even her name in small print. Our Italian opera singer story will never find credible support, there's no evidence we can use to silence the neighborhood kids. Paulina, Carl, and Nora are ready to take leave of our grandmother.

I was never convinced we could come up with some

wildly successful soprano in Italy. When the others told me about her, I felt an involuntary twinge of fear that I would be drawn into something from which there might be no escape. Our grandmother, I sensed, could still be troubling me when the other three had long since forgotten her.

But now that they all suddenly agree to give up our grandmother's story, something in me resists. An opposition so strong you would have thought the whole idea had been mine in the first place. A disappointment, a feeling in the pit of my stomach as if I were falling into an abyss, the same feeling I had when I first heard the stories about her. Surprising even myself, I try to talk them out of their plan. They are surprised, too, for I hardly ever spoke when earlier decisions were being made, and I have never tried to talk them into anything before.

Why should we bow to demands for proof? We can't drop the opera singer just to make the neighborhood kids happy, that would be like surrendering. It's our own grandmother, our own story, we don't have to share her with anyone. We've spent too much effort on this portrait to erase its contours now.

If photos of our own faces always seem like caricatures, if we don't trust them, why rely on photos of our grandmother?

We didn't need a photo of her Italian eyes, we already knew them better than any other eyes, because we saw them every day growing up. We still see them now, when we look at each other.

⏤

WE WERE NO LONGER children, and our visit to the record store represented a final, almost desperate attempt to discover something the way a child would: we dig through things, rummage about, pull a veil aside, and suddenly emerge with something surprising. We wanted to find the opera singer the way we found the fondant factory, but our grandmother was a totally different type of discovery, one of the sort I still make today: we were drawn to her precisely because she was invisible.

I doubt we would have paid any attention at all to a grandmother whose pictures were kept in a family album. Our parents might have tried to awaken our interest in the opera singer, showed us pictures over and over, repeated the same old stories about their parents. Every photograph, no matter how innocuous, points to an event we would never think to ask about. Our grandparents' story is all there in the photographs, we learn how they met, how the family wound up with the opera glasses, how they lost them during the war. We listen with one ear to the story of this or that expensive dress our grandmother wore for some performance in Berlin during the Olympic Games.

We know the stories about our grandfather, whose air force unit prepared for action in the newly completed Olympic stadium before the athletes arrived. We are no longer amazed that our grandparents watched the games being broadcast on television. The newly engaged couple met secretly in a television café in the city, nothing special for us today, it's lost all its excitement, we wait for the end, the going-away party for our grandfather on the eve of his departure for an unknown destination.

Our parents get so thoroughly lost in details, which they themselves must know by hearsay only, that we soon grow impatient and think we know all there is to know about our grandparents. It never occurs to us that each picture hides a secret, that every fact may conceal another.

Grandparents we could visit on holidays would have

differed little from the rest of our relations at the rare family gatherings. If our grandmother had not died young, or if we had at least known our grandfather, we would not have gone in search of an opera singer, and that search would not have led us toward further discoveries.

PERHAPS IT IS simply too late when we finally ask my cousins' parents about our grandmother. By then we have our own image of her, one we don't want to see blurred, let alone destroyed. And so we ask half-heartedly, scarcely paying attention, simply confirming that our parents can't offer any real help.

And yet they try their best. They can't help but notice how interested we are in our grandparents, our whispered conversations have put them on the trail, some sentence broken off when an adult passes by. Without prying, they understand, and look for some unobtrusive opportunity to aid us in our search. This becomes clear on our Easter outing, which leaves us feeling quite ambivalent. On the one hand we are aided in our quest; on the other, this strengthens the feeling that our parents can't be trusted, since they have clearly been spying on us ever since we discovered the photo album.

The outing is supposed to be a surprise. We head out into the countryside, almost at random, it seems, and we still haven't figured out what all the mystery is about when, in a perfectly ordinary village, my cousins' parents point to a large building—in comparison to the surrounding farmhouses, it seems huge. It is whitewashed from top to bottom, and some sections are tiled—the entire edifice set off, even at a distance, from the rest of the brick buildings in the village.

Here my cousins' father spent part of his childhood, perhaps barely two years, yet that period, which ended with the end of the war, remains clearly etched in his memory, more clearly than much that came after. Our grandmother's own uncle ran the dairy farm that stands before us, and other relatives on his mother's side lived on the premises and in the surrounding houses. The handsomest home was the dairy villa and garden up the street, where he and his mother moved after their apartment in the city had been destroyed in an air raid.

At home my uncle would have had to go to school, but no one worried about that here, he could watch the girls making cheese and visit the cows. And farms had cages filled with songbirds in those days. My uncle enjoyed his time in the village, even though the farmers viewed him and his mother with suspicion. The officer's young wife, an opera singer before the war, takes up lodgings with her son at the home of the richest family in the area. When everyone else was having to make do with a dab of margarine smeared on their bread, these urban refugees had butter every day.

We've seen the collapsed, rubble-filled house in the photo album. The model airplane in a later picture appears to dangle above the table in the living room of the dairy villa; perhaps the bomber still circles behind those curtains today.

We consider the pictures of this dairy carefully, the garden with its ancient trees rising over the roof of the villa, and the fields beyond the river as we pass. Lying in bed that evening, when we are sure no one is listening, we create a picture from those elements. And we know from the start that we won't share it with anyone, not with those who showed us the dairy, nor with the neighborhood kids.

In that village, in those fields, we see our grandparents meet again long after their youthful friendship. A chance encounter that surprises them both, but they seem immediately at home with one another. A summer day in the midthirties: no one will ever learn of it, no one is watching, my uncle won't arrive in the world for a few years yet, it will be another decade before my mother is born.

So we four are the only ones who know of this meeting. Our grandmother can no longer share those memories, and our grandfather has withdrawn into silence.

It was near this villa that our grandparents fell in love, discovered that they had always been in love. It was here that our family history began.

WE DISCOVER the fondant factory and the old photo album just after the start of the Easter holidays in 1977, when I am almost twelve years old. The time when boys and girls walked hand in hand now lies behind me. Paulina, who is only slightly older than I am, no longer spends time with boys her own age either. I am the only exception, and she would probably not admit it to her friends. Nora is well past this age; she may be holding hands again, but not so openly that we would catch her. Carl and Paulina know from the schoolyard how much attention Nora attracts, even among the older boys. Countless rumors abound, but none have yet been verified. Nora is reserved, no one knows what sort of letters she exchanges with her pen pal in France. Carl stands on his own between us, with hands neither young nor old: he doesn't fight with girls anymore, but he would not dare to stroke their hair.

There are profound differences among us, and it would be no surprise if we barely spoke to one another. Perhaps it is only thanks to our grandparents that we are in league: none of us could have thought up the meeting between the young opera singer and the young air force officer without the help of the others.

This mutual creation welds us together, but in retrospect it seems as if the story we invented was the initial step in the slow dissolution of our group, the origin of our increasing isolation as individuals.

We belong to the family of the scattered and silenced, other than our parents and ourselves we have no one to turn to. And now we are starting to distance ourselves from our parents, to withdraw, allowing no one to share in our inventions. Even our summer holidays together are spent over family photos, some of which have disappeared and some of which were never taken, and when I return home from my fall holiday at their place, everything has changed but our eyes.

First, we withdraw from our parents. Shortly thereafter Nora breaks with them forever. Then my cousins' parents divorce. This has been in the air for a long time—misunderstandings, suspicion, and a silence that makes my aunt accuse my uncle of behaving just like his father. Finally our group falls apart; I never hear from Carl or Nora again after that fall holiday. Paulina is the only one I'm still in contact with, we're the only ones in the family who haven't lost touch. We hold fast to the story of our grandparents, and perhaps that is the only thing that binds us.

IT'S NOT ALWAYS easy to make up stories we can all agree on. There are differences of opinion and arguments from the start.

There is a serious error in our grandparents' outing on the meadow, Carl explains to us. He is bothered by the description of our grandfather, but the rest of us like it the way it is. Carl just shakes his head: it might have been about the way we imagine it, the country outing, the field, the walk back to the dairy. But a soldier, and our grandfather was a soldier, after all, would never talk that much, tell so many stories, give impromptu speeches. It's a soldier's duty to keep his mouth closed, it's always been that way, and our grandfather would have been no exception. On the contrary, reticence was always his most striking characteristic.

And our grandparents aren't embarrassed that afternoon. It's a simple matter of honor, a solemn oath that fits our grandfather. As far as he's concerned, he's made a vow to our grandmother in the field that needs no repetition. In fact, repeating the vow would have weakened it. Had he done so, our grandfather would have undermined everything he had said.

As the two drive back to the city that evening, they say little—a few words about the sunset, the week that lies ahead. Then they slowly fall silent as they consider their work, their apartments, separately, just glancing cautiously now and then at their stained, rumpled clothing. Wordlessly, he drops her off at her house. They part silently, barely looking at each other.

But Carl sees a basic difficulty with this version: if the vow had been made just once, our grandparents' story would have ended that afternoon. Unless our grandfather repeats his declaration of love, there will be no wedding, no children, and the grandchildren, too, will remain mere inventions.

And on the other hand everything wouldn't have ended when our grandmother died. If vows had been so important to our grandfather, he would have stayed with his children instead of bringing a second wife home who forced him to break off all contact with his family. We would still be in touch today, our grandfather would tell us about the opera singer, we wouldn't seek in vain for our grandmother in the photo album.

But Carl still maintains that silence has marked our family from the very beginning. He's so devoted to this image that he's strongly opposed to asking the parents for further details. It takes great skill to elicit information from someone without revealing anything about yourself. We simply aren't clever enough to do so yet.

Nora, on the other hand, is bothered by our game of hide-and-seek, it makes her feel uneasy. We should speak openly with my cousins' parents: then they would have to be open with us, too, and that would be the easiest way to find out why the photos of our grandmother disappeared. In Carl's opinion, our openness will only lead to endless discussions that, far from clarifying our images, might veil them even more thoroughly. Nora should know her parents' tactics well, since on some evenings she is allowed to stay in the living room with them longer than the rest of us. The adults discuss a topic they disagree on and finally turn to Nora for her opinion. Everyone waits eagerly for her comment, each hoping for her support so they can nod to the circle and say, "You see, that's what I said," or, "Well, there's a completely unbiased view for a change." But they are soon at loggerheads again, none of them pay any further attention to Nora, and in the end she goes off to bed without having learned anything new.

Just listening quietly, however, sitting there silently, not only gets you somewhere but proves more reliable. Nora has her own secrets; if she hadn't, she would read us the letters from her unknown pen pal.

Before Carl and Nora can start to fight, Paulina and I suggest a compromise that, after some initial hesitation, they find acceptable: since I'm the youngest of the four and am just visiting, my cousins' parents can hardly turn me down if I take on the task of interrogating them.

Nevertheless, over the next few days I learn nothing more about our grandmother than what we've already imagined ourselves. I don't think their parents are hiding anything from me, but with every memory of our grandmother another figure enters the picture, a nameless woman who has driven our family apart: the Old Lady.

—

NOT SOMEONE WE'VE made up. A living person. Not from the underworld, nor the woods, nor the void. Just a few streets away from us. From a house at the other end of the neighborhood—undistinguished in any way from the others, except for the peephole in the door—she rules over all. She rules her front garden, the path to her house, the entire outskirts of town right up to our hill. She rules our grandfather, and through him she rules his descendants, and thus, in the final analysis, she rules us as well: she has ruled since time immemorial, since time itself was unknown, for her rule began at a time when none of the four of us was yet in the world.

The neighborhood kids have the bogeyman or the black cook; we have the Old Lady. Scarier than any other figure, no Huitzilopochtli can touch her. Even our parents fear her. This may be why they have never told us her name: speaking it aloud might conjure her up before us, like a spirit.

OUR GRANDFATHER has only recently married her, and the death of their mother is still vividly present for his two children, when the Old Lady attacks all three with an ax.

"I'll kill you all."

The children flee to the street, the neighbors stand at the front garden fence, called forth by the screams coming from the house. The noise comes from the stairs, or the hall, then is softened, muffled as the Old Lady moves into the living room. The splintering sounds indicate that she has attacked the sideboard or the wall unit with the ax. The neighbors wonder where our grandfather is—in the bedroom? locked in the guest bathroom?

"I'll kill you all."

The sentence is muffled, dies away, a neighbor has called the police. The children are safe, where is her husband? The police hesitate: they might fall victim to the blow of an ax. They could release the safety catches on their weapons and aim them at the Old Lady the instant the ax appears. Instead, they radio for a doctor.

By the time the ambulance arrives the police have sent all the neighbors back into their homes and the children are gone. There are whispers, everything is quiet, there's no more noise from the house. Because it's already dark, it's difficult to see much—just what the blue light of the ambulance strikes, alien, flickering, brief. Foreheads, the bridge of a nose. A doctor's smock, handguns. And finally, a straitjacket appears.

Over the next few days, things are cleaned up and put back in order. The children pick wood splinters from the living-room carpet: the vacuum can't get to them, it's only good for scraps of wallpaper and bits of plaster.

Our grandfather plasters over the hole by the door frame, brings the trestle table up from the basement. He holds the end of the wallpaper roll, the children make sure the pattern matches up. The three of them move the furniture outside to be taken to the dump. Together they try to buy identical pieces to replace them.

When the Old Lady is released from medical observation, they want her to return to a fully restored house. They want to give her the impression that nothing has changed since that early afternoon, that her outburst never took place. No ax.

THE IMAGE OF the Old Lady running through the house with her ax, screaming that sentence over and over, makes such an impression on our grandfather, my uncle, and my mother, that even my cousins and I feel as if we'd seen it with our own eyes.

My aunt never knew our grandmother, and the Old Lady made sure from the start of the marriage that no trace remained of her. My aunt didn't even know much about her father-in-law, although he lived nearby. She only met him a few times, secretly, in the city—that harassed man who spoke in a near-whisper and was scared to death of his Old Lady. His place at the table remained empty at her wedding, and at the subsequent baptisms of her three children.

My uncle left the house soon after those blows with the ax. Even my aunt never learned much from him about the time before that. Even now, he still thinks about his mother's death, and how the Old Lady turned up in our grandfather's life, and in our family. Although these events now lie twenty years in the past, they still seem so vivid to our uncle that they might have happened yesterday.

That's all my aunt can tell me: the Old Lady pushed her way permanently into the picture. Our parents were at the mercy of the image of the Old Lady and her ax, just as our grandfather was at the mercy of the Old Lady herself.

I ask my uncle, who never mentioned him at the village dairy, about our grandfather. He was serving in the war and didn't visit often; when my uncle was a small child he hardly saw his father. He was in the air force, that was all my uncle knew. Later, when he wanted to ask his father about it, the family's entire attention was devoted to our grandmother's illness. Nothing mattered but her and her future, there was no interest in our grandfather's past. When our grandmother died, talk was soon reduced to the bare essentials. And today my uncle no longer has a father.

The Old Lady pushes her way into the picture again: she wants to block out our grandmother entirely. Today my uncle can't even remember the color of his mother's eyes.

As far as I can gather from what he says, murder plots must have been hatched soon after the Old Lady came on the scene, since the entire family—perhaps even our grandfather—wished she were dead. At the time, no one would have considered this a crime. Various possibilities were thought through and rejected, for their attention was concentrated primarily on how to do it, and no justification seemed necessary: if they wanted to restore their family, or at least keep it from falling further apart, the Old Lady had to be killed. No matter how uncomfortable she felt in the family she'd married into, she had no intention of leaving it again.

These plans were never carried out, either because they were never fully developed or our parents could never get up the courage. Perhaps these old murder plans still weigh on them, give them a guilty conscience: What if they had managed to do away with the Old Lady back then, extinguish her from their family, their life, the world?

When I was small, I almost met her once. I must have been about three years old, and my grandfather was finally going to get to see his grandson, whom he'd known up to then only from photos. My parents had arranged a secret meeting at his office. We sought out the right floor and door in the office building. But before we could gain entrance by the prearranged knock on the door, my parents paused: they had heard steps on the stairs behind us. I was pulled into the next-best hiding place, an angle between two pieces of old office furniture. The look with which they warned me to keep absolutely still betrayed a fear I had never seen in them before. It wasn't until we had fled back into the street without having seen my grandfather that what had happened in the hall gradually dawned on me: my parents had recognized the footsteps of the Old Lady. We had barely escaped her.

A threat of deadly danger emanated from the Old Lady. And yet it's not at all clear to me what could have happened to us if we had met her there at the office.

Two or perhaps three years later, our parents take the four of us out near the redoubt to see the house where the Old Lady lives with our grandfather. This time the fear is combined with a sense of challenge, we park our car across the street, the motor is running, the Old Lady can't help but notice us. She will realize she is being spied on quite openly now, she'll know immediately who we are, even if she can't read our license plate through the peephole in her door. Our faces don't mean anything to her, it's been a long time since our parents sent photos of family and friends to their father. The Old Lady quickly discovered this secret channel and foiled any further exchange of information.

Our parents are dominated by their fear that the Old Lady will actually appear one day. Yet they are always talking about her, as if they needed to be sure she exists. The moment the conversation turns to our grandmother's death and the subsequent breakup of our family, the subject of the Old Lady comes up, for her very presence led to that dissolution. But in order to prove that their murder plans have come to naught, they must keep the Old Lady in sight: she still exists, she lives not far away, she maintains her power. She can't be dead.

We four are sitting in the backseat, taking turns looking out the side window: I had forgotten over time why we were there, but I can remember our mood to this day. Even then we probably didn't know exactly who we were looking for. Our grandfather's second wife: that didn't mean much to us, since we had never seen her or our grandfather before. Our fear, our parents' fear, might have simply dissolved if one of us had stepped out and rung our grandfather's doorbell. The door opens, an old couple stands there, saying nothing, a skeptical look, nothing special.

But the Old Lady, that unfathomable figure, couldn't be caught by such simple means. She didn't show herself back then, nor have we seen her since.

We must protect our grandmother from this figure. The Old Lady has no face of her own, she consists merely of a dark, faded spot that takes on the faces of others.

No one can remember the color of our grandmother's eyes. We should be happy that we didn't turn to our parents from the start. By the time we asked them what her eyes were like, it was probably too late to change the Italian eyes we had invented. A watery blue could not have masked the brown.

But nothing, not even a hint of color, shimmers forth from the faded picture. If we had not long since seen those deep, dark eyes in our grandmother's face, her gaze would have remained blank forever.

Whenever we speak of someone as having the powers of

a magician or medium, we always have in mind strange rituals with dolls and needles, blood and fingernails. Images of spiritualists sitting at tables in darkened rooms, the medium in a trance, nothing but cheap tricks. But perhaps it is words alone that make a difference. Anyone who knows how to release the undead from their spell, whoever can call forth the spirits of the departed, depends on everyone present believing what he says. Smoke, chicken feathers, or ancestral dolls may be there only to prevent a disturbing realization—perhaps a barely tolerable one, given its implications: Whoever wants to awaken the dead or dispense with the living needs nothing but words.

After her death, one sentence was enough to exile our grandmother from our parents' minds: "I'll kill you all."

<hr>

I DON'T HAVE a family album. No photo could show how the Old Lady tries to hide the face of our grandmother, how in response we put all our energy into banishing this dark spot from her picture, pushing the Old Lady out of the way. And how in the time that follows, instead of disappearing, the Old Lady begins to encroach on other, real figures around us: on the toothless woman who works as a supervisor, writes letters of complaint, and pulls our parents aside to grumble about us. A shadow flits across her face; while we watch her from our hiding place, her features seem to blur—the sunken lips, the deep wrinkles around her mouth—and the longer we watch this woman through the leaves, the more she resembles the Old Lady.

Or the mentally ill woman who lives in a trailer on the outskirts of town. She must still have been a child when her father supposedly chased off a policeman who had arrived to take the daughter to school. Others said they wanted to take her away to a home. She hasn't been seen for the last twenty years or so, she only leaves the trailer under cover of darkness. She might look something like the Old Lady.

The oddest person on the hill is the Pigeon Man, who lives next door to us, who has been in the area longer than anyone else. Originally, they say, there was no elevation in the landscape—just a garbage dump in the field, run by the city. The hill is the highest point in the area today only because the garbage finally piled up so high that a hill arose from the pit. The Pigeon Man was supposedly the first person to settle here on the hill, shortly after the war, when the garbage dump was used for the rubble from the destroyed city. Every day he stands behind his garden fence with a look that seems to say: "I'll kill you all."

What I do have is an object that we saw for the first time in that old photo album: a small ceramic figurine, apparently a dancer, with eyes half closed, arms over her head in an elegant pose, her dance costume slowly turning shabby, brittle, yellow. A figurine some tourist might have brought home as a souvenir. We called it the Spanish doll. But it isn't the one in the photograph, it didn't come from our grandfather. It belonged to the Pigeon Man.

THERE ARE NO pictures of our group on holiday together, and no photos from the time we began to drift apart: in those, each of us would have been seen alone, increasingly indistinct, blurred, until finally the names of Carl and Nora stand beneath blank photos, as if the photographer had forgotten to remove the cover from the lens. They fought a lot as children, they seemed to be totally different, yet they were hardly grown when they lost their way in the dark in similar fashion.

I don't know if Carl disappeared because he wanted to avoid military service or if he had already gone to Scandinavia to spend the rest of his school days on a horse farm in Denmark or Norway. Carl divulged so little about himself that I wouldn't be surprised if someone told me that he'd volunteered for the army at sixteen and was still a professional soldier today.

Nora apparently made her first attempt to break away from the family during the fall holidays, but her plans fell through without any of us or her parents ever finding out about them. She spent little time at home after the holidays, but her parents didn't notice until the school reported that she hadn't attended for weeks. One evening around Christmas she was brought home by the police. She had tried to run off to France with a friend, but they had been stopped at the border. Her letters to her friend were meant to throw her family off the track. He wasn't in France, he lived in town. Nora waited for her eighteenth birthday, then left home that same morning for good.

A few years ago I thought I spotted Nora in the audience at the opera. The back of a head in the stalls below, a woman's hands, the way she held the program, placed the opera glasses before her eyes. Everything pointed to Nora, but I had to see her eyes to be sure. As soon as intermission started I hurried downstairs, but the woman was not in her seat, nor was she at the side entrance. I searched the crowd, went to the bar, jostled other people, but Nora had disappeared. Perhaps she left at intermission, and I should have looked for her by the taxis.

In retrospect, it was not difficult to believe that Nora truly had disappeared. In the same year that her torturing need arose to discover the reality behind appearances, to remain alert and watchful, she had secretly begun to make herself invisible. Nora felt she must question everything and never trust surface impressions, but she could never do this to her complete satisfaction. She continued searching for the truth until her breakdown. She no longer trusted anyone: everyone around her seemed blind, a prey to incomprehensible lies. Her parents may have feared that someday, while waiting in line at the bank or at the post office, they would encounter Nora's gaze coming from some crude passport photo, and that her cold, harassed expression would differ in no way from those of the other wanted men and women on the poster.

Of the three, I had always been closest to Paulina, and even today I trust her more than anyone else I know. We used to pretend we were brother and sister, that our parents had only adopted us. Fear and an exciting tension were mixed in this fantasy, and we pursued our invented parents, our invented lives, until our Italian eyes drew us back.

My cousins always struck me as different from one another. They were certainly siblings, but each of them had such distinct characteristics that this fact seemed impossible. Still, they formed a group, two sisters and a brother. There was no need to dwell on this, except when I joined them. I was their relation, but as an only child I wasn't accustomed to being around other children. I was clearly different from them, and no matter how much I wanted then to be a part of their group, in retrospect I realize that I profited from always being forced to observe Nora, Carl, and Paulina from an outsider's perspective.

At that time my cousins' various characteristics struck me as incompatible, but now I know that in spite of their contradictions they melded together. I see this in myself as well: Like Nora, I seek the reality behind appearances. Like Paulina, I fill in pictures. Like Carl, I keep secrets.

ONLY ONE PERSON at a time can look through a peephole. The four of us tried it together once when we were visiting someone. We took turns, each looking out into the hall while the others stood guard us from behind. But this led to constant squabbles—one person saw something the next one didn't—and with the first hissed curses an adult would appear in the darkened hall, and we would flee.

I'm the only one of us four still there. I stand at the peephole and see things no one has ever seen before. I look beyond the hall, into the apartment across the way. Through the peephole, I see more than what presents itself to me at the moment, I see what happened before I stood at the peephole. But I'm not sure I want to see those images.

HIS WIFE THREW away the photo albums. The toys, the drawings, the comic books. She took the opera programs, everything she could find, and threw all of it in the trash—or in the stove, if the place was heated by a stove back then, we'd have to ask our grandfather, he helped build the housing development. I don't know how she got hold of an ax; it may have been used to chop kindling in the basement or garden, which means there would have been a stove for the photos, albums, and programs.

The Old Lady doesn't dispose of the photos and letters behind our grandfather's back; the things she can't burn she throws out in the trash while he watches. She, who has no interest in opera, pulls out one opera program after the other. If there's an opera on television, our grandfather must switch on the set in secret or visit a friend. He has kept all the programs in order of the operas' premieres or of his attendance, dated and tied with a ribbon. Now the Old Lady pulls the programs one by one from the bundle and tosses them through the stove door, because otherwise the fire might go out; paper doesn't burn well.

Programs with photos of his first wife, but the Old Lady doesn't look through them, she's already sure they have something to do with the opera singer, and she doesn't look at the rehearsal photos either. He stands by the stove, she stirs the fire with the poker, sparks rise, the stove plate glows, there's no other light in the kitchen, winter is coming, and they stand silently. The children—his children—have been sent to bed.

But perhaps the children are standing at the foot of the stairs in their nightshirts, in the dark, and are looking at the kitchen door. All they see is the red glimmer, a strip of light under the door, and it's cold at the bottom of the stairs, but they don't notice. They hear the sound of paper being torn, stuffed in, they hear the clang of iron; they don't hear anyone talking, but they know they're in the kitchen.

Perhaps it wasn't long ago that our grandfather looked at the rehearsal photos for the last time. The Old Lady gathers the albums without looking at them, the light of the fire falls on her hands, she takes family albums and individual pictures. Then there is indeed talk in the warm kitchen and the kids take off, they're heading upstairs. Where are the negatives?

The air, flakes, soot, sparks on the apron of the stove, a red glimmer under the door, no, a pale glimmer, I don't know if memories are in color.

I see the picture when I stand at the window in the night. It's one of those nights when I can't sleep, so I stare out into the darkness until the first shades appear, the gray of morn, then colors. Cardboard, not padded plastic: an album that would have been hard to tear up and burn. I stand at the window, it's quiet, it's snowing, I see the picture. The Old Lady's hate is directed at the dead.

The kids are still at the foot of the stairs, no peephole in the kitchen door, of course. I don't know if the Old Lady sees pictures in her hate. Black-and-white perhaps, too faint for colors to appear, or too quickly faded and gone. Colors perhaps, but not living colors.

At least one album escaped the fire, an entire period is not lost, of course she examined the pictures closely beforehand. The snowfall is heavier, I go out, the snow falls softly, I see the tips of my shoes, the snow will leave traces. Did he hand over the negatives?

Paper catches fire, photos crumple in the embers; they're flat for just a moment, then they blister, and a hand, its fingers curled tightly around a poker, impatient to shove in more torn paper, quickly. A picture no one could place in his family album. In the living room, in the hallway, drifting upstairs from the kitchen, a strange smell, the negatives. The soot, the smoke, and the stink, our grandfather put up with it all.

I don't know whether memories are seen in color, but in the dark you see only black and white. I see myself at night in the streets, I see the Old Lady in the kitchen, I stop, I look up at the sky, from which the flakes descend on me. The hand at the stove, the light at night, or is this hand and the heat and the sparks, wearing an oven mitt, an asbestos glove? And the opera glasses?

My hand, sinking in the snow—freshly fallen, with ice beneath, melted by day and frozen again in the night. My spread right hand: on its back, two dark points, barely visible, warts perhaps, and by the first joint of the index finger a short scar, from a bite when I was around eleven, the broad back of my hand, with fine hair on its side and no veins, no spots.

I slowly approach the ground, and my five fingers leave an imprint in the snow in front of my shoes. My fingernails have always been sensitive. The Old Lady has never seen my hand, just as I've never seen hers, not her hand as she grips the ax handle, not even her hand as she pulls the curtain slightly aside to look out.

Nor have I seen how her hand grasps the border of the curtain, how her fingers clutch the fabric. I've never seen this hand jerk the curtain down from the rod. Or how both, the hand and the curtain, perhaps the rod too, disappear below the sill.

I don't know if the Old Lady and our grandfather ever had a family album of their own. I watch the photos burn.

· messengers ·

SHE'S NOT SURE where her husband is when she hears the telephone ring. From her chair in the living room it's not easy to see into the hall. She can't tell if her husband is by the phone. Perhaps he's upstairs looking out the bedroom window. Perhaps he's in the garage with his car. She should know. She usually does. The phone is still ringing, but she won't go to get it.

Perhaps her husband has quietly descended the stairs, is standing by the phone, holding his breath so she can't hear him, staring at the dial, the receiver, not knowing if he should pick it up. He knows she's in the living room, sitting in her armchair. He doesn't dare answer it.

She should have known the phone would ring this morning, that someone would try to call. She shouldn't have gone to the living room, she should have stayed in the kitchen after breakfast, she can see the stairs more easily from there, even if it's only the shadow of someone on the phone.

It's not easy to see into the hallway. The telephone is in

a niche beside the door to the living room. She's tried all sorts of things, she's moved her chair, sat at the dining-room table reading a newspaper, but nothing helps: the telephone is lost in the gloom. A longer cord. But then it would ring right next to her. And she wouldn't see anything at all from the kitchen.

The telephone has finally stopped ringing. Perhaps her husband is not in the hall, perhaps he didn't hear the phone ring. She needs one of those mirrors to see around corners. Like the rearview mirror on a car, or mounted on a kitchen or bedroom window, the husband still in bed after the night shift, the wife standing at the sink, both keeping an eye on the front door.

She doesn't want calls. Sometimes the telephone rings and there's no one there. She doesn't know what that means. Perhaps it's the kids who go to a phone booth and waste their pocket money on anonymous calls. Just schoolkids, but it still seems menacing when they don't speak, when all they want to do is hear strangers answer, become frightened, give themselves away. Sometimes a whisper or a giggle, half-stifled, distant, in the background, as if the kids were covering the mouthpiece with a handkerchief. Or just a faint noise on the line.

Perhaps her husband was in the hall after all, perhaps he's still there, the telephone no longer ringing because he's holding it to his ear. She can't hear anything. He may be listening, listening to the person who called. Nothing, no sound from the hall, no one breathing. She's not absolutely sure. She doesn't get up, she doesn't go to see. She'll find out later anyway.

She hears the front door, hears her husband's shoes as he wipes them on the mat, so loudly that he seems to be trying to lead her down a false trail. He hasn't entered the house, he has simply opened the door from the inside and let it fall shut again. He knows how sensitive she is, that she feels the draft. From her chair she can't see as far as the coatrack, perhaps his jacket was hanging there just a moment or two ago.

She won't ask, "Who was on the phone?"

He would only answer, "No one."

In the kitchen she turns on the radio, low enough that she can still hear her husband's footsteps on the carpet, for there may be another call this morning. Even if it is only schoolkids. She's heard the cashiers at the supermarket talking about a gang of kids on the hill across the way who are causing trouble around the neighborhood, sometimes ranging as far as the redoubt. Women on the street clutch their purses when they hear a moped, a roar approaches from behind, the shopping bag falls to the ground. At night, the glow of fires on the hill, the sudden rattle of Venetian blinds, yells, howls, perhaps it's just a dog. And shots have been heard.

AT THE BEDROOM window she lightly parts the curtain, peers out at the slanting rays of the sun falling into the garden. It's still cold. Night frost, but no snow. A late spring this year. She sees the tree outside the window, her hand on the curtain. She can feel, close to the windowpane, that the glass is cold. The bedroom is never heated; she should remove her hand from the curtain.

At breakfast her husband was wearing street shoes, ready for work, his overloaded briefcase leaning against the table leg. She doesn't know what he drags to the office each day. He held the newspaper spread out in front of him; it was already light outside. It's been light for the past few weeks now when he leaves for work in the morning, the kitchen still cold, the radio on. Today he left the newspaper on the table, open to the obituaries, and said he would be back a little later than usual—he has a doctor's appointment this afternoon.

The ground in the cemeteries is gradually softening. She doesn't know whether her husband will visit the cemetery later that afternoon, doesn't know if he still secretly visits the grave of his first wife from time to time. She asked him, just once, early on, when his children still lived with them, and he answered, "No." That's all he said, no explanations, no evasions, not even a hint of fake astonishment—"What makes you ask that?"—tacked onto his "No." Not even a complete sentence. Just the one word. "No," and then he changed the subject. Or perhaps they both fell silent.

The days grow longer, and it gets lighter in the morning. She should release the curtain, the windowpane is too cold; she should start her morning chores, set the trash outside the door, go through the house slowly with the mop. She sees the spiderweb on the curtain rod—in the spring the spiders aren't fat anymore, they're worn, withered, if indeed they made it through the winter and aren't hanging dead and dry in the dusty webs.

He simply said "no." She doesn't recall if his children were there, and to this day she hasn't asked again. Besides, she thinks he's lying, twisting things, falsifying them, keeping silent out of regard for the dead woman. Even so, she has the right to know if he is prowling around the cemetery, through the frozen bushes, if he approaches the open gate the moment the street is clear, when no one is watching, no one is coming down the cemetery lane.

The gate has to be open. He would never open it himself—the rusty bolt might make a noise, betray him, the man who wants to talk with his departed wife. If the gate is closed, he'll walk past as if the cemetery were not his goal and return in half an hour, worrying that the gate will be locked: it's late in the afternoon, already dark, the cemetery hours are shorter in the winter.

Immediately upon entering the cemetery, he takes the same circuitous path to this grave of his first wife, walking without looking up: only when the border of the grave comes into his field of vision does he lift his head to the stone. He removes a glove and holds out his hand, he knows the dead demand a greeting, and you have to be prepared for them to touch you. He wants a response, he begs for one, implores, starts to move his lips; his hand hangs in the cold air, calls out to be grasped, while he tries to draw his invisible wife into conversation.

It won't be many more years, six at most, if graves are dug up after twenty-five years—she doesn't know for sure. She doesn't want to know, either; no one will extend the resting period. Or is it only twenty years? Then only one year remains for the grave her husband visits. She doesn't know whether he speaks aloud or simply tries to draw the dead woman into a silent conversation. It would be better if the time were already up. Or if there had never been a grave. But what would have happened then?

Her hand holds the curtain, then releases it. The curtains need a good washing. When everything is gray and the days are short, the dirt is hardly noticeable, but now, in the spring, you can see it. She will take out the trash, she pictures it: a piece of wax paper detaches itself from the rim of the open garbage pail, the cheese rind from last night's supper;

it drops to the ground and is blown along the flagstones, her flowered apron flutters in the breeze, while she, rigid, the empty pail in her hand, gazes at the pebbled concrete tiles.

———

THE BRANCHES SWAY, thick with foliage. We hide in the leaves and they obstruct our vision, but we don't dare push the branches aside. A trouser leg, a shoe, the back of his head, we can't even tell for sure if that dull band on his shoulder is a suspender or a rifle strap. The tree is filled with pigeons. They've left their cote and gathered on the neighboring branches, to spy on us as we spy on their owner. As if ready to betray us at any moment.

The Pigeon Man is standing outside, we've had him in our sights for half an hour. He came out of the house, walked up to the garden fence, and is now standing motion-less, like a dead man. He'll have to feed his birds at some point. But he may drop dead in the grass before evening.

I try not to think about the end of our Easter vacation. Instead, I'm looking forward to fall. Then we'll scour the hill looking for moldy homes. In fall the ground retains the summer warmth and the rain soaks it for days at a time, cre-ating a mass of water unable to seep farther into the earth, because the original garbage dump was sealed with sheets of plastic. The dampness oozes through basement walls, and mold appears overnight.

We descend into dark storerooms, crouching, shining our flashlights between shelves, behind worn-out sofas and boxes that might contain old photo albums. We take down a jar of last year's cucumber preserves, a fresh one of straw-berry marmalade; we check a damp sofa cushion, holding our breath so as not to spread spores through the room.

In hopeless cases we pause at the top of the stairs, shine

our flashlight across the shimmering, greenish blue cushion that has taken over everything, whole sections of wall tinged with sulfur yellow shading into black, then blue. There's nothing to rescue, no pocket money here.

More important, this is the time of year when people's homes are left open. My cousins tell me how they search in plain sight, in the bathrooms, closets, under the bed. To a practiced eye, traces of mold are easy to spot, leaving plenty of time for spying. The foliage has barely become thick enough to rustle at night in the spring wind, and I am already anticipating leaves rotting on the ground.

There's only one person on the hill who won't allow anyone into his house, not us or any other kids looking for mold: the Pigeon Man. As if his storeroom were spared by some miracle every fall.

None of us has ever exchanged a word with him, not even "Hello." Not that he acts as if he hadn't seen us. On the contrary, he stares. I keep my eyes down as I come along the path, because I feel the Pigeon Man's stare from a distance. Yet every time, as I draw within a few meters of his house, a feeling comes over me and I lift my head, look into his eyes. His eyes are sharp and emotionless, each blink the click of a shutter, as if taking a photo of everything that enters his vision. No need for a camera to record details. Nothing escapes the Pigeon Man.

Perhaps that's why we are silent around him. It never occurs to us to ask him about mold, or to try to talk our way into his home. We know there's no fooling him, he will catch any lie, deflate any exaggeration, dismiss any story. What's more, the Pigeon Man will soon squeeze out of us all the rumors we've spread about him on the hill.

———

RESPONDING TO SOME invisible sign, the Pigeon Man comes to life, turns to the cote where he keeps the feed for his birds. This is the signal for the pigeons to descend, and the next instant we're alone in the tree, while the pigeons crowd around their master on the grass. But instead of a bag of feed, the Pigeon Man has brought out the cages in which he takes his best pigeons to the races.

It looks as if we're being presented with an unexpected opportunity. The Pigeon Man loads a few birds into his car, and while we're deciding whether to crawl across the roof to the open hatch or enter by a window at the rear of the house, the Pigeon Man gathers up his things. To be on the safe side, we wait another ten minutes after his car disappears down the hill, then climb down from the tree.

Time and again we've kicked his pigeons off our property when he wasn't in sight, and time and again we've planned to get an air gun and shoot his pigeons from the roof at night. Now and then we find a red fleck on the glass door to the terrace; then we know we'll find a bird lying in the garden, its wings twitching. Time and again we've cursed the Pigeon Man, and now we have an unforeseen opportunity to go through his house. We've never broken in on anyone. Except for the kitchen, the entire ground floor is laid with carpet tiles, and our steps make no sound. The stillness seems eerie, the stuffy smell, the gloom.

My cousins tell a story about this man that gives even older kids in the neighborhood the creeps. The Pigeon Man arrived on the hill after the war, where no one yet lived, having sworn to avoid other people for the rest of his life. It never occurred to him that the garbage dump might close or that other people might settle there. The Pigeon Man sought complete withdrawal, wishing to die in peace and obscurity.

He's been living in this house with his pigeons for thirty years now. We glance into the kitchen, it's scrupulously clean, not even bread crumbs left from breakfast on the oil-cloth cover. The telephone is in the hall in a dark niche—we don't recognize it at first under its reddish velvet cover. The protective guard on the receiver is already greasy and worn—we're surprised the Pigeon Man uses the phone that much. In the living room, a suite of chairs, a television, a bookcase, just what one would expect of old people. There's nothing informative in the drawers, no papers, no documents, no secrets. A few books on pigeon breeding and a history of radio transmission, along with war memoirs and biographies, the dust jackets of which, however, serve as a cheap sort of camouflage, hiding collections of the sort of booklets we find on the redoubt. The whole house feels as if it had been unoccupied for some time.

The Pigeon Man is said to have several lives on his conscience. It's unclear what happened; people to whom we tell this can use their own imaginations. He may have commanded a firing squad during the war, but he may well have held his own pistol to the heads of defenseless civilians in some far-off village in the East. Perhaps he moved to the hill because his story spread through town; there may have been rumors from the start. Over time, all traces of the Pigeon Man's past have faded, and now he alone remembers the details. Not that anyone would call him to account, but he sees the dead every night. They can't be driven off, and the Pigeon Man fears for his sanity if the throng grows larger. There can be no more dead people, so he avoids everyone.

The bed on the first floor is neatly made, no dirty laundry in the bathroom or bedroom. No hint anywhere that the Pigeon Man has a secret life. From his bedroom window we can see almost as far as the redoubt: the view is blocked only by a distant row of houses, which must be the street where our grandfather and the Old Lady live. We stand for a while trying to spot their house, we don't say anything, we hear a clatter overhead, a scraping on the roof.

The Pigeon Man's stare, the suppressed trembling the moment anyone approaches his home, are signs of an inner struggle. He doesn't like doing it, but the barrel of his rifle trains itself involuntarily on the interloper, and if that's not enough to scare one off, he'll have to shoot.

We climb back out into the garden through the open window by the cellar stairs. Paulina is the only one who's taken something with her, a ceramic figurine, doll-like, apparently a ballet dancer. We all feel as if we've seen it before. Paulina knows where: the same dancer appears in a picture from that old album in our grandparents' living room bookcase.

——

BEFORE MOUNTING the tram to head home, he feels like taking a short walk. He clamps a briefcase under his arm as if it held secret documents. But it's just the usual things: lists, printed forms, his lunch, and paperbacks, spy stories, which he leafs through on his noon break, perhaps.

He stares at the ground as he walks through the park; he avoids eye contact, yet he sees people quite well as he walks along. A girl and three boys are sitting on the grass by the pond, then a few moments later they're on the back of a bench, it's growing dark, everything is quiet, he can't tell if they're talking. He would sit down for a while with his heavy briefcase if the young people weren't there. Not that he's afraid of them, and the dirt their shoes leave on the bench could be brushed from his trousers.

The dirt can be explained one way or another. It's the hour that makes him walk on; his detours after work are timed precisely, down to the minute. If he loses his way in the park, his wife will ask what took him so long. She won't need to drop hints—those times are past. He knows she will be suspicious. Perhaps he'll mention it himself. Perhaps he won't need to say anything.

She will suspect a secret rendezvous after work. He can say what he likes, or remain silent, for she still won't believe him. She'll be convinced he met his children. She actually believes he would. But there are no meetings, and it's been a long time since he's seen his children. Those times are past.

He might not even recognize them now, on the street, or even at some meeting place, here in the park, secretly. The last time he saw his grandchildren they were still little, today they would easily be as old as the kids there, in the twilight, on the back of the park bench.

Perhaps one of them resembles one of his grandchildren. But even if the girl leading the group were one of his granddaughters, he couldn't be sure. He hasn't seen them for twelve, fourteen, perhaps sixteen years. And there are no pictures.

AT NOON he unpacks his lunch and places it on the desk. He doesn't go down to the canteen, doesn't want to talk with anyone; instead, he opens his spy story and continues reading. Each of the stories is told in the same way, repeating expressions and entire sentences, and the structure and plot offer no surprises. Basically the various paperbacks are all the same, so he doesn't always read them from start to finish—sometimes he opens one right in the middle, flips on, jumps clear to the end.

Whose side was the first dead body on? Police inform-ers make inquiries, get in increasingly dangerous situations. When were arrests made, when was the first shot fired, what happened before then? It's taken for granted that an in-former is on one side, but he actually works for the other. Negotiations, pressure, threats, another dead body. One side thinks the next step will be the final liberation, the other speaks of unacknowledged surrender. First shots, then arrests.

Such stories hardly tire him, nor does his work at the office. Mornings he pulls out files, accepts or declines of-fers according to clear guidelines, stamps and signs, while the morning draws to an end. After lunch, holes are punched, dossiers filed, things tidied up, the shade pulled on the bookcase. He repacks his briefcase, locks his desk, steps into the hall. No need to say good night: his colleagues have long since departed.

But the informer sits up at night over his secret reports, writes in the gloom, can hardly make out the script. He mustn't confuse those dead bodies, bury someone from the wrong side—that might lead to another death. His report is camouflaged as an entirely fictional tale, written in the style of a funeral oration. Yet the informer doesn't fall asleep until dawn, for he keeps wondering how to get his report safely through the lines the next day.

IN THE PARK, he's still thinking about the story he read at noon. No one considers a spy an ally, no one trusts a spy, he knows that much. He clamps the briefcase more tightly under his arm, as if it might be stolen, and walks more and more slowly, as if he intends to miss the next streetcar, per-haps even the one after that.

He sees four kids, sits on a park bench near them, and glances over at the young girl and the three boys. He would like to stay with secret reports, flashing signals from windows by night, Morse code and smuggled messages, radio transmissions whispered anonymously into a set. He wants to occupy himself with mortal danger, but he realizes he has long since moved on to the opera singer and his children.

When he imagines an accidental encounter with one of his family he feels as if he were a spy, passing between the lines. He wants to turn up his collar, stay in the shadows. If he thinks about the opera singer, he betrays his second wife. If he's with his second wife, he betrays his former family. But there is no such thing as a former family, one that is past. Attempts to explain this to his wife have proved fruitless. She looks at him as if he were using some indecipherable secret code.

He looks around for the kids in the gathering dark, but they have vanished. He moves like a spy between his living wife and his dead one. No flashing signals, no Morse code. He can barely make out the hands of his wristwatch in the fading light; their luminescent paint is slowly flaking off. He should have been at the tram stop long ago: he jumps up from the bench, heads for the gate, and runs through the park, although both of his legs have gone to sleep.

He thinks he's being followed. Footsteps approach, his legs hurt now, and he stops in the middle of the path. The kids may have been watching him all this time from some hiding place. He hears breathing behind his back, he turns around, someone speaks.

"Your briefcase."

A figure emerges from the gloom: it's the young girl, with his briefcase in her hand. He reaches for it, starts walking again; the tram stop appears before him. He hasn't said a word. As soon as he's in the streetcar he'll check through his case. Something may be missing—the story he was reading that noon, perhaps. He'd planned to finish it on the way home.

It's not easy to trust someone, and he doesn't trust these kids. After all, they didn't call to him immediately when he got up from the bench. They waited until he was out of sight so they could go through his briefcase. But except for the paperback, nothing seemed worth taking.

Now they are sitting on the bench; the old man has finally left, and the young girl who is their leader pulls a spy novel out from under her jacket. All four wait impatiently for the park lamps to go on. In the dark, they can't make out a single word.

—

AT NIGHT SHE SEES his silhouette at the window. She doesn't call him back to bed; he thinks she is fast asleep. The first time, she thought he was coming from the bathroom and just taking a look out the window as he passed. But he stood there motionless. She started to speak to him, hesitated, said nothing. Since then she has been watching him every night. Is it the constellations, drifting clouds, a clear sky, snow, or simply the reddish glow above the city? Finally she realizes that her husband isn't looking into the distance: his gaze is directed at the tree. He sees his first wife there.

The dead are adept at catching the attention of the living, they demand a greeting, so he stands there, her husband, holds out his hand, waits, holds out his hand, and only reluctantly does he allow it to sink, in the course of the night, onto the sill, exhausted but ready as ever. The dead won't leave the living alone until the living, too, reach the end of their lives, and what holds for all the dead holds for his first wife too. Once you are near them, they'll never let you go. From the grave she will take all you have, that's what the dead say.

The dead touch you: you don't see them, but you feel it then, an itch where there's no sore, no insect bite. At first you're not sure, you look at your forearm, check your neck in the mirror, but there's nothing there. It can't have been an ant: there are no ants in the room. Nor a fly, landing quickly and taking off: the house is sprayed daily for flies. Nor a stinging nettle: you haven't been out in the bushes. Nor a drop of sweat: it's not hot—on the contrary, you're shivering.

It's unbelievable but true: I have just been touched by a dead person. He wanted to feel me but only brushed against me, repelled by my reluctance. He had not expected me to notice him so quickly. No trace remains today, but he will try again. Later, in old age, much later, the dots of countless contacts appear, flecks on the skin, on the hands mostly, but also on the chest and face.

She stands at the window as he sometimes does, motionless, staring silently into the darkness. A tree blocks her view, its crown covers almost her entire field of vision, its top branches extend far above the roof. Perhaps its roots already reach so deeply into the ground that they undermine the cellar. It should have been cut down long ago. At night her husband sees his dead wife among the leaves, she turns her head and their eyes meet; he hears her whisper, sees her draw near to talk to him when the branches sway, scratching against the windowpane.

She doesn't see the dead woman, only a tree. No other growing thing occupies her in this way: the dead woman does not sit on the mossy patch by the compost, nor in the pansies in front of the house, does not crouch in the uncut, frost-damaged, singed grass. Nothing occupies her like this tree outside the window, nothing.

SHE'S NOT ENTIRELY certain that he still talks secretly with the children from his first marriage; she doesn't ask him, and he wouldn't tell her. At first she caught him a few times telephoning his children when he thought she was elsewhere, down in the cellar, outside, upstairs making the bed. She would enter the hall from the kitchen unexpectedly, and her startled husband would put his hand to the mouthpiece and drop his voice to a whisper. He realized at once, however, that although this tactic might be useful at the front, facing the enemy or in an ambush, it did little good with his wife, and so he broke off the call, barked "wrong number" in an obviously feigned voice, and replaced the receiver so quickly that the lie was not actually spoken into the phone, but simply to the air.

Then silence. She knew what he was up to, and he was too cowardly to offer an explanation or excuse, let alone confront her with the truth. They stood in the dark hall, he at the telephone, she in the kitchen door, saying nothing. She wiped her hands on the dish towel while he examined the coat hooks on the rack one by one. He, who no doubt had the nerve to tell others that he couldn't risk saying another word to her for hours, days, all week.

That hasn't happened with the telephone for some years now. Not because her husband has become cleverer, or because her intuition for such things has weakened over time. On the contrary, it has sharpened, and she can tell from the slightest indications, from footsteps on the carpet and

the creak of his shoes, whether he's trying to hide something from her.

At first she wondered if his children had given up. She
soon realized that he no longer called them from the house
but instead went to a phone booth or to the post office, or
called from work. Perhaps he has grown used to whispering
on the phone even when she isn't around. She can't be sure.
After all, they don't call each other—they would need a
house phone for that. Over her dead body.

What do he and his children talk about, what sort of
conversations do they have? Probably he calls her "my Old
Lady" or, even worse, "the Old Lady."

"The Old Lady." Never her name or "my wife": she
knows that for sure, ever since she overheard the men in
the next room on a night when they'd gone to have supper
with friends.

"We almost mentioned your first wife and your kids. My
wife gave me a kick under the table and I bit my tongue in
time. I hope the Old Lady didn't notice."

"You wouldn't believe how hard it was just to talk the
Old Lady into coming tonight."

"It can't be easy living with the Old Lady."

It suddenly occurred to her that they were talking
about her.

She never brought it up. She never will. She knows he
will steadfastly deny it. He will regard this as steadfast; that's
how he'll think of himself, and he hopes others will, too,
but in fact he is hesitant, soft-spoken, he hangs his head,
slumps his shoulders, avoids her eyes, or, sitting opposite
her at the breakfast table, stares intently into the open sugar
bowl, as if he had no eyes.

———

HE'S CONVINCED she has been spying on him throughout their marriage. Since the day they met, he's lived in fear that she wants to know something he won't reveal. But there is nothing, she knows everything. For almost twenty years he's let her know he's convinced she will do anything to learn his secrets, and if she can't squeeze them out of him, she'll uncover them by constant spying. She has always been helpless in the face of this delusion, has never understood it. Nor has she ever been able to talk him out of it.

Presumably his delusions about spying have nothing to do with her, are not fixated on her, arose long before she entered her husband's life. She convinces herself, lets herself be convinced, only because she is interested in the man with whom she lives and will live for the rest of her life.

Over the years she has seen clearly the childish pleasure he takes in secrets, in code names, in concealment. There were hints enough from his side, but she didn't respond. He was always trying to involve her in his games: working together in the garden, planting potatoes soon after moving in, he would whisper: "Code name Potato."

She knows she was supposed to raise her eyebrows then ask what he meant, but she'd merely nodded, kept on digging. He had winked, then smiled like a boy breaking a rule: "Hansa Winter Exercises. We traveled using names like that. We were just a tour group, officially."

She knows he wouldn't have told her more, would have put his finger to his lips and referred to secrets. When they sat in the garden on summer afternoons and the bees circled the pastries, he would point at the sky, lean toward her as if to involve her in his conspiracy, and say: "Drones, apiary units."

She hadn't reacted, hadn't asked him what he meant,

just chased away the bees with a dish towel. She knew he would never involve her in his conspiracy.

From the start he'd enjoyed being wrapped in an aura of mystery, surrounded by secrets, and it never occurred to him that his second marriage might bring a wife who could not respond to that. Perhaps his first wife was attracted by secrets, but they don't awaken the curiosity of his second wife. She doesn't like the dark, she wants things clear. As a result, he treats her like a spy. He's even given her a code name.

If he never calls her by her real name when he talks with others, if she's always "the Old Lady," then he may have a code name for his first wife too. She doesn't know. She is unaware of the name he uses when he speaks to his dead wife. Hopes she never has to hear it.

—

OUR GRANDFATHER KNOWS how to withdraw from the world: to make himself invisible, he simply ceases to speak. We tried to call him from a telephone booth. It wasn't hard to find his number, we knew his address, and Paulina, Carl, and Nora share his family name.

Was it his breath or ours as we passed the receiver around? We didn't say a word. An old man's voice, far away, like a long-distance call. No name, just "Yes?"

Squeezed out, hissed into the mouthpiece, as if he were at some high altitude where the air is thin. Both sides listen intensely. We can't even be sure it's a man's voice. Again: "Yes?"

A moment later, he hangs up. We hesitate to try again. Perhaps we ought to keep calling, be stubborn, if we want to draw more out of him than this weak "Yes" and the sound of his breath.

The picture of a man who strictly adheres to his second

wife's ban on all contact, decreed long ago, as if it were a military command and refusal to obey would mean death. Up to now the Old Lady has learned about every secret meeting he's had with his children; she must have a network of informers stretching throughout the entire neighborhood, the whole city. A few neighbors who don't let the others know, our grandfather's colleagues, perhaps. But we can't imagine these spies reporting voluntarily: the Old Lady can't possibly have friends, people avoid her, everyone knows the story about the ax.

Under this ban, our grandfather has gradually fallen silent; he hardly dares speak for fear he might give something away, for of course he thinks of his children from time to time.

He no longer speaks, sitting in silence in front of the television set while the Old Lady offers a running commentary on the news: she's enraged, horrified, thrown for a loss by an assassination. A deadly ambush that the murderers call an execution, another picture in the rogues' gallery. The scene resembles a civil war, and the Old Lady struggles to find words for what has happened. But our grandfather is not upset, betrays no anxiety, lets the image of corpses in the intersection pass without comment.

The next day he notes in the newspaper photo the chalk marks outlining the bullet-riddled car, the numbers in several places where shell cases were found when the crime scene was examined. The Old Lady doesn't know what to think, she wants him to react, calls him cold-blooded, says he even looks cold-blooded, but our grandfather just shakes his head gently.

———

HE KEEPS SILENT. As long as he says nothing, he's safe. From his wife, from his children. He thinks no one has caught on. He hasn't reckoned with his grandchildren.

The ballet dancer put us on the track. There's nothing striking about it, it's an ordinary souvenir. You visit elderly people, you glance at the display cabinet filled with kitsch, a little china dog, shot glasses with greetings from abroad, dried gentian blossoms, perhaps, and beside them a Spanish figurine. A figurine like that might be anywhere, you think, shrugging your shoulders—who knows how many there are, even from the same manufacturer? The doll from the Pigeon Man's house is so ordinary, it can serve as a secret sign.

In the old photo, too, Paulina recalls, the Spanish dancer in the living-room cabinet looked quite ordinary. We go through the album again, leaf backward from the doll, page by page, note locations, dates, feverishly re-creating the path to this figurine. When does it appear for the first time, who brought it, is it really from Spain, where was it purchased?

None of us knows as much about the military as Carl, but it is through Nora that we stumble on our grandfather's secret story. The doll disappears into the dark past, yet Nora deciphers a handwritten caption on a picture we linger over, even though this picture of a young man in uniform is much like the others: "Back from Spain: Summer 1937."

Carl should have noticed them right away, the decorations on the young man's chest, the base metal reflecting the light; in fact, he may have but said nothing at first. Did he think our grandfather had vacationed in Spain, innocently toured its cities? A man in uniform, a pilot, a professional soldier, lying all day on the beach while a civil war raged? Doesn't Carl know that the rebels could never have defeated the Spanish Republic without the secret support of the German air force? Do the words Condor Legion mean nothing to him?

Nora reproaches herself for not having figured it out sooner. If any of us had ever read a single book by one of her favorite authors, we would know everything about the Spanish Civil War, but we don't even know the writers' names. It was against them, too, that our grandfather went to war.

—

THE TELEPHONE will ring again today, just as it has every morning this week, regardless of whether her husband is home or not. She hasn't answered up to now. She's not expecting a call.

Why do his children insist on calling? What's the point? What do they want to know? Isn't it enough that he calls them secretly from a phone booth, from his office? Isn't it enough that she has to watch her husband hoard his coins, thinking she doesn't notice? When, with his solicitous look, he suggests that they keep their change on a saucer on the hall stand, claiming that all those useless coins just make his wallet bulge? Isn't it enough that she hears the clinking and knows her husband is by the saucer in the hall, sorting out ten-pfennig pieces, and that when she goes through his jacket pockets before going to bed, she knows he'll phone his children the following day?

Isn't it enough that she guesses why he's sometimes overly friendly toward her, helps with the dishes, runs the vacuum awkwardly through the living room, places a coverlet over her legs while she sits watching TV in the evening? Must his children call on top of all this?

When she cleans the house she polishes the phone. She places the receiver beside it, hears the distant dial tone, broken only when she presses on the cradle with the dust cloth, or works on the dial, the damp cloth wrapped around her finger. She wipes off the perspiration stains left by her husband's hand; the fingerprints aren't hers, for she rarely uses the phone. The dial tone sounds closer, then is muffled again by the cloth. The mouthpiece takes the longest; the most dangerous dirt lurks in the tiny perforations, where germs nest invisibly.

Once when she had just replaced the receiver, the telephone rang. As if they knew she was at the telephone at that moment. As if they wanted to scare her to death.

She might as well have the phone line removed. She doesn't need a telephone anymore, she never needed one in the first place. The line was already installed when they bought the house, that is probably the only reason they have a phone. The housing development was provided with phone lines, the lines on the other hill were laid at a much later date, and they say some houses there still don't have a phone.

For years she hasn't been to the other hill, where new development has supposedly appeared. It used to be just a few houses, shacks, really, small gardens with toolsheds where a few people lived. Even the garbage dump was still there. She probably wouldn't recognize it today. But there's no reason to go now—that's where the son from his first marriage lives. She hasn't seen him since he left home, nor met him in passing on the street. She'll try to make sure that doesn't happen.

She hears only rumors and gossip about the area now, silly things in the supermarket where customers and checkout girls try to outdo each other with stories, each less believable than the one before, whispered behind cupped hands but loud enough for everyone to hear. The roar of mopeds, the sound of blinds being lowered, the glow of fires in the night. What is that gang of kids on the hill? Who are they after?

SHE HAS A mental picture of splinters, wood, destroyed furniture. It must have been at the outset of their marriage, not long after they moved into the house. She can hear the splintering, the breaking; it must have been the back, seat, and legs of an old chair that she chopped with the ax. She doesn't see it clearly, isn't sure anymore whether it was at night—that would have been strange, all that noise with the children already asleep. She sees the splinters, it's dark, why destroy a chair inside the house, chips, kindling everywhere, covering the carpet.

At first the house was heated with stoves, and on cold nights she would stoke the one in the kitchen so the embers would last through the night. She stood alone, in the dark, her husband rarely there, or if he was, he had already washed his hands and didn't offer to help her. That must have been the first, second, or at most third winter; after that they had installed central heating.

Sometimes there wasn't enough fuel, and she had to think of something on her own. When the coals and briquettes ran out, when the last piece of kindling had been brought in from the shed in the garden, she would go through the house and try to figure out how to keep frost patterns from forming on the kitchen windows. She sees herself on the cellar steps, holding an ax, she sees herself standing in the living room, looking around, hesitating— the lights are out—sees herself mount the stairs, go into the attic, into the icy cold. They had to burn everything at the time, even items they treasured, particularly things her husband and the children liked.

Did they heat with a stove? Was there an ax? From time to time the pictures blur, and other figures push their way in. There are things she's no longer sure about, although she saw them with her own eyes. She gets angry when she thinks of all the things she let herself be talked into. Her husband with those fantasies about spies that he insisted on so stubbornly, no matter how solid the evidence against them. She should have contradicted him from the start. If you let ideas like that pass in silence, you may begin to believe them yourself.

The things she let herself be talked into. Now she couldn't trust her own memory. Who held the ax, and what happened? She had to defend her memories with all her strength against the others. She sees the ax fall on her husband's desk, steadily hacking away at the wooden desktop. The filing tray jerks back toward the edge, pencils, paper clips, erasers bounce out, the paperweight falls to the floor, she sees a blotter ripped apart by an ax blow, but the more closely she looks, the less certain she is who holds the ax.

Not kindling for the kitchen stove. It must have been blind, destructive rage. She sees four people standing in the room, herself, her husband, his daughter and son. The image gradually sharpens, the shadows dissolve, and slowly it dawns on her what happened. And it becomes clear why this memory was buried so deeply, why it could be dragged forth only gradually, with the greatest of effort: this was why her husband's children left home. First his son, perhaps that very day, and soon thereafter, his daughter.

Now she sees the children again, hacking at their father's desk. His son must have swung the ax, the sister watching, shielding her brother, so no one could stop the destruction, the rage. Their father withdrawn in a corner, doing nothing, allowing his desk be chopped to pieces by his own children. Perhaps he puts his hands in his pockets or covers his face. She can't see clearly, she has to cover her eyes to avoid the splinters, all four of them in the room. No one speaks.

She immediately grasps the situation; she has no choice but to intervene. In his frenzy the son might lash out at other family members. She knows she must wrest the ax from his grip, even if it seems foolhardy, since he's so much stronger.

Then everything happens so quickly that the image blurs. She approaches the raised arms from behind, his son is about to deliver another blow when she grabs the ax at just the right moment, and jerks on it; the son hasn't counted on that, his arms are pulled back and he's about to lose his balance, is in danger of falling backward on his head. He releases his hold.

Her husband is still in the corner, his son on the floor, motionless, the daughter between them, all three staring at her. She holds the ax in her hands. With this the picture goes dark.

—

THE SMALL WRINKLES around his eyes and mouth are accentuated by a deep tan—intense sunshine over several months has left its traces, hints of how his face will change as he gets older. We concentrate on the pictures of our grandfather taken shortly after his return from the Spanish Civil War, to get some sort of idea of how he might look as an older man, today.

It's possible that furrows now run from the sides of his nose to his chin. Or has this young face softened in old age, if only because it has filled out slightly? Are there two deep vertical lines on his forehead that seem to extend the bridge of his nose, or do countless horizontal lines appear the moment our grandfather laughs, or recognizes someone, or is surprised? And which characteristic of his eyes will persist— the alertness, the constantly harried look, the ability to view everything with detachment, the guilty curiosity, or his infinite openness to all things?

We run our fingers over his face, mentally connect a few weak points on his cheek so that they form a sharp line. But depending on where we start with these extensions from forty years ago into the present, a totally different person appears.

We're looking for a man who doesn't say much, that's all we know for sure. An old man, for example, in the parking lot outside the supermarket, staring into the trunk of his car, almost lost, as if he'd discovered something strange next to the repair kit, the spare tire, the extra blanket. Another man, standing outside a telephone booth, already impatient, although the woman inside has just lifted her hand from the dial. He looks around him as if about to summon a policeman: the woman speaks quickly, in clipped phrases, and he seems to find her suspicious.

But the more closely we observe them, the more similar these old men appear: they don't talk much. The bald man we help onto the tram, the man in the coat and tie sitting before us, staring quietly out the window, making smacking sounds, as if his dentures don't quite fit. To pick out our grandfather from among these men, we would need to see them react to something unforeseen, to a police interrogation, for example: which one speaks curtly, who is speechless with fear, who starts talking excitedly to the uniformed men.

The tram stops between two stations. A murmur arises, questioning looks, then the driver tells everyone to exit the tram and wait by the barrier. Now we see flashing lights on the pavement, nail strips, sandbags piled high on the sidewalk with a machine gun barrel sticking out of them. Armed men in black leather jackets, probably in bullet-proof vests. They hold their weapons calmly, but when we see two of them up close at the barrier, we notice a tense flicker in their eyes.

Our grandfather must have experienced this sort of thing in the civil war: he still remembers what it's like, and the standard responses come back to him. A combination of superiority and fear can prove dangerous; one must never allow a uniformed man to sense contempt. Our grandfather may be tempted to make some disparaging remark, these youngsters shouldn't act as if they're facing death, they have no idea what that's really like. But he knows you have to keep calm, even though you want to break out in rage.

Not far ahead in line stands an old man whose composure had already struck us as we exited the tram. He has his I.D. out, hands it to the policeman silently. Just when he thinks he can pass, the policeman grabs his arm and points to his briefcase. He must open it and empty the contents carefully onto the ground. It contains nothing suspicious: an appointment book, ballpoint pens, paper clips, a photo. The police are about to let him retrieve the contents, but the old man shakes the briefcase again as if to prove his honesty.

At this, a small plastic case falls out and bounces along a step or two on the pavement; the hollow sound each time it strikes the ground seems to reverberate between the buildings. Suddenly, they all hold their breath.

The police spring aside, release their safeties, and train their automatics on the white container. It's only an empty denture case. But why does he have one at the office? The man wears false teeth, but he doesn't take them out during the day, only at night.

The old man remains calm, clears his throat, shrugs. The police see they won't get anything more out of him. They lower their guns and let the man gather his things. We don't dare help him. A few paper clips still gleam on the pavement as he finally passes through the barrier, and shortly after, we're waved through, too. We don't want to lose sight of him. Nothing has disrupted the old man's composure; he reacts calmly to dangerous situations, and we're close to believing we've seen our grandfather.

Until we hear him speak. We follow him to a café where a young woman is waiting, a girlfriend perhaps. They greet each other with a kiss, and even before he sits down the man begins talking excitedly. With sweeping gestures he sets the young woman laughing, he bends over, almost as if he were looking for something under the table; he smiles broadly with false teeth, and we see at once how little resemblance this man bears to our grandfather. We're disappointed.

WE CUT LIFE-SIZE birds of prey from black adhesive film, birds with outspread wings and sharp beaks, then distribute them evenly on the glass door to the terrace, so that the pigeons will stop flying into it. We have no idea if the Pigeon Man has noticed that the Spanish dancer is missing; if he has, he gives no sign.

He now lacks the secret identification that allows members of the Condor Legion to recognize each other. They don't have to mention the Spanish Civil War: when one elderly couple visits another, all it takes is a quick glance at the living-room cabinet. While their wives are still expressing surprise that the same Spanish doll is in both of their homes, an unusual figure, much prettier than the little dogs and donkey carts, the men go outside to smoke a cigarette and swap stories about the places they were stationed, the planes they flew, their confirmed hits.

But no one visits the Pigeon Man. Our grandfather never has guests, either, we can't imagine his life otherwise, nor do we know if a ceramic figurine with curved arms still waits in his living room to be recognized by a former comrade. We mustn't pretend: even if our grandfather shops in the same supermarket we do, we'll never be able to tell him apart from the other old men.

Nora plays with the idea of just going to the Old Lady's place and ringing the bell until our grandfather comes to the door. Even if the Old Lady is right behind him with the ax, Nora will have seen him for once in her life. She thinks the story of the ax may have been invented to protect our grandfather. Blame everything on the Old Lady, so no one will think to ask about his secret past.

But there's one thing Nora hasn't thought of: the peephole in our grandfather's front door. The Old Lady will never open that door if she spies someone with Italian eyes standing there.

The only person who can lead us safely and discreetly to our grandfather is the Pigeon Man. Of course our grandfather will never visit him: he would have to pass our house, and the Old Lady would be sure to find out and make trouble. He avoids this area, doesn't dare climb the hill, fears he might see a member of his family even at a distance. But if we dog the Pigeon Man long enough, we're sure to get close to our grandfather at some point. We just need to be patient.

One day the Pigeon Man will again cage up his best birds and leave the house as if heading for one of the usual carrier pigeon races. No one on the hill will think anything about it, but we won't be fooled. On this weekend the Pigeon Man will not attend the race, no one will admire his birds' unusual homing ability, no one will receive a message delivered by one of them.

The Pigeon Man drives to a sheltered spot in the fields and parks his car among the bushes so that the birds won't die if the sun comes out. Then he walks down the hill into town, enters a certain pub, and disappears into the back room. If the waiter blocks our way, throws us out of the bar, we won't resist—we might just as well wait in the street. At some point the veterans' meeting will end, at some point the old men will grow tired of telling tales, they'll have re-created their war stories once more in living color, they'll have sung all their songs—our grandfather perhaps loudest among them.

At last he emerges from the back room with those of his comrades still living, their pockets bulging with medals, each one heading home on his own, as if he were just a tipsy pensioner. When they part, one of them will be noticeably hoarser than the rest; apparently he's not used to talking so much, and now he breathes heavily, says only, "Yes."

We will recognize him: we just have to be patient. At some point the Pigeon Man will show us the way.

❧

HAVING READ THE obituaries, she slowly leafs back to the front page. There too she finds only dead people these days, another death early that morning, the dead just won't go away. The stains on the street, the blood on the pavement, the polished concrete, the death stains can't be pasted in the family album.

Such pictures cause her almost physical pain: several cars stopped in the middle of an intersection, an open door on the driver's side, a wool blanket on the ground nearby, shielding a corpse from the eyes of strangers. She feels like doubling over and falling to the ground herself, for the dead man is not completely hidden from bystanders after all—a hand, a shoe, a bloody head, as if she were expected to piece together the dead man's body.

She tries to distract herself by focusing on the shattered windshield, the fragments still clinging to the rim, the web of bare lines on bare ground, but she's unable to see inside the car. The sunlight is caught by the splinters of glass on the ground, and in the grassy banks by the road are shiny areas—motor oil, or is it blood, reflecting the rays of the sun? She follows the trail of shattered glass back to the wool blanket, is pulled insistently toward it, as if forced to crouch beside it, doubled over by pain, to jerk the blanket away and reveal the dead body beneath.

She can't look any longer, she puts the paper aside, the dead won't leave you in peace. She takes out the trash: the pebbled concrete, a dead man on the pebbled concrete tiles. A scrap of paper falls off, the cheese rind. The dead want you to watch for them, keep listening for their movements. They insist you stop in the middle of the path, in the park, when you shop, when you carry out the garbage pail. You stand stock-still beneath the trees, in the supermarket, tilt your head and listen. Or by the garden fence, motionless, engrossed: was that a dead man's greeting you nearly missed, rigid, your gaze on pebbled concrete, the empty pail in your right hand?

The memories of the living are always tied to the dead; only of them do images remain. Apparitions are created from the ashes of the dead, from the earth in the graveyard—the gravel surface, the flowers on the grave, suffice for images to arise. Yet a living person moves unseen among the living. She knows that should she disappear overnight, her husband would retain no image of her.

She has never seen a dead person. In photos, yes, but not in reality. Even in war she has been spared. Not one hand emerging from a pile of rubble, nor a shoe with a foot still in it; no bloody head. She was always fortunate enough to close her eyes at the right moment, to turn away. Nor did she view her parents after they died. No victim of an accident, no drowned body. She has avoided the dead as if guided by invisible signs.

She's never spoken about this with her husband, but he must have come into contact with countless dead, in addition to his first wife. His first death, who would that have been? Was it a stranger or someone he knew? Was the body lying in the street, barely covered by a wool blanket, or totally exposed, staring blankly into the clear sky? A civilian, an enemy soldier, or, earlier on, an old neighbor who died, a young man hit by a car?

The blue light flashes across the pebbled concrete; it shimmers in his hair and eyes. She sees herself standing there; the picture has reappeared, but the ax is no longer in her hands; her husband's desk is destroyed, but the danger now seems averted. Her husband, and his son and daughter, no longer stare. Now it's the neighbors outside who surround an ambulance. All eyes are directed at her, she is led exhausted to the garden gate by the ambulance team. She hears voices but can't understand what they're saying, she's lying on a stretcher, and suddenly, everything is still. She doesn't know what happens next.

When she comes home they behave as if nothing had happened. No split desktop, the paperweight back in its place, not a single splinter on the carpet. The ax is gone as well. They have decided to fool her, to make her lose faith in her own memory. She can't defend herself against them.

To this day, no one has said a word to her about the incident. But there are rumors. Crazy stories have been circulating in the neighborhood and throughout the city since that afternoon—the ax in her hands, the emergency doctor, the police, the departure of the children soon after. In the supermarket she senses that people wait for her to leave. The moment she's outside with her shopping bag, the whispering begins. About involuntary commitment, no doubt: the cashier rolls her eyes, a customer pities her poor husband, another simply shakes her head—how could he have missed the chance, why didn't he sign the papers? No one dares confront her openly with such lies, no one gives credence to her view, afraid that the stories they've made up would instantly collapse.

The flowered apron flutters in the breeze, a scrap of paper falls from the rim of the open garbage pail, the cheese rind from supper, but she still stands there, her head tilted like a sick bird's, listening for a message from the dead telling her to lower the pail so that her hand is free to greet them.

The dead never return a greeting, but you must extend your hand, expect their hands, demand them. When you're outside with the trash, no one greets you. It's not snowing, hasn't snowed for a long time, summer is on its way. And yet there are flakes in the air. Perhaps she's only seeing spots before her eyes, a flickering, a faint uneasiness. She breathes in something sweetish, the air seems thick, enriched with some unknown substance. It's hard to breathe, as if, when she no longer expected it, a dead person had drawn near after all, unnoticed.

She retreats to the house. Without turning, letting the door fall shut, ignoring the peephole. If there were snow on the ground, it might be possible to recognize other, unknown footprints beside those left by her slippers.

—

HE CAN'T ENDURE it much longer, it will unhinge him: to work in the morning, then straight back home to his wife in the evening. He needs to see others at some point; he has almost forgotten how to talk. The same dialogue every day, the same old words, in his files, in the paperbacks, with his colleagues, at home. He can't join a club—his wife doesn't want him going out at night. He needs someone to talk to now and then; he can hardly breathe anymore.

He posts a note on the supermarket bulletin board. He doesn't really expect an answer, but at least he's finally given a sign. He'll tell his wife about it later, she'll find out soon enough anyway. He's seeking tutorials in French, an hour of conversation every two weeks, evenings or weekends.

He'll find it easier to speak in a foreign language, he'll feel more comfortable, especially with a stranger—even thinking about it brings back memories he would never mention otherwise. He spoke French quite passably once, he always had a talent for languages, he even remembers a few phrases in Spanish.

The usual questions and bland remarks of a tourist abroad, but also a series of phrases he'd best not use in conversation. The military terms are of scant interest anyway, but given all the off-color jokes among his comrades, he'll have to watch out—a few words still come to mind he's no longer sure about.

During his first foreign mission he actually met a spy, or at least someone who made every effort to seem like one.

Of course he knows his spy stories have little in common with reality: the life of a spy is not nearly as interesting as the uninitiated think. Inconspicuous agents carry out mundane tasks for the most part, write reports, punch holes, file them away in a cabinet, and wait for a call. He sees them sitting in their offices: a commercial office center, quite similar to the one he spends his day in. You can't envy a spy. The entire air of mystery is maintained only because the secret service is afraid someone might discover how boring their work really is.

The spy he met over forty years ago seemed obsessed with appearing mysterious. His primary goal in conversation was to conceal the monotony of his everyday life by omitting everything routine about it. He dropped vague hints, changed the subject, and awakened in his listeners the impression that most of what he did was not intended for strangers' ears.

But in those days everyone wanted to be a spy, and he doesn't deny he would have found it fascinating. In Spain, high-ranking officers even had code names, and he would gladly have gone by some alias himself to begin with. He soon realized how ridiculous it all was. Men with code names went to brothels where they met young women who also had code names, soft-sounding, promising, just right for the whispered tones of an afternoon lair.

No one back home would ever know how impressed they had been by the feigned sighs, the false lashes and wigs. When he saw his comrades step back into the street wearing conspiratorial grins, he felt a slight uneasiness, his first doubts. How much could his part in this secret assignment mean when his comrades' idea of a secret was a visit to a brothel?

He can't stand secrecy now. Secrets repel him. So it's

doubly unfortunate that his wife leaves him no other choice. It worries him. Someday she will have a heart attack thinking about his first wife and his children. She's announced one often enough, even threatened it when he made tentative attempts to contact his children openly. An outsider might think she hoped for an attack.

He would like to see his grandchildren, but it's clear he can never actually meet them. A photograph, perhaps, a group portrait of the four of them, he would be satisfied with that. He could do something silly and look up a certain former comrade in the phone book. An unpleasant fellow who settled on the opposite hill, shortly after the war as far as he can remember. They had always avoided each other, but now that so much time has passed, perhaps he could ask a favor of him. Without having to explain himself in detail. He would surely have a camera. In any case, it would have to wait until one grandchild visited the other three, and the picture could be taken from some safe hiding place.

He's standing in the hall, the telephone in its dark niche. A number has been dialed. Just a whim. No reason to hurry.

HE'S FORGOTTEN to check at the peephole first. Now the door is open, and he's face to face with a girl he doesn't know, just two steps away. He has no idea what she wants: strangers don't ring at their door. She introduces herself politely, and now he remembers his message on the bulletin board at the supermarket. He had an older woman in mind for these conversations, not a schoolgirl.

She says she lives here in the neighborhood, so she just came by without calling first. She pulls her school certificates from a folder and points to the relevant lines: her grades are uniformly good in languages; she speaks fluently, she says, error-free. He can't judge that. She pulls out her French books, saying that if he doesn't like the way the lessons are set up, she can prepare exercises suited just for him.

He still hasn't said a thing—just nodded "yes" now and then. The schoolgirl repeats a few sample sentences so he can check her accent, but he's no longer listening, he hasn't been listening from the start.

There's something about her, and he's trying to figure it out. Is it her chin, something about her mouth, is it her voice? This schoolgirl resembles someone, but whom? The girl with those kids in the park a few days ago? Or a face from the past?

He slams the door shut. He doesn't mean to, it almost closes itself. He presses his forehead to the wood, sees her eyes through the peephole. The eyes of his first wife: he should have recognized her at once.

She's still there, she rings again—at any moment his second wife will be asking why he doesn't open the door. He peers through the peephole into a puzzled face, he barely breathes, he waits, he can study this face another moment or so. It's true.

She mentioned her name, too—she must have said her name when she greeted him. He waits until she puts her textbook and certificates back in her bag. She turns around, pauses at the garden gate, looks back, shrugs, wads up the note from the supermarket, and throws it into the bushes. Then the eyes are gone.

—

ONE OF THE BRANCHES almost touches the house: the dead sit in that tree. She's shaken out the covers, made the bed, shut the window again, and she still can't see anything. Perhaps it only happens at night, perhaps that's when the tree shows the dead, while the branches sway gently against the dark background.

Then they move slowly into the foreground, and his first wife takes shape—he sees her face and her hands, the outermost branch stretches toward him. Then nothing remains but his dead wife and himself. He's forgotten everything else.

He is unaware that his second wife is lying awake just a step away, that she's heard him put on his slippers and approach the window. He never dreams that her eyes have been open and trained on him from the moment he took up his station to await the appearance of his dead wife. He thinks she's fast asleep. Otherwise, he never would have left the bed.

When the light is off and no further word is spoken, they can hear each other breathe. A sleeping person breathes more slowly; she knows how her husband sounds once he's fallen asleep. And he knows her breathing pattern, too. She pauses longer between breaths, takes a few deeper breaths— she knows that her husband is listening. After a few minutes, during which her breath has become almost imperceptible, he pulls back the cover and quietly gets out of bed. He never speaks of it, he has never even hinted that he stands by the window at night to watch for his first wife.

Perhaps she can't find the dead woman in the tree because she can't picture her face. She's never seen his first wife, except in photos, perhaps, early on, but then she didn't want to see the woman who had died a few months before. And now there are no pictures—her husband has taken every opportunity to spirit away all his photo albums, documents, and souvenirs to his first family. He has secretly removed even the most inconspicuous keepsake from the house, because he wants them all safely in the hands of his children.

Almost none of the things he had when she first met him remain—only two or three worthless items, ones he never gave away, although she can't see why he still hangs on to them. Cleaning out the basement once, she found a model airplane. At first she thought it had belonged to his son, but then she remembered that the boy had never cared for military toys. Her husband must have told her that early on: they were just married, and he'd assumed she would want to know about his first family. She didn't learn it from his son, who never would have spoken a word to her on his own.

Then there was the doll that stood for years in the living room cabinet, in a case beside the books. A female figurine made of plastic, or perhaps ceramic, with long legs, one on the ground, the other in the air, her arms stretched over her head. She wore a short dress, a costume of real cloth, the skin shimmering through the bright glazed surface. A souvenir, perhaps: the dress was Spanish, a Spanish dancer, with knotted hair and half-closed eyes.

She had no real face—her vague features melted into the glaze—and yet she seemed to look out into the living room as if keeping watch on everything. This figure, this face, was what she imagined when she thought of his first wife: vague, blurred, but with a penetrating gaze.

THEY'RE CALLED FADED so that they can be given—must be given—life by filling them in with bright colors, like the man on the hill who died last night. As long as he was alive no one had cared about him: a pigeon fancier or veteran, cold, laconic, hardly friendly. No one noticed him, for the neighborhood was filled with people like him, but now his death brought him to everyone's attention. Presumably he had anticipated that, had meant to leave a gap behind. They would be talking about him in the supermarket for weeks to come—what sort of a person was he, what terrible experience had driven him to live alone with his pigeons, why was he always on guard at this fence with a gun? What had led to his death?

Each word about the dead brings the living an imperceptible step nearer to death. Without realizing it, in discussing the dead they are practicing making their own voices heard in death, they are listening to their own dead voices. She decided early on to say nothing about the dead. And she's held fast to that: in all her life, no one has ever heard her say a word about a dead person.

Her husband always had a detailed image of his first wife's face. Almost twenty years after her death, he knows the set of her mouth, knows what lines appear with what expressions, what each smile means, knows her every look.

If photos still exist of the singer, they're with his children, and he can ask about them anytime, in case his dead wife fades from the tree. He slips the coins into his coat pocket, is preoccupied with the phone call he plans to make, forgets to take precautions. After all, she can see the change missing from the saucer. And she sees the bulge of his jacket pocket when he leaves home in the morning. This doesn't occur to him; he doesn't think of her for a single moment.

Perhaps it's not true that he hasn't seen his children for years. Perhaps she's mistaken in that assumption. She's let herself be fooled—he's not headed for the post office or a telephone booth, he's going into town to meet his children.

In a busy café, perhaps, where he won't be noticed, where no one knows him, where he won't have to worry that someone might spot them meeting secretly. Perhaps he meets regularly with his son. They may not even need the quiet corner of a pastry shop, her husband will go straight to his son's house on the opposite hill. In the end they are both laughing at her because she still believes the silly story about secret phone calls.

But if that's the case, then the calls in the morning are not from his children. Someone else is calling. She doesn't know who else would be calling, she doesn't ask, hasn't mentioned it. She doesn't tell him that the phone has been ringing for over a week now. Perhaps he's not trying to hide anything from her, perhaps he actually did spend the weekend in the garden and didn't hear the phone ring. Perhaps he knows nothing. The calls aren't for him. They're for her.

SHE COMES FROM the supermarket, she's at the garden gate with her overloaded shopping bags, she digs the key out of her coat pocket, she hasn't reached the door and already she hears the phone ringing in the hall. She lowers the bags, turns the key twice, leaves the groceries outside, the door open, the key in the lock. She's in the niche by the phone, it's still ringing. She lifts the receiver.

· spies ·

FOR NINE MONTHS she hasn't see her fiancé. She's always on the road, playing in various cities, but she's beyond provincial halls used the rest of the year for other shows: brass bands with troupes in national dress, peasant farces, junior gymnastic meets, dances for veterans of the Great War. And the local rabbit show, the smell lingering in the building, straw, animals, sweat, no matter how hard they scrub the floorboards to transform the place into an opera house for the evening.

Behind her now are those halls lacking even an orchestra pit, where damp stains on the stage, invisible to the public, attract her gaze against her will. There she sang not to the heavens or to her lover but to those water spots, avoiding the direct glare of the spotlights. The lights were mishandled, the trapdoor squealed, the stage creaked at every step, the prompter's lips twitched all evening.

She hasn't had to endure those evenings for some time. Now she sings only in established houses, and from the moment she arrives at the railway station in Frankfurt, Hamburg, or Munich, she keeps thinking she'll see her lover's face among the soldiers on the platform. The laughing men crowd around in their identical uniforms, waiting to be directed to a car in the special train.

On a few occasions she realizes she has unintentionally brushed against one of these uniforms in the crowd, when, with a side glance at the soldiers in the station, those meeting her ask if the train ride has been comfortable and without incident. She nods and smiles, explains that the rank and file don't come into first class, as her purse strikes someone's elbow by chance, and her welcome bouquet inadvertently brushes a shaved neck. The soldiers suddenly break off their conversation, stop laughing, and all turn toward her. She hears a polite apology as she herself begs their pardon, all the soldiers' eyes trained on her for a moment as they pass, but once more her fiancé is not among them.

In the evening, just before the performance, she peers as always through the peephole, searching through the upper and dress circles, checking the faces in the stalls: perhaps her fiancé will surprise her, perhaps one day he'll come back from somewhere with a promotion and be sitting unexpectedly in one of the better seats. The lights go down, she pulls back from the curtain, she couldn't find her fiancé, but there are still some empty seats. It might have been impolite to leave his promotion party so soon, perhaps he won't make it until the second act.

Then she leans once more against the plywood wall, stands once more beneath a tree of papier-mâché bark, she sings her aria in the second act and sweeps the audience with her gaze, takes a few steps toward the apron: darkness beyond, no face, no empty seat, and no fiancé.

Trees shed their leaves, stand bare, new buds appear, she hears the rustle of silken leaves upon the ground, and still she strokes false foliage in despair, asks in despair through what landscape her fiancé moves in silence, unseen, through what true foliage?

IN ADDITION to the usual rehearsal photos, the first portraits by well-known photographers begin to appear. She has learned to gather with the others in the wings for a group portrait, she has grown used to striking a characteristic pose for the house photographer, like the other leading players. And of course there are portrait photos by her fiancé, on an outing, under the open sky, in her summer dress.

But these sessions are different. She is invited to an appointment of her own, with no colleagues to complain that the light isn't right for them or that the photographer is giving them less time than she's getting. The atelier has none of the opera house's depth, there are no empty rows in which she can visualize an audience, and no fiancé stands backlit before her.

The photographer seems to almost whisper his instructions to his assistants, who change film, set the spotlights, work on the shadows under her brow, on her neck. The rest of the room is darkened, curtained off with heavy black swaths of material, swallowing all sound. She lifts her head, stares into space, at the heavens, as she does nightly. She draws a deep breath and even opens her mouth, but no note is heard. No song, only the release, the aperture, the shutter.

In profile as a young woman, her hair loose, in a peasant dress, she gazes at an earthenware jug she has apparently just put down, the expression on her face at odds with the exaggerated liveliness of her artificially reddened cheeks.

She seems to be listening, as if something might appear at any moment, as if something were stirring in the jug—not just water or wine, but a spirit.

In another photo, she holds a walking stick festooned with ribbons, she gazes from beneath a broad feathered hat, as if she wanted to give herself a touch of the demimonde—one could almost take her for an inscrutable mistress, a police chief's murderer, or a beautiful spy. But she may simply be bothered by the feathers in her field of vision, blurred white streaks that tremble with every breath she takes.

But there is no point to all this finery in the silence of the photographer's studio. Everything intended on stage as decor, complementing and supporting the song, drawing the attention of the audience to the voice's source, seems false here. It might be right for other singers, who seem to be dressed for the stage even when they aren't performing, but it doesn't suit her.

Toward the end, the photographer wants to try something else. No wig, no makeup, no flowing dress; her eyes struck him right from the start, and now he wants just the eyes, her face, lightly powdered, and nothing else.

He needs no dramatic gestures now: her hands relax on the simple dress, the tension dissolves from her limbs, the line from her throat to the orbit of her eyes no longer reveals the length of the shutter time, and her gaze loses its mistrust of the viewfinder. A calm look gradually emerges, penetrates the lens, seems to enter the body of the camera and touch the film, as if she'd discovered someone on the other side, as if there were space for someone else there, someone invisible whom she now observes in alert silence. She has already decided to keep a copy of this picture for her fiancé.

She has colleagues, she has friends, she's not alone. There are enough people around her—that's not it. Her parents are always there for her, too; they clip reviews from newspapers and magazines, conscientiously collect photos and programs in an album. But she would love to know what he thought of this or that evening, are her performances becoming more and more overpowering, as everyone else seems to think, or does she sound a bit tired now and then?

She would like him to be near her when she has to decide on a new role. He wouldn't have to speak; she'd just like to see him sitting there on the stool, as he used to, with a libretto spread out on his knees.

When she feels restless, she looks at the earlier photos he had taken of himself. In every training session, on every field exercise, he found time to press a camera into a comrade's hand and have the film developed, and each time a picture reached her from some new place.

A few of them are indistinct, because his comrade doesn't know how to handle a camera: her fiancé on a sandy path, bushes and a picket fence in the background, each grain of sand in focus, but his face blurred. In other pictures you can hardly see him—a landscape, a snow-filled forest of pines, and there, at the edge, in a white winter uniform, someone on skis is waving his ski pole, and if you look carefully you can see a distant smile.

She keeps these photos in her purse, looks at them in her dressing room before each performance. She pulls one out again at night before she goes to sleep, her bedside lamp already off. In the dim light her fiancé seems slightly faded, indistinct: a clumsy photographer blurred the picture, or it's too dark, or she's not seeing clearly. At a restaurant she rises from the table, excuses herself, takes her purse to the restroom. Once she stops in broad daylight on the sidewalk, and while people push and shove by, she rummages through her bag, but the smile in the snow-filled photo disappears in the blinding sunlight. On the train, she holds a photo behind an open magazine, taking a last look as the train enters the station, as if she needed to memorize the face before comparing it with the ones on the platform. Her fiancé used to send her a photo from every destination. She's been slightly worried recently that these photos might, in fact, become mere memories.

—

SHE SENDS HIM no picture as a keepsake, none of the photos in which she sits calmly in a photographer's studio. She was going to, with her very first letter, when he finally wrote. But she removed the photo from the envelope, she doesn't know why—perhaps for no reason at all. She may send one sometime; there will be plenty of letters. Nor does he send her new pictures of himself. He and his comrades have ample spare time after field exercises, he writes, but they aren't allowed to take photos, he can't be more specific, she'll just have to understand.

The entire correspondence goes through a cover address. She was startled the first time she saw an unknown return address on the envelope, but now she sends each letter as a matter of course to Herr Max Winkler in Berlin. She knows the mail is inspected, and she can't help feeling a twinge of nausea each time she realizes that every letter from her fiancé has gone through a stranger's hands, that every word has been pored over by someone else's eyes.

She has always managed to read between her fiancé's lines, hints about clandestine missions and the air force, but now she realizes that she's rebelling inwardly against it, that she doesn't want to understand.

She no longer has the feeling, as she sometimes did about earlier letters, that he wants to slip something past the censor. She doesn't expect him to reveal professional secrets in some coded form, those don't even interest her, but there are things that touch just the two of them. They don't have to be secrets, they can be simple descriptions meant for her and her alone. Her fiancé knows she needs to visualize things, the weather, his clothing, his face, the landscape—that's why he sent photos. Now that he can't photograph anything, he should send written descriptions, so she can gain some idea of his present life.

But he hasn't yet devoted a word, in any letter, to his surroundings, nor can she read anything between the lines. He could at least give some hints about the weather, how long the days are, some indication of local geography: she would seize on that at once, they could develop a sort of secret language in their correspondence with seemingly ordinary phrases. But nothing of the sort.

It's possible that he has no clear idea himself where he is or what he is doing, and it appears he's paid no attention to the weather for days. He never changes the subject, breaking off a thought because he realizes that he has to be careful or his letter won't ever reach his fiancée, and he knows she can fill in the rest on her own.

There's nothing to fill in, nothing to see, no sentence to be censored. Secrets remain so well hidden that even the recipient can't unveil them; the censor's office takes no pleasure in them either, and the man's letters soon cross the table unread. It doesn't seem to bother her fiancé that the picture she is given is unclear. For the first time she has the feeling that she will have to piece things together on her own, from scratch, without the slightest clue. She still doesn't feel like sending a calm portrait of herself to a cover address.

THERE ARE RUMORS. She doesn't hear them from her fiancé, they're brought by colleagues. Friends hint at what her fiancé's letters omit. He's been gone all winter, and field exercises don't normally last that long, she can figure that out for herself. But he still sticks to his story, as if it never occurred to him that she might grow suspicious over time.

She can't ask anyone, can only listen to what others whisper on the sly. On one occasion, a tenor who makes most of his living crooning famous arias on luxury cruises tells how he lost a job last fall. Mediterranean trips had been temporarily suspended because naval vessels were cruising the Straits of Gibraltar to monitor the civil war, and then, overnight his invitation to sing on a Scandinavian cruise was withdrawn without a word of explanation. He was convinced they just hadn't wanted him for the job, and that annoyed him. He checked around to see who was going to take his place, then learned to his relief that the entire trip had been cancelled.

Another colleague claims that steamships have been removed from service and reassigned: in the harbor at Stettin men are being taken on board, but not the usual soldiers heading for East Prussia. Instead, they are dressed in civilian gear, some in shorts even, with sun hats, as if they were off for the holidays in midwinter. Tour groups consisting solely of men, but why is there no entertainment? No one knows of a single musician who's gone along, so these men must be choral groups.

A friend returns from Paris: they're talking about Spain

there, too, and someone recently come back from Madrid can't understand why so many men there are speaking German in the street.

"I haven't seen your fiancé for a long time, either. Did he finally have enough of the opera?"

"He's on field exercises."

She doesn't want to connect him with the rumors, she avoids drawing conclusions—the cruises, the ships in Stettin, the all-male tour groups, and the German spoken in Spain. Perhaps she's overexcited, seizing every chance to call up the image of her fiancé, and in any case the thought that the German air force is participating in the Spanish Civil War is out of the question.

She's almost ready for the foreign stage. A first offer arrives; she can tell her friends, discuss it with her parents, she knows no one will try to talk her out of it or hold her back. But the only person she wants a reaction from is her fiancé: she wants to know what he thinks about his future wife's possible career. She makes no mention of it in her letters; she imagines surprising him face to face at a performance in Milan or Rome.

She postpones her decision, asks for time to think it over, but in her position she can't afford to take time to think things over, she tries to put them off for a week, something she can't really afford to do at her age. She hopes field exercises won't last much longer, she counts the days and nights, sees her fiancé entering her dressing room any moment, but in fact he doesn't return in time, and she won't be going abroad.

His letters continue to sound so distant, it seems as if he hasn't been writing to her at all. He might just as well be writing to someone else—the same innocuous phrases in letter after letter, the conspiratorial tone they once shared has disappeared.

Now his letters read as if they had been written to someone long since abandoned. She doesn't want to believe he's in Spain, there are no grounds for that, but the only other possibility she can imagine is that he's writing his letters in the presence of some other woman, one who might walk in at any time and ask him whom he's writing to, who might even look over his shoulder and read a few lines, since he has nothing to hide.

As a young opera singer she, too, is approached on occasion, very respectfully, and quite innocently at first, but she can quickly tell if an admirer is interested in more than her voice, in which case she extracts herself politely. It's the extravagant bouquet, the champagne in the dressing room, a certain phrase in the congratulatory note, a phone call far too late in the evening, at times simply an unguarded look in a restaurant.

Perhaps a Spaniard after all, because he likes dark-eyed women. And that's why he writes in such a reserved tone, with no deeper connection—or: he abandoned his fiancé long ago, she just doesn't know it yet. He hasn't found the right words, but she may still believe he's on a secret mission, on field exercises, and he can't leave her in total ignorance. It's time he finally told her the truth, the Spanish woman insists on it, he's promised he will.

⌐

THE HEAT OF the spotlight, the energy expended as she sings—she dabs her face with a handkerchief before removing her makeup. She sits in her costume in front of the dressing-room mirror, exhausted. The handkerchief dabs at her temple, wanders to her forehead, it's already flecked, damp, spotted with makeup, but she doesn't stretch out her hand, she can't move, doesn't want to ask for a new one, she's too tired to speak. So she keeps on dabbing at her eye shadow, her rouge, her perspiration. Her eyes are burning, and she can no longer tell that the handkerchief was ever white.

She shakes it out; that doesn't help, so she flaps it to evaporate the moisture, she fans herself to cool her face a little. A handkerchief covered with spots, smears, as if it were not makeup but grass and pollen. She feels the heat again, smells the flowers in the field, and hears the rustling of the leaves, as close as they were last summer, when she lay with her fiancé in the country meadow.

Now she must turn to the mirror, the bright light: the cotton wool and the cold cream lie ready. She tilts her head back, she has to close her eyes; in some places the makeup is embedded in her pores, in other places it has crumbled off. She holds her face still and flaps the handkerchief weakly.

The air was mild that afternoon, that evening, as they drove back to the city together. A handkerchief was torn from her hand by the airstream; she made no attempt to hold it, she let it go, a gesture of farewell, but from what? The summer before last her fiancé was not yet in uniform, and now she hasn't seen him for months, she never thought it would be like this, there was no way she could have guessed. She no longer smells hay, she smells alcohol: the makeup is almost gone. The handkerchief may still be clinging to a bush along the highway.

So many times she's imagined him sitting on the stool by the dressing-room clothes rack after a performance, he's all she ever sees as the final applause rings out, as the audience cries out in enthusiasm, as the final curtain falls, on the way to her dressing room. But his image is blurred—in what uniform should she picture him, with what expression on his face, is he squinting slightly, has he narrowed his eyes, blinded by the harsh sun of distant steppes, is his hair bleached, his skin tanned, or is he snowbound, somewhere in the north, in a winter coat, gloves, and earmuffs, in the crackling cold?

But she needs him in the dressing room, needs to know he's there when her costume is hanging on the rack and her wig has been removed, when she leans her head back and closes her eyes, when she finally pulls the curtain aside and takes her everyday clothes off the hanger. She no longer imagines her fiancé sitting on the stool, she has hidden him instead behind the curtain, among the piles of costumes. He watches, listens in on the dressing-room conversations, smiles, furrows his brow, or nods when he sees a visitor approaching.

AN OFFICER with a monocle, hair cropped short, and the sort of mustache popular twenty years ago, which a few soldiers are now wearing again in emulation of their Führer. She looks toward the curtain, is not sure if she sees her fiancé nod as the visitor pays his compliments, awkwardly kissing her hand. Other than the usual clichés, nothing seems to occur to him: after "a triumph" and "incomparable" and "moving" he doesn't know what to say, and yet he makes no move to leave the dressing room. Instead, he lights a cigarette and asks if he might be permitted to sit on the stool, then waits, as if it were now up to her to keep the conversation going, as if she had called him in because she had something to say to him.

He clears his throat, and the wardrobe mistress leaves the room, perhaps to find an ashtray, or perhaps he's bribed her. The officer takes another look around, as if someone might be hiding, listening behind the curtain. She wishes he would leave, but doesn't say so, and yet a moment later she's all ears as he speaks her fiancé's name. He has come on her fiancé's behalf, to deliver his greetings; he's doing a comrade a favor, they were together not long ago, and today he was in town by chance and saw her name on a poster.

He begs her pardon: what must she have thought of him waiting until the wardrobe mistress left, the silly conspiratorial air, but the situation was indeed a bit complicated, and it would be best if she didn't mention his visit: no one, no superior officer should learn that her fiancé had sent him. She doesn't know what to make of it, she sees no smile, no nod among the costumes, and she hopes the officer will tell her more.

And he does become more talkative, gets friendlier and more confidential as he goes along, digresses, but she doesn't dare ask where her fiancé is or what she should make of all this highly unusual secrecy; she's afraid any question she asks might harm her fiancé in the end. But this officer isn't coming back to the matter on his own, either, he sticks to other subjects, he was in an opera dressing room last summer, in Bayreuth during the festival, but it wasn't a young singer with eyes like hers sitting there, it was a delegation from the south.

The whole story is told out of context, and she finds it difficult to follow the hollow formulations. He speaks of the Führer in a difficult hour of decision, dealing with the civil war in Spain and the Red Menace—the country can't be allowed to fall into communist hands. The negotiators had been on the road for days—Seville, then Marseille, finally Berlin. But they were not content with that: they requested, insisted on, a personal interview with the Führer, and the result was the Bayreuth Accord.

But what this Bayreuth Accord consisted of, and what role the officer had played in the discussions, is never entirely clear. Much as she doesn't want to hear about it, he long since passed on to the terrible winter weather, he misses the sun, the warmth, how pleasant it would be to spend the dark months in southern climes.

He has nothing to report about her fiancé. Perhaps he's never seen him, she herself can no longer see him behind the curtain. She starts to put on her coat, her colleagues are waiting, and the officer indicates again that their meeting should be kept in strictest confidence and takes his leave with a wink—or else his monocle is bothering him.

AFTER A LATE supper, in bed at the hotel, she avoids looking at any of her fiancé's pictures in the dim light—the officer who visited her might push his way into them—the same uniform, but with his ridiculous monocle and airs. She wonders if her fiancé is equally affected around other people, hinting things, speaking in confidence, with feigned respect and secret arrogance. She has never known him to be like that, but she has no idea how much he might have changed in the meantime.

She can't fall asleep. She doesn't want to think about the officer anymore; she wants her fiancé. She should have overcome her reluctance, asked the officer specific questions about him: with the slightest clue, she could have filled in the picture for herself, and his image now would have been far less pale.

No, he wouldn't wear a pince-nez—he's always been

proud of his keen pilot's vision. And he wouldn't pick friends like that among his colleagues. He would never have entrusted this man with carrying a message to her: neither of them can stand such braggarts. That was no friend, and it was not just some awkward, innocent admirer. On the contrary. Someone sent this officer to the dressing room to see what she would say; he must have been put on her trail.

The story about an airplane and Bayreuth and Spain was only a ruse, a makeshift ploy to see if she had any idea where her fiancé was. If she had filled in any of the gaps, if she had smiled when Spain was mentioned, it would have been clear that her fiancé hadn't kept his secret, that she was aware of his covert mission. She has given nothing away, she couldn't have given anything away, and now she can take pride in her fiancé: he, too, has remained silent. She can laugh and shake her head at the whole business of sending a spy, as if, were she to perform in another country, she would immediately tell everyone about her fiancé's secret mission.

She's not proud, she doesn't shake her head, she doesn't smile in the darkness, and she doesn't fall asleep. Now she knows. She no longer has any doubt. This so poorly concealed arrival of a spy in her dressing room has revealed everything, the conspicuous secrecy has only reinforced the rumors. No lover, no other woman. He's in Spain.

They must have offered him a choice: either stay with his fiancé or take part in a covert mission for an initially unspecified length of time without saying a word about it, even to his closest friends. While the two of them were still making mutual plans for the coming months, for Christmas, perhaps for a winter holiday together, for a wedding the following year, he had already opted for secrets; he knew already then that one evening, before long, she would no longer see him through the hole in the curtain, sitting in his usual place.

—

SHE KNOWS HER fiancé is in the sky, with an aviator's cap, a microphone at his mouth, wearing a pair of goggles, his ears hidden by headphones—that way, no one can recognize him. But she knows he's in a cockpit, or the fuselage, wherever the radio operator sits in the aircraft these days. She knows he's in the sky.

She's not interested in fighter planes, nor does she know much about aviators who fought in the Great War. She doesn't want to hear about them, and yet she pricks up her ears now and then when someone at the next table mentions Moreau or von Richthofen. She can't help listening in on the conversation of strangers, although it's basically nothing but places, names, abbreviations, and various aircraft types, none of which make much sense to her. Only the vocabulary of heroism, by which the veterans are carried through life, knits together the meaningless recitals.

She learns nothing from this, can't determine what lies behind it, loses the thread. If she listens to the war stories at the next table for too long, she may even begin moving her lips silently on the way home. She mouths the air force jargon, a steep glide through a veil of mist, strong turbulence, repeating words she never intended to say aloud: air patrol, nosedive, ack-ack guns. She wonders if airplanes will circle the skies again for Persil this spring.

At her aunt and uncle's farm she takes a stroll through the fields alone: new grass, buds appearing everywhere, the first pollen in the air, light, shapeless flakes that dissolve in her hand to nothing more than a resinous, slightly coarse film. She's not entirely sure whether she's caught anything, she's not even sure if these flakes are floating in the sunshine or if they are inside her eyes. Just a faint cloudiness, dots, light; she's noticed it several times recently.

Perhaps it's her circulation, or perhaps she's under too much stress. Sometimes when she looks at something, the image seems to slowly coalesce from separate dots. She holds her head still, concentrates on the freshly plowed ground, first the furrow, then a strip of sand, and the image is clear, the flakes have disappeared. She almost feels dizzy.

A slender shadow stretches across the fields. She sees the silhouette of an airplane approaching, the rounded nose, the wings, the tail rudder, and she recognizes the type, even though she's never paid attention to such things. She looks up at the sky: she was right. The shadow passes over her, then the plane is above the village—perhaps she didn't need to see its outline, perhaps she would have recognized it even from the sound of its engine. She closes her eyes, listens, yes, she sees a figure.

SHE KNOWS HER fiancé is in the sky, but she doesn't want to picture him flying toward cities in Spain, sitting in the cabin reconfirming the flight plan, giving target coordinates or time remaining before the planned drop. She doesn't want to imagine the crew pointing out a cloud formation, reflecting light, or the moon in a clear sky, or hear them joking or making plans for the evening. She doesn't want to listen to anyone complaining about the air at that altitude.

She hears the cries and sirens as the German squadrons approach, distant dots in the sky at first, almost invisible. She hears the sound of the antiaircraft guns—or no shots at all, only sirens, because there are no antiaircraft guns. She hears the low hum, slow, soft, as if all the sound were in her own body, in her throat and stomach, hands, and knees.

She doesn't want to see her fiancé up there, on one of the calmest flights in recent weeks, with no turbulence, no cloud banks, no perils. Altitude, wind speed, the city barely visible below. She doesn't know if the conversation dies away when they reach their target, nor what the orders sound like when it's time to prepare the drop. Those exchanges in the final moments—are they still comrades, or do they speak like strangers, are they suddenly shouting? Can't the click of the release be sensed even under the headphones, a faint metallic sound that vibrates in their temples?

She doesn't want the whistling in her ears that seems to come from all sides, doesn't want the blasts and explosions, the pandemonium under which all other sound is buried. She doesn't want to feel the deafness as she peers up through the dust and smoke and rubble to where her fiancé can no longer be guessed at in the cabin of a plane that swerves away.

He has seen nothing, neither village nor bridge. At the decisive moment he cannot follow the bombs as they near the earth, turn to dots above the village, barely visible, and, as one squints to see them, little clouds that billow up into the air.

But the camera on board records each step in individual frames. The moment the rolls of film emerge from the canisters, the moment the first prints are dry, the pictures pinned to the wall, the staff gathers around to admire the completed mission. That's the payload released over the landscape. You can see shadows of other planes. Then a clear, calm picture, nothing but the familiar dots. And then smoke, flames, rubble. It was supposed to be the bridge. It turned out to be the village.

Her fiancé can see it clearly, too, although aerial photographs require a good eye and some practice, for the distance between the camera and the subject is substantial. He sees the torn-up streets with lines of cars, burning buildings, and countless fresh craters, but he doesn't see the dead.

AT SOME POINT her fiancé will have to see a dead body. He's not had to deal with death till now; he's only twenty-five, and his parents are still far from death's door. He'll encounter his first true corpse in Spain: not someone confined to bed at the end of a long life, with no strength, no wish to go on, but a human being who stood there a moment ago, who left a street corner to cross the broad square, a mistake, since there was no cover, and now perhaps a surprised look on his face.

She sees her fiancé seek shelter in the alleys of an unknown city: out on a day's leave, strolling through the old quarter with a few comrades, and then they're fired on, from a rooftop, they think, there must be snipers' nests up there. At first they duck behind pillars, but as soon as the attack lets up, they want to withdraw from the line of fire. They just need to reach the corner of the next building, and he estimates how many strides it will take, scrutinizes the empty square, figures the angle the shots are coming from—should he crawl forward or run?

He checks his bootlaces again—a loose one could be his downfall. Only now, as he bends over, under cover, slowly, and finds his boots still tightly tied, does he see that the tip of his left boot has been touching a dead man's shoulder. His comrades had spotted the dead man on the ground long ago.

His first real corpse, a man alive a short time ago, and now the blood on his ear gleams in the sun. Her fiancé wants to move his foot, but he remains motionless, feels his left leg, his knee, his toes; warmth seems to penetrate his leather boot from outside. The man's eyes are opened wide, as if still trained on the narrow strip of sky, the edge of the roof, a figure outlined against the sun.

The lids immobile, the pupils small, the eyes bloodshot, the lashes touched by the sun. Soon her fiancé will no longer be standing in shadow, either; it's been quiet for some time, and now one of his comrades gives a sign and they begin running.

He's determined to clean his boot, they've reached the intersection, shots ring out again, they've made it to a street they know, they want to get back to their lodgings as quickly as possible. He curls his toes as he runs, still feels the warmth in the leather, he just wants to stop a moment and wipe off the tip of his boot, he always carries a clean handkerchief, they have to reach safety. The handkerchief is white, he doesn't dare take it from his pocket, unfold it, use it—that might be misunderstood.

She sees her fiancé run—unevenly, he seems to be favoring his left foot, as if he has a pebble in his boot, as if he'll soon be limping. He's out of breath now; the attack is behind them, and he hears nothing but his own panting, the squeaking of his boots. She sees him outside his lodgings at last, no longer running. He takes the handkerchief and crouches down, cleans the dark leather, polishes the toe of the boot till it shines, until the handkerchief turns gray and his fingertips are black. He could have shined his boots inside, with shoe polish, brushes, and rags, but he had to do it out here in the sunshine. The heat has let up, the handkerchief is useless now. Her fiancé checks his fingertips: the ridges are filled with dirt, the nails rimmed in black.

He can't remember whether he drew his foot back, whether he accidentally kicked his first dead body; he doesn't know if the man fell face down, if blood flowed from his mouth, if there was vomit on his lips, or if it all just appeared so in the noon light.

His boots are polished, but something still clings to his hands. His comrades have brought beer, are eating salami sandwiches in the shade. What's that on his hands? You can see something. He didn't touch anyone. His skin is dry, slight calluses starting to form from carrying equipment; his skin is brown, dark hair on his fingers and the backs of his hands, he has to use hand cream, that's all. Tinned meat, brawn—they cut the bread crusts off with their pocketknives. He didn't touch anyone, there should be no trace on his hands. Nothing has changed. He doesn't want bread and butter, or pickles, and in spite of the heat he's not thirsty. He just runs the radio, transmits reports, sits with his headphones on. It would be crazy to think you could see something on his hands.

—

WHEN SHE FINALLY sees him again, he's wearing leather gloves. It's the fashion; they're not meant to keep his hands warm, it's high summer now, July. Soldiers wear gloves, and anyone in the air force. It's been hot in Rügen recently. The bright sunlight, a cool breeze off the Baltic, hands sunburn easily, and even operating a radio can be painful if your skin is sunburned. He strips off his gloves: his hands are almost milky, pale, yet his face is deeply tanned. Yes, he's been out of doors a lot, they even spent some time sunbathing on the beach, he's mentioned that in letters.

He was stationed in Rügen, and now that field exercises are over he can tell her. Yet something's not quite right: his gloves, his tanned face, his slightly weathered skin, the sun wrinkles around the eye. She can see that his tan won't fade completely, even over the course of the coming winter.

But he almost seems to believe his story himself—the chalk cliffs, the marram grass, the sea-buckthorn schnapps—and he seems to linger over his winter exercises in Rügen, which lasted all spring and into the summer. After nine months they feel a bit like strangers, of course—they've never been apart this long, and they barely knew each other when he left. Letters don't make up for that; no matter how often you write, something is always lost. They have to overcome their shyness first, perhaps a new intimacy has to develop between them, and then he will tell her where he was and what happened.

He would gladly have brought his fiancé a few photos as keepsakes—she can imagine it must have been hard on him, since he always carried a camera, but personal photos were strictly forbidden during field exercises. Those who didn't understand, who thought it couldn't be all that serious, had their cameras confiscated prior to departure, and some comrades were annoyed and preoccupied by this. And if someone did manage a photo or two, his film was seized. Anything that didn't bear the staff film department stamp disappeared immediately, and although they said the rolls of film were destroyed without being viewed, everyone knew, and it bothered some, that they took a look at the negatives first, just to make sure nothing forbidden had been photographed.

So he has no pictures to show. And they have a gap in the family album before they even have a family. For a while, a few pages on, she's the only one present: in costume, her gaze calm, onstage and with her colleagues. Her fiancé carefully arranges the photos, pastes the corner mounts onto the black card paper, looks the page over, exchanges a picture: he doesn't like to see her look so serious.

THEN COME the wedding pictures. A garden party with countless guests, so many you can hardly find the bride and groom. He's invited his friends and comrades, and she's on the lookout all afternoon for an officer with cropped hair, and a monocle, she thought he would turn up in her dressing room a second time, but she's never seen him again. She was right, he can't have been a friend, they just wanted to sound her out, and she has never even told her fiancé, her husband, the story.

Sometimes she would look out at the audience and think, *They're all spies this evening,* as in a thriller or a bad film. *They have no interest in music,* it's just a cover, *they'll exchange information discreetly during intermission.* They sit shoulder to shoulder as she sings into the darkness, and she alone knows they are spies—each spy thinks those on either side of him and in the next row are music lovers. They'll never learn who works for which side, who is in counterespionage, who is a double agent. At intermission they disappear into the crowd, although their contacts can still spot them, and those who spy on spies.

Several cast members are at the wedding; it's a farewell party, too, this is her last season for a while. Partners from love scenes banter with each other, as they sometimes do after performances, calling each other by their stage names, having pressed their cheeks together, felt the thick makeup, its fragrance, the vibration of their temples during the duet. She has died in the arms of one or two of these tenors, too, thrown herself on his breast for her final aria, her last sigh, singing unto death.

And her friends have arrived; they were always there to cheer her up or console her, but never pressed her about her missing fiancé. Some did a little spy work of their own to figure out which stories could be trusted, where the officer with the mustache and the monocle came from, how long the training mission would last. They sit in a circle on garden chairs, whisper, poke each other, sneak a look at this or that man in uniform.

Nothing this afternoon recalls the intense argument she and her friends had one spring evening at the home of another soprano, after someone returned from Paris with the story that German air force units had destroyed a village in Spain. The air raid had been unlike any before. No stronghold, this Guernica, no arsenal, of no strategic importance, the bombs had fallen in broad daylight, and the victims were civilians, women and children unable to defend themselves.

Some said it was unthinkable, it must be propaganda—that was clear from the very fact that Germany wasn't even involved in Spain's civil war. Others maintained, incensed, that the very existence of a German air force was the most shocking revelation, and a quarrel ensued—some thought the proof was clear, others wouldn't believe a word of it. She belonged to the latter group: regardless of what she believed, she had her fiancé to consider.

When he came back, she didn't ask about the report; perhaps her doubts had faded. Given his long absence, they didn't wait long: they had already set a wedding date and then repeatedly postponed it, and now it was finally time for the preparations. They've had to establish a new intimacy, and with a lifetime to share, they can return slowly to the past, to the months they were apart.

Before evening falls, her husband calls the wedding guests onto the lawn for a group photo. The two sets of parents and relatives, their colleagues, friends, and comrades break up their smaller group conversations, put their glasses down, appear between the trees or emerge from the house. She asks who will take the photo; she doesn't realize at first that it will be her husband, who is already fiddling with his camera. He polishes the lens a second time, turns away from the sun with the light meter, closes his left eye and peers through the viewfinder. She has to accept the fact that he won't be in the picture.

He's excited to be taking pictures again, and one moment he's out on the lawn, concentrating on the camera, unaware of anyone else; next he's calling out and laughing—it looks like everyone's there, and he arranges the pose. She'll be the focal point, along with their parents and the witnesses. He moves the children to the front and the women pull up garden chairs; he has someone kneel, motions another a bit to the right, inserts a uniform among the summer frocks, checks the viewfinder, moves them back a step. Now everyone's in the picture, and he cocks the shutter and says, "Smile, hold still a moment."

———

THINGS GO ON as before, except that she no longer stands onstage while a wind machine offstage blows paper leaves across the boards, propelling them into the wings, piling them up; no loud rustling as the crepe-paper surface of the rocky cliffs begins to tremble, while the prompter coughs from her little box, clears her throat, rubs at her eyes, twitches her lips. No more visits to her dressing room after performances, no spies dropping by. She no longer lingers in the empty hall after rehearsal—the seats turned up, the exits closed, the lights dimmed, the stage piled with props, a garden table by the willow. She no longer wanders through the spacious hall with its somber light—alien without its song—puzzling over things, listening, replacing opera characters' names like von Moreau, von Richthofen, perhaps Warlimont and Sander, with murmuring, singing softly to herself, trying to work in unfamiliar phrases from somewhere, from some other lips, matching them to the flow of the melody, Red Menace, Bayreuth Accord.

Her husband taking courses again as he did before he left, reconnaissance, flight safety, radio practicum, along with his comrades wherever they're stationed. Everything goes on as before, the morning fog off the chalk cliffs is no longer mentioned, the seagulls are not a topic of conversation—how they perched on the driftwood, peering into the calm waters. All invented, perhaps, she's still not sure, she shouldn't trust rumors. And if she asked her husband about Spain, it would mean accusing him of concealing the truth from the start, as if he hadn't been honest with her even after the wedding. She can't accuse him, and she doesn't want him to think she distrusted him all along, that she was less than honest herself, sending out her spies to discover how far his accounts could be trusted.

She doesn't want to see hints where there are none, when he squints at the sun or complains about the heat, nor detect innuendos when he talks with certain comrades as if they alone shared some special friendship. She's been convinced often enough by some phrase or pause in the conversation: *This is the man with whom my husband saw his first corpse.*

SHE'S NO LONGER onstage, but she still sings an aria or two to herself at home, just as other people talk to themselves when they're alone—or think they are. But she's not alone; her son has just started to walk, taking his first steps, then clutching at his mother as she stands at the sink or the ironing board, singing. He looks up at her and she looks down into his eyes, her lips moving.

He hears the song and he gazes at her as if he knew it doesn't matter whether the words are meant for him or no one in particular. He absorbs the tones while a white sleeve sways before his eyes; he stands motionless and the tones pass through him. The words mean nothing to him yet—the farewell aria, her half of the duet.

She knows how the other half sounds, but not the text; she gets mixed up on certain lines and about what comes next, then puts the iron down and goes to check the correct wording. She picks up her son and carries him into the living room, runs her finger along the shelf—the librettos are in no particular order. She opens the script directly to the right place: the dialogue and duet and her marked lines. Now she is silent, while her son hums and plays with her hair.

She's never paid much attention to the text before, but now, as she reads a few pages closely, she's struck by the fact that passages here and there are slightly silly if not sung: the intensity, the hyperbole, the constantly repeated images. Reading the text by itself, she can scarcely believe that music could emerge from these banalities. It's as if a mystery barely perceptible to the human eye lies in the script. Even she can't understand the basic nature of this mystery, although she is well aware of how to solve it: she forms the words, slowly her voice gains strength, and soon there are no silly words, there is only song.

EVERYTHING MUST HAVE been prepared in secret: the travel guides and holiday reading disappear overnight from the shop windows, and by morning the displays are dominated by war memoirs. The books are stacked in piles in the stores the moment news of the end of the Spanish Civil War arrives—the veterans have been writing in secret, but now it's official, the rumors can be confirmed: German volunteer units helped Franco emerge victorious, and members of the Condor Legion are proudly feted everywhere.

Her husband was a Condor Legionnaire too; he had exchanged his long-sought dark blue uniform for a drab khaki one without hesitation. He brings one of these war memoirs home, hands it to her, is proud that he, too, was one of the volunteers, that's his plane on the cover. He presses the book into her hand, she can read in detail what happened to him, it's all there in black and white. No keepsake photos from Spain, but here's a whole book, he still can't quite believe it, a book devoted solely to him and his comrades—he never dreamed that one day they would be considered worthy of an entire book.

Although it is emphasized now that it was a secret operation, even if that secrecy was one of its main attractions, he is still happy that he no longer needs to hide anything from her after having to conceal his mission for so long. He has always wanted to tell her everything, and at first he didn't know where he would be sent, but he wanted to give her at least an idea, some sign to let her know how long it would be, although even that was forbidden.

She can surely imagine how at odds he felt: he wanted to tell her everything, and the pressure of secrecy gave him the oddest ideas. In his very first letter he thought of simply telling her where he was, writing in large block letters about Spain so that everyone could see it, but he knew she would be the last person to receive such a letter, if she ever did.

From the very start he was tormented by the secrecy, by the letters he did send, all of them false, and at times he could barely restrain himself. If he lost control for even one moment he could wind up in the guardhouse, he knew that. He admires her courage, the way she accepted everything without complaint. What must she have thought when he left her hanging that way, what unpleasant images must have come to mind, he didn't even like to think about it.

He meant to tell her everything the moment he was back, but he was still afraid. If something had come out he would have been demoted at the very least, possibly even accused of treason or, worse, spying, and they would have lost any chance for a stable life. After all, it was his part in this secret mission that had allowed him to build for both of them. They wanted to get married, but their plans might have dissolved into thin air: she might not have married him if he had been a simple handyman or an electrician.

Nor could he bring himself to talk about it on their honeymoon. The secrecy, the dishonesty continued, and at some point it seemed too late to explain, too late because he feared she would blame him for not having spoken openly sooner.

But that's all over now, thank god, the tension has been released. He's happy now, he can breathe easily again. She can ask anything—she can read through the memoirs, and if anything is missing or unclear, if she still has doubts about something that doesn't seem to square with reality, or she just wants to be sure, she shouldn't hesitate to ask. He will give her a full account.

—

HE GOES TO the wardrobe and rummages through his socks. He returns with a small package, a gift he brought from Spain for her, hidden in his drawer for two years. How he has waited for this day, to see her eyes when she opens the box.

She unwraps the gift carefully, for it seems fragile—a doll, a figurine perhaps, made of clay or porcelain. It's a Spanish dancer—he searched a long time for the right gift—with a dress, or rather costume, made of real cloth—he never found an opera singer—arms extended, hands touching above her head—the markets were full of cheap goods of course, but then he saw this dancer, with her knotted hair and half-closed eyes, and luckily she survived the journey home intact.

Her son stares, wants to touch the Spanish dancer, and reaches out; he seems to like her, a new toy perhaps. He's allowed to stroke the costume with his finger, the surface beneath, the bright, cool skin. But he can't include her among his stuffed animals; she's fragile, and if something happens she can't be replaced. It seems wise to place the figurine in the living-room cabinet—it will be well displayed, and her son can examine it from a safe distance.

How lucky that she never rummaged among his socks during the past two years and found the gift: the hiding place was well chosen, the package rolled up in a pair of heavy winter socks, but now they can stop keeping secrets.

ALMOST THREE YEARS of secrets. From November 1936 until the following July she waited for explanations, then, for two more years, hoped that the mysteries would resolve themselves. Now it is midsummer of 1939, and the secrets revealed, she can now ask her husband anything. But she no longer has questions.

She glances through the memoirs from time to time. She can't read them for very long; she doesn't really care whether her husband was in Seville or in Ávila. He may have been pleased by the palm trees, but it doesn't matter to her whether he attacked Teruel or only Madrid, nor is she interested in Franco's memory or if the war has taught him a lesson.

In any case, there is nothing in these books about her husband's first exposure to death. That's the one question she might ask, but she does not. She's afraid he might reply in the same tone that dominates these memoirs: overblown, cheerful descriptions, a silly, forced breathlessness marked by short sentences and frequent exclamation marks. Like a series of shouts.

She doesn't need these books. She's as happy as her husband that they can stop keeping secrets, she's glad her fears were unfounded. Her fiancé's overnight disappearance had nothing to do with being engaged, there was no indecision, no second thoughts with a Spanish mistress, no bachelor life to atone for, however one might imagine it, brought to an end with "I do" on the day of the wedding.

She doesn't need these memoirs, they offer no new insights—that's what so absurd, shocking, even disappointing about them. Everything was just as she had assumed. No alternative story opens up before her, no surprises, no unexpected explanations for his absence. Regardless of how unpleasant a surprise may have been, it would have offered some relief, all the scenes she had imagined dissolving before her eyes, the whole thing simply a case of overexcitement, a delusion.

But now, in retrospect, everything she imagined is confirmed in detail by reality. Her husband kept silent and she came to the truth on her own, without his help. No expression, no squint, no shadow crossing his face will alter that now, when he recalls these stories. No hint from him was needed to unleash her imagination—that was provided by the stiff, too closely shaved, unknown officer who appeared in her dressing room.

PERHAPS HER SON will read the memoirs someday, perhaps, when he's old enough, he'll be interested in this phase of his father's life. A time will come when he will ask about the family history, become interested in his own childhood and what happened before he was born, but that's still a long way off. If he wonders then why his parents were separated for nine months before they were married, he can read these books.

But as she thinks it over, picturing her young son with one of these books, sitting in the garden, devouring one page after another, enthusiastically adopting their tone, she can't stand the idea, simply can't bear it. Even now, the thought of those Spanish memoirs on the shelf beside her librettos bothers her.

The length of a secret mission can become a new secret. She can leave it at that with her son. What has been revealed can be concealed again without great difficulty.

The Spanish figurine remains, and the boy has grown fond of it, constantly begging to have it taken down from the cabinet so he can examine it more closely. But the books haven't yet caught his attention, he pays no heed to the plane, the antitank guns, or the uniformed man that decorate the cover. He knows nothing of all that. The books can be quietly removed from the shelf, from the apartment, disappear, be put somewhere in the basement.

Her husband has no objections. She's a little surprised, she's relieved, and her husband seems almost happy to have a new secret so soon after the revelation of the old one, this secret pact between him and his wife that no one will ever know about. She suggests it, and he agrees at once: they'll never mention it to their son or future children. His role in the Spanish Civil War will remain a secret forever.

AFTER THEY'VE SEALED the pact, there's a look in his eyes she thought she might not see again. An occasional wink, a conspiratorial glance when they talk, gestures, hints made in the certainty that there's something they alone share. There's a new intimacy when they walk through the fields and their elbows touch by accident, when he takes her hand unexpectedly on the street or rubs her neck in the dark.

He even abandons his quirk about leather gloves, seldom thinks to put them on when he leaves the house; they lie all day on the dresser, and once he almost forgets them in a local garden café.

She thinks about the gloves more often than he does. Before his departure for the Condor Legion's victory parade, it was she who placed the gloves in his suitcase so he'd be sure to have them: he would have missed them in Berlin, when he joined his comrades. And afterward, when they all marched past beneath the eye of their Führer, when he received his Spanish Order, he could not have saluted without leather gloves.

Hands to their foreheads, hands stretched out in the

German salute. She could have gone to Berlin, but she didn't want to see those hands. While the Condor Legion was celebrating the action in Spain as if it ensured peace for the foreseeable future, there was already talk about the next war.

Perhaps in the not-too-distant future, new memoirs will dominate the window displays: new theaters of operation, more dangerous air battles, yet greater victories. And Spain will be forgotten.

· messengers ·

I GAZE OUT the side window into the darkness the whole time, among the trees, into the undergrowth by the roadside. From time to time I spot an animal. I've seen a few foxes, apparently lying in wait for prey, even a lynx, once, disappearing into the ditch by the side of the road. But I can see no farther, barely a meter beyond the edge of the traffic lane, where everything coalesces into a black wall.

I focus on the outermost twigs that emerge from nothingness, then disappear; I watch for shining eyes. Perhaps I might see more if we were moving more slowly. Our speed makes it difficult to scan the landscape at night, and the motor is so quiet I can't even judge how fast we are going.

When I drive alone at night, I have to concentrate on the road, watch the shifting speedometer before me, but now I'm sitting beside Paulina in her station wagon and can ignore the gauges. She keeps her eyes on the center line but motions to me now and then. Far ahead, deer are crossing the road, an animal lies on the asphalt—bundle of fur, blood and innards flashing past. A fox will find it eventually.

Cars have always played a different role in Paulina's family than in mine, and when I visited my cousins I was infected by their interest in sunroofs, cup holders, and adjustable seats. I learned the technical terms for the newest features, but at the same time I saw it all as an outsider. I was never able to push the buttons and press the levers with the same self-assurance as they did. No matter how hard I tried, this never changed, and dealing with cars has remained foreign to me. In the same way, the notion of making love in a car always intrigued and repelled me in equal measure—the cramped interior, the stale smoke, the stuck zippers.

We've been driving through the dark for over an hour now. We've left the woods behind, an endless road stretches before us, the glow of the instrument panel tinges Paulina's face with a deep sea-green shimmer. We sit in an aquarium's night light, and it doesn't smell of sweat or perfume here, but of new car. I once saw spray cans at a gas station with the matching fragrance for each and every make of automobile.

At first we discussed the station wagon: its color, seat covers, electronic system. We imagined a scene: a fuse blows, something mysterious happens inside, and all at once a ghostly hand locks the doors and we're trapped. We touched on horror stories we used to tell—one about a trip at night, a car parked in an open field, a knock from above, an invisible figure crouching overhead, rhythmically pounding on the roof above the passenger seat. Then we moved on to stories about uncanny experiences from our childhood.

I'm around four years old, five at the most, and alone, waiting for my parents to come home or at least call. Darkness is slowly falling. I don't play or draw, nor do I turn on the lights. I sit close to the telephone, which shimmers when the sun sets, as if reflecting a last remnant of daylight. Finally it rings. I lift the receiver at once and say hello. But it's not my father or mother on the line. There's a click, a low hum, I say hello, my name again. There's another click, then the busy signal, followed by the dial tone. I hold the receiver in my hand, I can barely make out anything in the room, and I can't reach the light switch.

Paulina says, "I know, that happened to me too. Always in the early evening. It was odd, because whoever called never apologized. A person usually says something, Sorry, wrong number, particularly when a child answers the phone. Those calls always frightened me—I didn't want to tell anyone about them, not even my brother or sister. We've never talked about it, but we may all have received those calls. Do you know what I used to think later?"

It might have been our grandfather calling. He'd never seen us, never spoken with us, but perhaps he just wanted to hear our voices for a moment, perhaps that was all. He didn't dare ask for anyone because his wife was always nearby. Even today, when someone hangs up without saying a word, I think it might be our grandfather.

Paulina says, "At times I even thought I could hear something, far away, as if someone were speaking through a handkerchief. We'll never know if he actually wanted to talk to us. I picture him choosing his words carefully, dialing, then being so excited at the prospect of speaking with his grandchildren for the first time in his life that he can't find his voice. He hesitates, is about to speak, but it's too late: the child at the other end has become nervous, has pressed his finger down on the cradle in fright. Perhaps, without realizing it, we were the ones who prevented the contact."

Before I can ask Paulina what she means by that, she slows down, bringing the car nearly to a halt. I look out again: we are on a country road. I can see nothing but underbrush, but Paulina has seen something off to the right, and she shifts into second gear and turns into a narrow farm lane.

It's not easy talking with Paulina about our grandfather, I have to be very careful. The life our grandparents shared is still safe territory, we can always make up new episodes, add new variations, I don't have to watch my every word. Since our grandmother's death, however, things have become increasingly difficult; I have to be sure to refer to the Old Lady only in passing, and the closer the story gets to the year we spent the holidays together, the more hesitantly we speak. What we said about our grandfather and the Old Lady in those weeks, about two elderly people living in our neighborhood, remains taboo. Not a word. Those terrifying images, stories, and intentions—they simply never existed.

On the other hand, in the past few years we've often spoken about the time that followed, and I was usually the one who tired of hearing about it. Paulina is firmly convinced that we have the Old Lady on our conscience.

I know how stubborn the images we create can be: they overlie what we see, and if at first we perceive them as a veil easily removed, they are soon firmly attached, have penetrated our vision, persisting there at a deeper level. Sometimes it seems as if spirits guide my vision, as if I am moved by a mysterious force to see something in a person or a landscape that isn't there.

When I was traveling through Morocco years ago, I saw a place where our grandfather once stayed, in a region I had never been to before. I was traveling to Tétouan in a shuttle bus, and the highway stretched northward through an otherwise unremarkable plain between Er Rif and the Mediterranean. Dry undergrowth, scree, and dust whirl up behind the taxi; I gaze out the dirty windshield, exhausted, squeezed between the other passengers. And all at once I think I see something out there on the plain.

Looking more closely, I make out a landing strip, along with the oil drums, fences, and hangars found only on airfields. But if our grandfather joined the Condor Legion in November of 1936, he can't have already been here in the summer; when troops were being transported for Franco, the Condor Legion didn't exist.

I know that he never set foot on Moroccan soil, and yet I can see our grandfather standing on that airfield; I can't help conjuring that image. A souvenir photo, never taken, underexposed, causing the bright midday scenery to look as if it were an image of the night: our grandfather as a young man, watching the Moroccan soldiers at the edge of the field. It's his first time in Africa, but the heat hardly bothers him; he's pulled the brim of his cap far down on his forehead. He's there again with the next squadron, and then the soldiers board the transport planes, cross the Straits of Gibraltar, and shortly thereafter set foot on European soil for the first time in their lives, their legs still wobbly from the rough flight.

But for our grandfather it's a matter of turning his plane around and heading back to Tétouan as quickly as possible; he knows how important this transfer of troops is: the Spanish army is for the most part solidly behind the Republicans, and without the Moroccans, Franco's efforts would be in vain. My gaze is directed by spirits, and I'm defenseless against their whispers: this is where our grandfather took off and landed as a young pilot, and I hold fast to this, in spite of knowing better.

Perhaps it's for this very reason that I shy away from taking a trip to Spain. Since I have no clue to where my grandfather may have been stationed, I would be asking myself on every street corner if he ran through a hail of bullets at this very spot; perhaps I might even duck involuntarily, watching the overhang the shots came from. Like a tourist who apparently can't take too much sun, perhaps I would stay in the shade, and beneath the acacias I could not help but recognize the exact spot where our grandfather saw a dead man for the first time.

I didn't take a photo of the airfield at Tétouan, but in my mind's eye, I can can still picture it in full detail. A photograph would show nothing—only the meaningless stones, branches, dust, not even an old airplane in the sun that one could speculate about. What sort of a family album would that provide?

Now we're driving very slowly, not talking, and looking at Paulina's face from the side, I can tell she's trying to locate something specific, she's focusing on something—a crackling inside the car, an electric discharge, a sound from an unknown source—but there is nothing but the deep hum of the motor and, now and then, the faint blow of a stone against the undercarriage.

I worry about Paulina sometimes, because she's obsessed with the stories we've invented. We didn't kill the Old Lady, but Paulina insists that we did. I keep trying to convince her by constantly questioning the reliability of what she considers valid evidence. But I've never been able to disabuse Paulina of her notions, and now the story is behind us; today we no longer speak about it.

For several years, Paulina has been tending a grave, one she's convinced is the Old Lady's. And when we're talking on the phone and Paulina says, It's about that time again, she doesn't have to say anything more: I go to her and help her tend the grave site—she doesn't want to do it alone.

We weed it regularly, put flowers on the grave, and replace the memorial candle, not wanting to get in trouble with the cemetery administration. We've managed it thus far, though tending the grave is a lot of work. Perhaps it's due to the soil, or the old trees surrounding it, but the flowers wilt more rapidly there than on the surrounding graves, and even the moss doesn't do as well—we've had to change it several times. I've given up trying to convince Paulina that the Old Lady can't possibly be buried there; I simply go along until she's satisfied with the way the grave looks.

The lane narrows, I hear twigs scraping along the car's shiny finish, we're both concentrating on the ruts before us. Then Paulina points at fresh tire tracks.

She turns off the headlights and dims the aquarium green of the lights on the dashboard. I place my hand on the spotlight by the windshield, so I can turn it on the moment Paulina gives me a sign. We watch both sides for pull-offs in the undergrowth, for a lane leading to the fields. We wait for the tire tracks to end.

WE'VE GOT THEM. The car is angled off to the left, one side in the muddy ditch, the other on the grass-covered ridge; it will be hard to get it back into the ruts. Paulina stops, she gives me the sign, and our hood is flooded with light—along with the twigs, the foliage, the mud flaps of the other car, its bumper and trunk.

The handle of the spotlight heats up quickly. I aim the

beam of light at the rear window, and the foliage and twigs appear as a dark pattern against the exterior of the other car blurred by the condensed moisture on the glass. As the film evaporates in the intense light, the shadows become clearer, and a hand appears and wipes away the moisture from the inside of the window.

The hand is followed by a man's face, his eyes narrowed above the backseat. Squinting, confused at first, then angry, his flat, damp hand balls into a fist. The man can't see anything with the light in his eyes, he yells something, we say nothing. He shields his eyes with his hand, and I remove my hand from the searchlight, but it stays in position. He pulls up his other arm and braces himself, something moves beside or beneath him, but he doesn't look away, he stares into the light. The man stops yelling, pauses, listens, almost as if someone is talking to him.

Now things move rapidly. The face disappears. We see two pairs of arms, two pairs of legs. We see knees that don't match. We think we may have seen two pairs of underpants. We don't speak. A shirt appears, the car rocks slightly, and the man climbs forward into the driver's seat. He reaches under the seat, groping for car keys on the floor. There is no further movement from the back.

He starts the engine, turns on the lights, tries to steer, directing the car back into the lane with awkward jerks, giving it too much gas, spinning the wheels as he lurches forward.

Paulina shifts into first. We follow the car slowly; it can't handle this country lane, and we catch up, we're right on his bumper. I see Paulina's hand on the steering wheel; she holds it loosely, her other hand equally relaxed on the gearshift. Her palms are still dry. Her hands have scarcely changed at all over the past twenty years.

The interior of the other car remains brightly illuminated by the spotlight. It stays that way until we reach the highway, but we never get to see the second face.

I remember how surprised we were back when the Pigeon Man died. He had been standing by his garden fence that evening with his penetrating gaze, but at noon the next day, as we returned from an outing on the hill, we saw a hearse approaching along the narrow path to our house. We ducked into the bushes to let it pass; the stiff, dark gray curtains swayed at the windows, and we knew it had to be the Pigeon Man lying behind them.

We had spread the rumor that the Pigeon Man had moved to the hill in order to die in peace, but now we could scarcely believe that he was dead. Never again that pitiless gaze that missed nothing. The entire set of observations that he had lined up in his mind in a chain of evidentiary photos was suddenly dissolved. We no longer feared that the Pigeon Man would see through us.

We'd never read the newspaper before, but in the days that followed we waited impatiently for my cousins' parents to finish reading the paper at breakfast. We turned straight to the obituaries and looked for the Pigeon Man. On one hand we were furious with him, because he could no longer lead us to our grandfather; on the other we felt sorry for him. He had isolated himself from the outside world, kept in touch with no one, had never given any sign of real life, yet he deserved at least a memorial death notice.

It sounds crazy, but we may also have felt guilty. Perhaps the Pigeon Man hadn't been able to cope with the loss of his Spanish dancer. We didn't even know if he had relatives. Day after day we searched the newspaper in vain—we were almost ready to submit a death notice for him ourselves.

The spotlight has long since gone off, and we slowly lose interest. The car races along on the highway ahead, fleeing through sleepy villages, through moribund industrial areas. We haven't lost sight of it for the past forty-five minutes, we've followed all its feints, its tricky turns; it slows to a crawl at a taxi stand, and the back door opens a crack, but then it takes off again at full speed.

We no longer care to know where they live. It would take all the fun out of the chase if we finally recognized the woman in the backseat, it would be banal and embarrassing; perhaps one of Paulina's neighbors is cowering there.

On the open highway we let them to pull away, and Paulina coasts to the side of the road and turns off the lights. The cool night air, a gentle breeze across the fields, no other sound. In the darkness ahead we see a pair of taillights disappear into the hills.

—

SHE NEARLY DIED of a heart attack once. The image comes back into focus, emerging suddenly from the bluish beam of light that flashes across the faces above her, feeling its way across the concrete sidewalk, making her eyes blink frantically. Then she recognizes the two blue lights on the front of the ambulance, feels the cool air. Unable to stand on her feet, she is lying strapped to a stretcher. Two medics carry her out from the kitchen.

She had tried to get up from the kitchen table on her own, but she'd felt a pain so sharp that she doubled over, and the newspaper fell from her hand. She was lying there on the kitchen floor, heard voices saying things she couldn't understand, the medics coming through the door, her husband talking to the emergency doctor, who knelt beside her and reached into his case, then looked for something in his pocket.

Outside in the blue light, she gazes up at the sky; the tree by the bedroom window has lost its leaves in the past few days. The medics walk carefully, then the harsh light is on the ambulance roof above her. And suddenly it's quiet. She sees herself in the land of the dead.

It was the worst scare of her life. And yet the day had started like any other; she hadn't been prepared, particularly on this autumn morning, to be killed. She should have been on the alert. She still can't forgive herself. Having briefly glimpsed the realm of the dead, she won't let herself be talked into anything again, she'll stay on the lookout, she won't allow herself a moment's blindness until the inevitable end. Now she knows that they're always after her.

As usual, she had cleaned up the kitchen after breakfast, then sat down at the table to read the paper, turning automatically to the obituaries, as she does every morning. Many elderly people live in her neighborhood, and she constantly comes across familiar names. Not long before there had been an obituary for the Pigeon Man from the hill across the way, with a tasteless bird in the corner, its wings outspread and a line through its beak that was evidently meant to represent a twig, along with the usual expressions of sorrow, in a similarly tasteless vein. And at the bottom a list of his heirs.

A scribbled dove of peace for this man who was always said to be a gun lover—how outrageous. If she ever writes a will, she'll forbid the placement of any such announcements. No one will use her death to polish his phraseology. When she finally dies, no one will need to know about it, and she certainly doesn't want anyone to read about it in the newspaper. She can just picture the neighbors, the cashier in the supermarket, perhaps even strangers, reading her name with satisfaction, breaking out into smiles then laughing with relief; at last they will be able to show their contempt for this woman openly.

And while she's still envisioning this in vivid detail, the newspaper turned to the obituary page, the unthinkable occurred: she was cast out from life. She discovered her own name listed on the page.

She shut the paper, opened it again. Her name. There could be no mistake. It was her.

Her vision flickering, she felt a pull in her left armpit, but she composed herself, read the notice carefully. The date of death was Thursday of the previous week. No date of birth, just her age, eighty-eight, but that's was not right; she's was nowhere near that old. Hoping she'd misread it, she looked at the name again: it was still the same. No signature, no burial date, just a line of fine print stating that the modest funeral has already taken place.

She felt her heart pounding, saw spots in the air before her eyes. She had to do something at once, look in the phone book for a woman of the same name, call the classified-ads department at the newspaper, but first she had to show the announcement to her husband—didn't he notice this nasty piece of business? He too reads the obituaries before anything else. Where was he, anyway, was he at the bedroom window again, while she read her own death notice? She stood up, grabbed the newspaper, called her husband's name, but she could no longer hear her own voice over the loud roar in her ears. Darkness.

———

WHEN SHE'S RELEASED from the hospital she learns that her husband has done nothing about all this in the meantime, he has not called the newspaper or the police. She came within a hair's breadth of dying, the doctors have made clear to him that he should treat his wife with care for some time, so he doesn't want to do anything to excite her. But she knows that he simply doesn't care, a brief phone call on her behalf was too much trouble. She wouldn't have been upset; it would have calmed her, it may have just been an innocent error, and a letter of apology would have found its way to her mailbox the following day, a messenger would have brought a gift, a book, pralines, a bouquet of flowers.

Now it's left to her to try to clarify the situation, and that means she'll get excited again—humiliating phone calls to the registrar's office, conversations with the local authorities, with the cemetery administration, where she will be brushed off by bored assistants. It will take all her willpower to give her name twice to the unknown person on the other end of the line, first as a living person seeking information, then as the dead person on the list.

In fact, she doesn't get far. She's dismissed or put off; she meets with silence. They don't believe her, they hang up on her. Sometimes she thinks she hears a hand move to cover the receiver while someone tries suppress a giggle. Then the pain returns, and with each call she feels as if her heart will give out. She abandons her inquiries, perhaps it's for the best, who knows what she might have learned?

She imagines a doctor on the line, noisily rustling through his papers, announcing after a brief pause that he's found the death certificate. The name is correct, and he's not responsible for the age listed in the announcement: he gives the date and place of birth, the cause of death is listed as heart failure due to advanced old age, everything is in good order, he has not been remiss in any way.

She sees herself returning from the mailbox with a form letter addressed to her husband. She tears open the envelope, skims the brief text as she walks into the kitchen. A formal apology—her husband is being advised at this late date that because they were unable to locate him in a timely manner, through a clerical error, his wife has already been buried; the lot number and location are enclosed, followed by an ungainly signature and nothing more.

Her husband is still sitting at breakfast, leafing through the newspaper, when she waves the letter in his face, then reads it to him twice. He looks at her with that cold-blooded gaze. She grabs the table's edge for support, the letters on the page grow fainter, slide into darkness, her husband remains silent. No, she couldn't take the excitement—one more heart attack and she's done for.

SHE COULD HAVE looked for the grave and checked to see what name was on the cross, if there was a cross, or a headstone. But she doesn't visit graveyards on principle; she would never set foot on the decorative gravel, on the yielding earth of the dead.

The plot must still exist, if it ever did, overgrown by now, or simply an untended patch of grass. The twenty-year period during which a grave cannot be disturbed has not yet expired, as far as she knows. It must be twenty years, or have they shortened the period again, and is it only for seventeen years that the dead are left in peace?

Her husband could easily have done it for her. But he didn't lift a finger, even though he always enjoyed visiting cemeteries, never missed a chance to wend his way through the headstones, reading the inscriptions, breathing in the unbearable smell of box trees and pansies, even watching the widows wield their watering cans. He certainly sneaked off to the graveyard often enough when his first wife was still buried there.

But he has no desire to look for his second wife—that would be too much trouble. She knows he will never visit her when she's truly lying in her grave, and he'll ignore her final wishes and announce her death on the obituary page. That will be the end of it as far as he is concerned—not another thought, not the faintest memory will remain.

WE WIND UP in an area that Paulina doesn't know very well, either. We look for a gas station and survey the night landscape for bright spots, for red, green, or blue lights.

Paulina says, "There's something else you should know."

I sense suppressed excitement in her voice. I know this tone, it's familiar, and can mean either joy or uncertainty. I've known it since childhood and have never been able to predict which of the two it means.

She says, "I don't know exactly how to tell you this. I've met with my sister, just think, I've seen Nora again."

The uncertainty is gone. Paulina is happy about this meeting, and pleased that she can tell me about it. I hope she can't read the skepticism in my face, by the light of the deep sea-green shimmer. Fortunately, Paulina keeps her eyes on the road, and I simply wait for her to continue.

"I was so excited, but at the same time I was a little uneasy when I recognized her in the supermarket. She was wearing sunglasses, and her shopping basket filled with groceries of the sort only old people eat. I thought because of her sunglasses, that she might not want to be seen—she was examining the shelves so timidly. I went over to her, she looked up, and she seemed confused at first, as if she hadn't slept well."

I'm not clear what I'm supposed to make of this story. I haven't seen Nora since we were children, but I can well imagine that a certain bitterness would be evident in her features. Her face was already changing while we were on holiday together, becoming harder, more determined, more desperate. That might be why she's wearing sunglasses these days.

"There we were, her shopping cart between us filled with pureed vegetables and frozen chicken strips, as if she had stomach problems. I suddenly realized she hadn't called me. What was she doing in town if she hadn't come to see me? If we hadn't happened to visit the supermarket at the same time, I would never have known about it. Perhaps she visits the city all the time without telling me. And why stock up on food, as if she were living here? But we didn't bring that up. Not in the supermarket."

I don't say anything, but I sense that something isn't right. Nora dropped out of sight for years, and now Paulina runs into her by accident. Nora wanted that to happen, I'm convinced, otherwise she wouldn't have been shopping in that store, she would have gone to some other neighborhood. She must have been waiting, hoping to run into Paulina. I don't know what's going on, but I'm certain this meeting is part of a plan. Nora is up to something. But Paulina is apparently so happy about seeing her sister again that she hasn't figured this out yet. Now she thinks for a moment.

"I can understand her reluctance, we hadn't seen each other for such a long time. But of course she was happy to see me, too."

Paulina sounds hesitant as she speaks. Perhaps she's not entirely convinced, herself, or perhaps meeting Nora has made her think back on our past, those holidays we were not supposed to talk about. We fall silent.

I never thought much about Nora's disappearance, and over the years I seldom wondered what her adult life might be like. From the moment Nora broke with her parents, she seemed a little strange to me. I couldn't have explained it back then, but I was careful to maintain a certain distance from her. A precautionary step, perhaps, so that it wouldn't hit me too hard if Nora decided to break with the rest of us.

The intensity of her battle with her parents disturbed me, particularly since the whole thing had been occasioned by a passing remark. And I lacked Nora's steadfastness, her fidelity to principle. Once she had announced that she would not speak to her parents anymore, she stubbornly kept her word. Paulina, Carl, and I were the only ones she still spoke to at home. The most she would give to her parents was a curt "yes" or "no," said softly and rudely, and now and then a brief phrase, almost formal, as if she had prepared it in advance and learned it by heart. Nora, who had always been the child closest to her parents, felt that they had betrayed her. And that feeling has apparently persisted to this day.

I no longer know what outrage evoked it. I remember Nora sitting with her parents in the living room: they're watching the late news, and the rest of us are hiding in the hall, listening. The sound of the TV conjures up the images. It's no problem for us to picture the blocked-off streets strewn with debris, the iridescent pools of blood, the rust red footprints of thick shoes on the asphalt, the dully gleaming upholstery of a bullet-riddled car, nor to envision the armored cars or the heavily armed policemen standing in the midst of this scene, apparently unmoved.

They'll be reintroducing the death penalty soon, Nora says. It sounds like a passing remark, but as the conversation continues she grows more agitated, spurred on by her parents' denial. Nora raises her voice, claims they favor bringing back the death penalty; they just won't admit it. Her mother gets upset, tells Nora she shouldn't talk to her parents that way. From the hall we can hear every word they say.

The news report has long since ended, replaced by the sound of violins, accompanying a movie made for television. When her father finally speaks again, it's in a calm voice: Surely Nora must know that he opposes killing any human being, whether through assassination or by legal means. He opposes the use of force in any situation, and he has always tried to convey that to his children, all three of them have been raised that way. But he can't calm Nora down.

"You don't even care that your own father was in the Condor Legion. As far as you are concerned, you don't even have a father. You go to a museum and stand in front of Picasso's *Guernica,* and everything's fine and dandy."

For a moment the room is silent: even the TV seems to have paused. So silent that I'm sure my cousins' parents never had the slightest idea about our research. So silent you could almost believe they had never heard a thing about our grandfather's secret story.

IF THE PIGEON MAN hadn't died, the rest of us might never have looked at Nora's favorite books, and if we had never met our grandfather, we might never have become interested in his role in the Spanish Civil War. A chain of suppositions that can be extended right up to the present, for if we had not eavesdropped on the three of them we would not have heard what Nora said, and perhaps today I would not see a northern Moroccan plain as an airfield.

I don't know whether it was in Münster, or in Halle, where he was later stationed, or in Bergen, where he set up radio transmitters, that the brightest images appeared to me, a feeling in the pit of my stomach, as if I were being pulled back into the past at a high rate of speed. The airfield at Bergen appeared on the TV screen, first from the perspective of a helicopter, then from that of the tower: flying taxis transporting workers from the Norwegian mainland to their drilling platforms in the sea. Shrugging my shoulders, I saw structures that my grandfather helped build almost sixty years before.

The other places he was stationed at while he was in the military were never a secret; he may even have told stories about them when he met his children in a department store tearoom. Just for coffee, for fifteen minutes during his lunch break, and he tries to keep the conversation going with tales from his glider days, and from the war, because there's hardly anything else they can talk about. They were just two or three strangers sitting next to each other at a Formica table in the cafeteria. Perhaps he simply couldn't bear to talk about our dead grandmother.

Nora had read a memoir from the Spanish Civil War that covered the precise period in which our grandfather was in Spain. The author must have written it in the same month our grandfather was preparing to return home. The perspective was from the other side—poorly equipped volunteers fighting for the Republic, who had joined up in hopes of adventure, not realizing how alike all wars are. The author complains about the boredom in the trenches; over the course of three weeks he was able to fire only three shots at the enemy, and slowly he lost all hope for a life-and-death struggle, which was, after all, the only reason he had had volunteered in the first place. If it went on like this, it would be twenty years before he killed his first fascist.

We shared his longing for the first firefight, sweated with him as he encountered the first heavy fire, wished he had more ammunition. And while we imagined the first man he would kill, the image of our grandfather kept coming to mind—perhaps he had passed over this man's trench on one of his reconnaissance flights; one day his plane may have strayed into the sights of the volunteer. But the deadly bullets remained unfired.

Had the story turned out differently, we would have gone to the cemetery today, looking for the grave of a stranger who had died as a young man. The boxwood interment, giving off a repulsive odor, pansies perhaps, the stone covered with tendrils, the weathered inscription deciphered with difficulty, only to reveal the usual wartime clichés. No, that's impossible. I have to keep reminding myself that we couldn't have been at our grandfather's grave in any case.

NEW-CAR SPRAY is not limited to various makes; the smells differ according to model and year. I might buy a can for my car—I know the make and model. Though I'm not certain about the year. I pick cans of spray from the shelf at random and read the labels: I don't want the smell of some other model in my car.

Apparently I've lingered too long in the gas station convenience store; the night cashier isn't letting me out of her sight, but she could watch me just as easily on the screen right in front of her eyes. The car has been filled. Paulina wants to use the restroom, and gets the key from the cashier. A strange custom, I don't know why restrooms are locked these days—as if the gas station attendants might recall a face if a hostage was found tied up in the toilet.

The new-car smell I want is no longer available. Paulina's car is locked. I want to smoke another cigarette before we leave. The cashier's eyes follow me as I leave.

I have to talk with Paulina about her sister, and soon, on the way home. Tomorrow it will be all about the visit to the cemetery—Paulina is always worked up from breakfast on, although we never go till evening. We want it to be as dark as possible when we enter the cemetery, and in the summer we have to watch for just the right moment before the gate is closed. We don't want anyone to think that we might be the ones tending the grave. It lies not far from the Pigeon Man's grave; apparently this end of the cemetery was newly laid out back then. We are tending the grave of a person we don't know and have never seen. The stone bears no name, only an inscription: "We will always remember you."

Nora is up to something, and I have the feeling that if I knew her plans I wouldn't like them much. I can't make head or tail of what she had in her shopping cart—she must have changed a great deal. On the other hand, I can't imagine that her determination has lessened, her severity with herself and the world, her unrelenting search for the truth. Perhaps Nora has turned up simply because she wants to accompany us to the cemetery. I have no idea how I would react if Nora, too, wound up claiming we killed the Old Lady.

I have to try one last time to convince Paulina that our grandfather and his second wife still live just a few streets away from us, that nothing has changed. It may be that Paulina has simply had a hard time grasping that fact.

Everything is still the way it was twenty, even forty, years ago: Our grandfather remains silent, there is no contact with us. Even though he may once have rebelled against the notion of a life without that contact, we have to realize that he and his wife have long since come to terms with it.

—

THE YEAR THE Pigeon Man died, the Old Lady must have gone crazy at some point, for she did something unthinkable. At the time she thought she was being courageous, but in reality it was mere foolishness. Never before had she recklessly abandoned one of her basic principles, nor has she done so since. When she recalls this now—how she walked from one hill to the other—it seems as if she were observing a totally different person, and any similarity between this person and herself is a mere coincidence.

It was the summer shortly before her heart attack, which afterward overshadowed all other memories. The calls began around Easter. The telephone rang nearly every day, as if to wear her down. At some point she couldn't take it any longer and picked up the receiver. She listened intently, said hello several times, but there was no response, only silence on the other end. Just as she had expected. Then whoever was calling hung up.

She thought of the silly stories about a gang of kids. No one had ever seen this gang, and yet there were rumors that they had something to do with the death of the old man who kept pigeons. She paid no attention to the gossip of the cashiers at the supermarket. They had invented the gang simply to draw attention to themselves.

But another thought occurred to her. She knew that her husband's children had families of their own, and she tried to figure out how old his grandchildren might be by now.

The years had passed so swiftly. She still thought of them as small children, but today they must been teenagers. Those anonymous calls. Perhaps it was those youngsters calling, hoping their grandfather would answer sometime.

The calls resumed in the summer. Not a sound from the other end. Finally she realized she would have to do something about it. Calling back seemed impossible, and the police would not believe her. There was nothing to do but write to them. She had written very few letters in her life, none of them long. The ballpoint pen by the telephone was gone. She remembers how she rummaged about in the drawer for a pencil, then looked for paper; it couldn't be one of those cheap squared sheets fit only for grocery lists. In the attic she found some old stationery—who knows how it got there—sheets imprinted with various hotel letterheads, along with matching envelopes.

She put only her first name on the envelope, and addressed the letter to his son's wife, a woman who had also married into this strange family and therefore the only person who might feel a tiny spark of understanding. She no longer knows exactly what she wrote—no return address, no signature. Just the words: "Leave us alone."

She sees herself coming out of her house and taking the path toward the hill: a venture with unknown consequences, she has to be sure that no one is following her, that she's not seen, even from a distance. She has turned back several times before, waited for a better opportunity.

The path up the hill, probably in the noontime heat, when it's quiet, people at work or asleep, no one in sight. If someone she didn't notice had seen her—even she, had she seen herself, as she now does in her own memory—that person would have recoiled from the stare, the unsteady walk, the head, held tilted as if its owner were listening to something, to a voice, perhaps, that only she could hear.

She knew it was the next-to-last house. Doors aren't locked this far outside town, and she listened, slipped inside, and laid the envelope on the kitchen table.

But the calls kept coming. She had to formulate the next letter more precisely, and as she had the first time, she tried to disguise her handwriting: "Leave us alone, let my husband and me live our own life in peace."

Now she knows the way well, and the quiet periods, when no one is home. She never spies about, doesn't want to see anything more, just lays her letter hastily on the kitchen table: "And tell your children, too."

She doesn't want to hear the telephone ring again, so she goes further, adding in her disguised script: "He is no longer your father, father-in-law, or grandfather, hasn't been for a long time now."

In her excitement she almost forgets to add the period to the end of the sentence. Only after she has been forced to climb the other hill once more is she at peace: "You know that."

She has never received a reply to her letters, nor has she expected one. But the telephone harassment stops soon after this last letter.

—

WE'RE DRIVING through the hills and fields, the highway leading straight as a string to the next patch of forest. We pass through villages with unfamiliar names, through future industrial parks consisting only of asphalt, sidewalks, and streetlights.

Slowly I grow accustomed to the smell in the car. As if

I were the first person ever to sit in this passenger seat and stare out at the landscape. As if Paulina had always taken her night drives alone. That hardly seems likely, but I've never asked her about it.

When I returned home from the summer holidays with my cousins, it was always Paulina's image that stuck in my mind most clearly. I used to ask myself what her days were like now, what she was doing with her girlfriends, who else was in her life. It was like my enthusiasm for cars, the final holiday weekend, the first days of school perhaps. Then other images arose, of other girls.

Later, too, Paulina's image sometimes would surface unexpectedly—mostly when I watched girls I didn't know, girls I would have liked to get to know. I saw Paulina as a schoolgirl, standing beside a friend in a phone booth, laughing, looking around, not placing a call. She let her fingers glide along the metal cable, lifted the receiver, hesitated, and finally dialed when her friend held up a crumpled piece of paper with a telephone number on it. I knew they were calling a boy.

I see Paulina in profile, her forehead, her nose held as if she were concentrating on a single point. The long car trip has tired her, perhaps I'd better wait until tomorrow to ask about her sister, to try again to talk her out of the Old Lady's death.

It's not far now: we've reached the outskirts of town, and in ten minutes at most, we'll be home. People are still sleeping; the only light gleams through the blinds of a bakery. I roll the window down, hoping to smell the fresh bread from the street, but the stubborn new-car spray still dominates. As if I didn't have a smell of my own. We're in the valley, driving along the river, an empty flower shop to the right and the former munitions factory to the left. If the sunroof were open, I'd be able to see the redoubt up above us.

Once, when I was in town with my parents, I noticed a group of boys in the park, gathered around a girl. It was getting dark and there seemed to be a tension in the air, as if the boys were waiting for a sign from their young female leader, who sat totally relaxed on the backrest of a park bench. That's how I pictured Paulina, and I wanted to be one of those boys, but at the same time I knew that I would never spend that kind of a spring evening in the park.

As we approach our destination, we see a delivery truck being unloaded outside the supermarket, crates of vegetables under neon lights. After we've passed the old farmyards, Paulina shifts into second gear, and the road mounts steeply upward over the final stretch of the hill. When I arrived, late this afternoon, I noticed new ditches lining the freshly tarred road, and now it seems as if the cow pasture on the left has also been totally altered.

Paulina says, "They've torn everything up, you can't imagine what it looks like here in daylight. They're supposed to be building a new development, but while they were digging the ditches for the sewer lines, the soil seemed strange, a porous mass. Then the first construction workers fell ill; they coughed for a few days, and a week later they could hardly move."

We turn onto the path leading up to the house. Paulina drives slowly, and in the red glow of the brake lights I see the security tape shimmering at the edge of the construction site. The entire area is a cordoned-off pit.

"They had already laid the sewer lines, but the water was undrinkable. If they go ahead with the development they'll have to start over from scratch. First all the dirt will have to be carted away. You'll never guess what the mass turned out to be—I couldn't believe it myself at first: a mushroom. A gigantic underground mushroom, a single organism, that had spread throughout the entire hill. I've never heard of anything like it. They think that this underground growth was produced by the former garbage dump, maybe caused by the plastic sheets; they say the mushroom may have formed beneath the covering layers, which gradually disintegrated."

At night everything looks black and white, so I ask whether this mushroom has a distinct color by day. Paulina shakes her head: the stuff is gray, about the same color as the rest of the soil, otherwise they would have noticed it much sooner.

She turns off the engine, and we come to a stop in the driveway beside my car. After the divorce was final, and first her father and then her mother moved to another city, Paulina took over her parents' house. Today she's the only member of our family who still lives near our grandfather. The Pigeon Man's house stands empty; it has been unoccupied since after his death.

"Actually, the residents were advised not to go outside without a protective mask. Everyone here has a mask, but over time people stop using them."

Paulina says that after the discovery of this incredible mushroom it dawned on her why there were always so many spores in the air by the hill. She asks if I remember how we used to go out together looking for mold in the fall.

"No, I don't remember anything about that anymore."

We scraped the mold from the cellar walls of all the houses in the area to earn a little extra pocket money. During fall holidays it was a source of extra income that wasn't available to the kids farther down in the valley or over on the other hill—there was no mold there. Paulina wonders if maybe I missed out on that.

"I do remember digging potatoes in the fall."

But surely I must remember the spores that floated in the air at dusk. The flakes that enveloped the hill on certain evenings. We even called them spores, although no one knew anything about the mushroom back then.

"Maybe I've just forgotten about it."

I can't think why I don't remember anything about the mold. But I remember clearly how after the death of the Pigeon Man the birds seemed to wait for his return. No one came for them, and they continued to live in the cote and fly over our gardens. It was almost as if their numbers were increasing, as if some, released from distant points, were only now returning, too late, ruffled and worn out by the rigors of their long journey. The roof of the neighboring house, its lawn, its polished concrete walk gradually disappeared beneath a layer of white. We knew that pigeons carried diseases dangerous to humans, and sometimes we wondered if it might not be better to get a gun.

I still remember that the police used to ring at the door and distribute leaflets with photos of wanted men. One of them bore a certain resemblance to my cousins' father, but I was probably the only one who noticed that.

We had always suspected the Pigeon Man of being a police informant; we saw it in his eyes. Since he never spoke to anyone, what else would he use his telephone for but to pass on slander about any strangers who came too near his property?

I remember the shell casings we looked for on the redoubt, and the invisible shooter, whom we suspected of being the Pigeon Man. We were on the wrong track, it seems, for we kept finding new shells long after the Pigeon Man was buried.

ONE MORNING the four of us are awakened by a ringing voice, a metallic, nearly unrecognizable sound, the words almost unintelligible, and only after the phrases have been repeated several times can we make out what is being broadcast over the entire hill. All inhabitants are being instructed to stay in their homes, to remain calm and keep away from the windows.

Shielded by the curtain, we spy out into the garden. The bushes shake slightly: men in uniform are hiding there, wearing helmets. We run over to the other side of the house, but we don't dare go into the living room—we might be seen from the outside, through the windows. Paulina crawls a few feet into the room and sees a row of dark green vehicles on the narrow path. The loudspeaker announcements were coming from them, but it's been quiet for a while.

Our parents may still be asleep; we don't know how late it is. No one seems to be at home but us—perhaps my cousins' father has long since left for work and their mother is out shopping. If the entire hill is going to be cordoned off, they may be standing at a police barrier now. It's eerily quiet, just the sound of a radio in the distance now and then, a soft rustling in the foliage.

I don't know if we're safe here in the semidarkness of the hall. Paulina looks worriedly at the floor, Carl seems to be carefully counting all the coat hooks, one after the other, and when I glance at Nora I see an incipient look of triumph, as if she always predicted this would happen. As if she knew that at some point the special forces would touch our lives too, and she was preparing to spit in the face of the police and then be interrogated all night. In spite of her exhaustion she will remain steadfast, in spite of all the threats she will not reveal any names; she is already pressing her lips together, yet in her triumph she doesn't look any happier than Carl, Paulina, or me.

Then we are torn out of this tense silence by a fluttering, a rush of air that suddenly passes over the house. The next moment we are in the kitchen, listening to the sound fade away. There is no longer a bird to be seen on the Pigeon Man's roof. Only a few feathers, a fluff of down in the air. The pigeons have been driven off.

The special forces have worked their way to the other side of the fence, they lie there mired in pigeon droppings, they have released the safeties on their guns. A silhouette flits by an upper-story window. A chair falls over, perhaps a table, then we hear the dull sound of upholstery being slit open, desk drawers opening, and a trampling on the stairs, shouts.

The men in the bushes rise to their knees. One of them appears at the front door and lowers his weapon. He wears a helmet, vest, and the black uniform, to which down still clings.

They actually believed that the Pigeon Man's house was a secret cell, that they would find terrorists there. At a signal, the forensic team approaches the people by the security line, we recognize them by their cameras. Weapons—guns and pistols—are carried out of the house, along with belts packed with ammunition. Now they're convinced that they have smoked out a nest, while in fact it's only the gun collection of an old man long dead.

I remember the weapons gleaming in the sun as if it

were yesterday. And how a policeman removed his helmet and his hair was damp with sweat. Then a few moments later, another announcement came over the loudspeaker, the all clear signal.

From that day on we could never find another empty shell on the redoubt. Of our search for mold not the faintest of images remains.

I'M NOT SUPPOSED to go barefoot. I wait until Paulina has fallen asleep, and when I hear her breathing evenly, I get up. I can't be expected to wear shoes in the apartment in midsummer.

Paulina has furnished the house according to her own taste. The walls have been repainted another color, new furniture has been moved in, but the basic floor plan is, of course, unchanged. Even the record player is in its old spot in the living room. I can almost see our breath on the windowpanes, as if we had never grown older.

The black film falcons, with their uneven wings, faulty beaks, and misshapen heads, have long since been scraped off the large window looking out on the terrace, and replaced with commercial decals of birds of prey. The part of the garden beyond the deck has been fenced off with security tape; there are even signs bearing the skull and crossbones; the ground has been dug up and all the old junk under the deck carted off. There must have been some things that belonged to the four of us, too—booklets with glossy photos, now rotted away, unrecognizable. We used to store such things secretly under the deck.

They're still not sure, they're waiting for the analysis, but it's possible that the subterranean mushroom has spread as far as Paulina's house. But that's true of any parcel of land on the hill, they are digging everywhere. The security tape and the warning signs are only there as a precaution. Until they have more information, there's no reason to worry.

Our car picked up a few scratches during tonight's chase—Paulina was planning to have it washed tomorrow anyway. We won't be able to sit in the garden in the afternoon because, strictly speaking, there is no garden. I stare at the piles of dirt, the exposed perennials, the furry gladiolas. I discover scraps of plastic foil, screws, blackened Styrofoam containers, bits of toys, and other trash. A calf's thighbone, a shoulder blade in the loam, apparently buried there by dogs.

Early in the evening we'll go to the cemetery. The garden tools have been laid out, the rubber boots, and Paulina will buy fresh flowers. Earlier, as I was watching her apply lotion to her hands after brushing her teeth, she looked at me in the mirror and announced that she had a surprise for me tomorrow evening, after everything had been taken care of. She wouldn't say any more.

The first gleams of light appear among the clouds, the sun will soon be up. I decide not to lie down. I wouldn't be able to sleep anyway.

—

SHE NO LONGER stands at the bedroom window; those days are gone. It's difficult for her to stand for any length of time, and she sits in her armchair as often as she can, with her numb feet raised. Her knees are less and less reliable, her legs simply give way beneath her. Perhaps it all started with her heart attack, when she collapsed on the kitchen floor—perhaps the first slight unsteadiness may have set in then. She sits in the living room, the hall as hard to see into as always. She no longer makes any calls. Now and then she hears the telephone ring, and her husband goes to the phone and lifts the receiver.

He no longer spends his nights waiting for the dead woman to appear in the tree outside the bedroom. Not that he gave up voluntarily—not that he had seen enough. He would still be standing there today, his hand stretched out in greeting toward the dead woman, if it weren't for the blinds. Back when new terrorist attacks were expected daily, when banks were constantly being robbed, and cars stolen, and dead bodies lay in the streets, when the fear spread that even houses in quiet neighborhoods would be broken into, they had installed heavy blinds at the windows, blinds made of an artificial material that shut out every trace of light at night.

Soon after he retired, her husband took up photography again. Perhaps he just wanted to take his mind off his dead wife, whom he could no longer see outside the window. There's no other explanation for it, for there's nothing worth photographing here at home, and they have no visitors, they don't go anywhere on holidays. Basically her husband is just wasting film; she doesn't even want to see what sort of pictures he's taking, what he puts in his albums. He goes through the house and snaps pictures of the same spots, the flowers on the windowsill, the kitchen, he even aims his camera at the living-room suite.

When the pictures come back, there are countless shots of her armchair; some show her in it, some show it empty, but the chair itself is nearly always the same. As if her husband sees things that aren't there. As if he's driven to capture something invisible, as if he's in search of ghosts. Sometimes he stands outside the house and takes pictures of the front door. Why does he want photos of the peephole?

Perhaps he even roams through the house at night, snapping pictures of total darkness.

No moon, no constellations, no streetlights, only a black plane beyond the pane; now that the blinds are fully lowered, you can't even hear the rustling of the leaves.

She used to start up in fright at night because she thought someone had broken into the house and was standing by her bed to catch her in her sleep. She heard footsteps, the creak of the stairs, the soles of shoes on the carpet, and each time it was merely the twigs scratching against the window pane. Since the blinds were installed she no longer has such dreams, but she knows it would be a mistake to be lulled into a false sense of security. If someone is out to murder you, blinds will not stop him.

You don't have to get close to the victim; after all, you'd be placing yourself in danger as well. She knows an easier way, one that leaves no trace, no clue. The murderer will never be found; no one will even guess that a murder has been committed, and the death certificate will indicate heart failure due to old age.

You can kill with words. She's well aware of that—after all, words nearly sent her to the land of the dead. The obituary had been no error. Someone intended to do away with her in the vilest fashion. Someone intended to give her a heart attack. There had been no confusion. She had been the target. She still was.

She, too, knows how to kill people with words. She's never mentioned it to her husband, they don't talk about such things. People would lend no credence to her if she expressed her fears. Paranoia, they would say, she should be in therapy, or, with a simple shrug of the shoulders, The

Old Lady always was a bit off her rocker. No one would take her seriously: meanwhile, her murderer has forgotten nothing, he is waiting to strike again.

She must be increasingly alert to the lurking danger. She has stopped reading obituaries altogether since that day. Magazines only with extreme caution. Books not at all. She has always approached the phone with the utmost doubt in any case. And when she still was able to go to the supermarket, she wanted to plug her ears so she wouldn't have to hear the gossip. In fact, she did press her hands to her ears when she heard someone whispering in the aisles. You don't really need obituaries or anonymous phone calls. Rumors are perfectly sufficient.

If, for example, she learned that word was being spread around the neighborhood that she, the Old Lady, had blood on her conscience. If it turned out that people had been saying for years that the Old Lady had totally withdrawn, screened herself from the world, because she feared someone might die at her hand. If everyone assumed she had come here to die in the first place. Then, she thinks she would surely have faced another heart attack, her last.

She is amazed to this day how quickly she was able to discover the murderer. She had expected to encounter greater cleverness, a better cover. False leads, even shady characters, but nothing of the sort; everything took place right before her eyes. She simply had never really looked before. She'll never tell anyone who it was. She has sworn that to herself. She'll take the name with her to the grave.

—

THE PITS and the signs with death's head, the bare skull and crossbones, they look hand-painted, but I know they're factory-made. I examine the barriers more closely, out in the fields, while it slowly turns light. I've put on rubber boots but not a face mask. I should probably be wearing rubber gloves too and, to be on the safe side, even a plastic hood.

I won't touch the mushroom. I let the security tape glide through my fingers a moment in the twilight, then crawl under the barrier. I slide down into the shaft, and the earth is not crumbly, as I thought it would be, given the summer heat, but almost muddy, damp.

I keep thinking about Paulina's surprise. She spoke of it as if she weren't sure whether I would be pleased. She had that tone in her voice, the one I can't quite figure out. The surprise may have had something to do with Nora, I think. Maybe Paulina has arranged for her sister to come by, maybe we'll meet for supper, because Nora would like to see me again too.

I should have questioned Paulina more closely about it, perhaps even forced her to reveal the planned surprise ahead of time. She hinted that the meeting in the supermarket hasn't been their only one; perhaps the two of them have met several times since then, or have been in regular contact by phone. And if Paulina goes to the car wash later in the day while I stay home alone, maybe the phone will ring.

I can't tell where the sound is coming from—I look everywhere for the cordless phone, then find it in the corner of the couch, still ringing. I lift it and say, "Yes," then wait. I give Paulina's phone number, say, "Yes, that's right," but in the same breath I add, "but you've still got the wrong number," and push the button that shows a receiver with a line drawn through it. When Paulina comes home, the first thing she'll ask is, "Did anyone call while I was out?"

I'll have to think about how to respond. On the way to the cemetery, Paulina will say: "My sister called earlier; she tried late this morning, but evidently there was a problem with her telephone, a mis-connection. Even though she knew she had the number right, it was there on the notice."

It will turn out that the characteristic tone slipped into Paulina's voice because she didn't want to tell the whole truth right away. Maybe I'll find out by breakfast time that Nora and Paulina have been in contact with each other much longer than I've suspected, that they met in the supermarket months ago. And since Paulina didn't know how I would react and thought I might be upset, she didn't say when I was there at Easter that they had been secretly seeing one another for a long time.

When Nora broke off contact with her parents, Carl found his judgment confirmed, and I could see the satisfaction in his face. Nora fled from the living room, while her parents remained sitting there without saying a word, the rest of us having long since withdrawn to our own room. Then Nora threw herself on her bed, repeating softly: "I'll never speak to them again."

In the end, Carl had us all on his side; even his older sister was convinced that we had to keep silent. When I think of Nora now, I realize that she always struck me as strange. I have no desire to see her again.

The ground is soft, and my rubber boots are covered with mud. I follow the course of the shaft. Soil samples have been taken everywhere; it looks as if long-distance lines are being laid on the hill.

I recall a passage in Nora's favorite book, in which the author claims that on some fronts during the Spanish Civil

War a megaphone was much more important than weapons. Since it didn't seem possible to kill the enemy, and they might never get to shoot a fascist, soldiers started shouting back and forth between the trenches. The enemy was worn down with words rather than bullets, as well-situated volunteers exchanged their practically useless guns for megaphones and took on the role of advocates, shouting mostly set phrases at the enemy, trying to encourage some worn-out soldier to desert.

One simple phrase from the megaphone repertoire impressed me in particular: "buttered toast."

The propagandist who spoke of slices of buttered toast through his megaphone hoped the Fascists would believe the Republicans were still supplied with peacetime rations in a trench warfare zone. And even though he knew there was neither toast nor butter for him and his comrades in the trenches, the author admits at the end of the paragraph that his own mouth watered when he heard the false words.

I picture a rugged ravine near Regone, dark and soundless, a cold sky, rocks, each side lying in wait for the other, and through the darkness those two words—"buttered toast"—ring out again and again, until it is impossible to know for sure where the cry first came from.

Only now do I realize that there are no mosquitoes on the hill this summer. Perhaps the whole area has been sprayed to hinder the mushroom's growth. Nor is there a scent of grass in the air, or of dust or fresh soil.

It would be strange to discover that Nora is still frantically obsessed with the truth. She may suggest it's time we went to our grandfather's house and rang the doorbell: as grown-ups, we should no longer be afraid to confront him. She won't let up until she has convinced Paulina. What do we have to fear? she will say. If we confront our grandfather with facts, we can put an end to our snooping around once and for all, and ask him to tell us the details of his secret story.

Things would be simpler if Paulina hadn't lost touch with reality. We could work on Nora together, counter her plan somehow. But I can't count on Paulina; she doesn't see the danger, she's convinced that the Old Lady has long since departed this life.

How could we have organized a burial when we were still youngsters? Where would we have found the money? We had no experience with such formalities: a death certificate, the burial plot, even picking out a coffin would have been beyond us. How could we have chosen among earth, urn, and sea? None of the four of us had ever been inside a mortuary.

Why are we the only ones ever to have heard of her death? Surely her husband would have known about it. Someone would have told our parents, perhaps suspected something and questioned us. Does Paulina recall a visit from the police, an interrogation, a verdict, any time spent in a juvenile home? But no matter how hard I argue, Paulina always winds up saying simply, "But still."

I've reached the edge of the settlement without ever having left the shaft. Here the darkness of the surrounding heavens swallows the red glow above the city at night. The sun has long since risen, but I remember clearly that from this point one can see the reach of the light above the city and its suburbs, and where it ends on the slope along the fields.

Paulina was right when she noticed that Nora's purchases at the supermarket were more suitable for an older person, but I doubt this had anything to do with stomach problems. I just can't imagine Nora warming up chicken ragout with rice for herself. In the end it will probably turn out that Nora is caring for our grandfather and the Old Lady. If so, the meeting in the supermarket was certainly no accident. Perhaps Nora has come back to this neighborhood to arrange things comfortably for the twilight years of these two old people.

Perhaps she felt sorry for them—our whole story may have suddenly struck her as one of neglect of our grandfather and his second wife. The Nora I know would be moved by an attack of conscience to become more and more deeply involved, until she saw no way out but to drop all her reservations and get in touch with them, cautiously at first, then on a more regular basis, to ask how they were, and finally to offer her help. Trips to the doctor, health insurance forms, a visit to the drugstore—over time Nora draws closer to the elderly couple, they gradually lose their shyness, forget their earlier misunderstandings, their mutual dislike based on no real knowledge of one another, the torment of so many years.

Nora has come to understand some things better in the meantime. She can empathize with the couple's radical views, and when one day while seated at the coffee table they play with the possibility of Nora's moving in with them, so she won't have to travel so far each day, she is prepared to follow certain rules. Naturally she realizes that one must show consideration for the views of old people, even if some of them strike her as odd. To this day she doesn't understand why they had forbidden any contact, but there was no point in trying to change the minds of people of their age now.

That would explain the meeting with Paulina in the supermarket. Nora couldn't get in touch, that was impossible, but nothing stood in the way of an accidental meeting—she could hardly be held responsible for that. Our grandfather and his wife suspect nothing, know nothing of the secret meeting with Paulina. Nora cooks supper for the couple, helps them wash up, and puts them to bed; then she leaves the TV on low in the living room until she hears the slow, steady breathing of two old people. She goes up to the bedroom again to make sure they are asleep, then throws on a jacket and pulls the front door shut—she's learned to turn the key soundlessly.

The shaft comes to an end; the dredgers stand ready, but the excavation has yet to begin. Poles marked with red and white chalk have been rammed into the ground every few meters, marking a construction line from the last house down to the depression. The air has something milky about it, flakes are floating over the field, they could be the spores Paulina mentioned.

If the planned surprise turns out to be a reunion with Nora, Paulina may try to awaken my curiosity, so I'll simply forget my resistance to the meeting: "We can even find out if it really was our grandfather who called when we were children. You know, those strange calls when no one said anything. You could ask my sister, and perhaps she can ask him sometime, he may still remember."

Across the way, on the opposite hill, the excavation is already complete; all that's missing is the connection between the two sections. Over there, of course, barriers—waist-high plastic mesh—have been installed, like the ones that line the highways in winter to keep the drifting snow off the road.

What if I were to get in my car, let it roll slowly backward out of the driveway, and disappear before breakfast? Paulina would go on sleeping, would notice nothing. Before she could draw me into this craziness, I'd practically be home. I could call her on the way, so she wouldn't worry. I could say, I'm sorry, and she'd have to go to the cemetery by herself for once.

Normally blackbirds and larks would be singing now, but even at sunrise, oddly enough, I heard nothing. I turn around, glancing back for a moment to see how the barriers are placed on the other hill. The cordons start straight up, then seem to veer off and disappear between the houses, where, on the closest street to the right, the old couple's house must be.

· silences ·

THE SEAGULL by the boardwalk seems to be eyeing the others attentively. It's been sitting nearly motionless for a long time now, just turning its head, following the line of flight of its comrades across the water. It's probably ill, otherwise, it would take off when someone approached. Once, I would have gone up to inspect it—perhaps it's crippled—but I know now that injured birds shouldn't be touched. In the November light its feathers seem to glow from within, in contrast to the snow at the edge of the road, which remains a dull gray. All day I've felt that darkness might fall at any moment. A glimmer of sun in the snowy sky this morning, and when I stepped out into the street after breakfast, it seemed as if several hours had passed unnoticed and that the sun would soon be setting.

A pleasant light. It's probably too dark even for pictures, you'd need highly sensitive film. This sort of twilight reigns all winter and is said to cause depression among some who live here. I probably couldn't stand it long myself. It's my first time in Stockholm. I've never been this far north before.

Once, as a child, I stood with my parents by her grave. We went in secret as darkness fell. I didn't understand the point of all the secrecy, nor did my parents' nervous glances down side paths, our ducking behind box hedges, turn it into an adventure. The whole atmosphere was oppressive. We weren't spies. It felt more like flight.

When we found the grave, we stood there for a few minutes: there was a headstone, low-maintenance greenery, but no memorial candle or fresh flowers, if memory serves me. It wasn't long before we had to turn back: the cemetery would be closing soon, and a course of false turns and diversionary maneuvers through the maze of gravel paths lay before us, until we would finally reach the gate.

I can't have been very old, for I didn't realize then that these precautionary measures had to do with the Old Lady and our grandfather. The confusing detours inside the cemetery were meant to ensure that we didn't run into our grandfather, who sometimes visited our grandmother's grave after work. In the end, we barely made it back to the main entrance before it closed for the day.

There was no snow on the ground, no tracks. I'm not even sure it was winter. My main worry was that we would be locked in and have to climb the gate or scale the cemetery wall between two headstones. One thing, strangely enough, remains lodged in my memory: the path my parents took to my grandmother's grave. I could retrace it step by step today, though back then I had no way of orienting myself as we walked through the darkness. The graves all looked alike, nor would the shrubbery or ancient trees have served as points of reference, if I had been sent back to the gate alone.

In that oppressive atmosphere my gaze must have sub-consciously registered barely perceptible and otherwise ordinary signs. And yet in retrospect it seems as if the child consciously memorized the complicated path, then over the years repeated it in his mind's eye before falling asleep, so that the adult could retrace it once again. The grave at twilight put me on a trail. Thirty years later, I'm still seeking the woman who was our grandmother.

It's snowing again, the flakes fall wet and gray, the image turns grainy. The boardwalk is empty. I can't spot the seagull, it's left its station, so it must not have been crippled after all. The other birds won't circle much longer, either, and some of them are already settling on the water with a strong beat of the wings. Snowflakes whirl for a moment, are caught by a wave, and disappear.

Outside my window a few gulls float up and down amid the drifting snow, as if keeping an eye on the hotel—or seeking shelter. The glow of their feathers gradually fades, no longer bright white in the falling darkness. Perhaps the single gull has long since perched on my windowsill, waiting for the snow to stop.

I'm in Stockholm because of Carl. I always pictured him as a soldier, in part because in the military a person can disappear without a trace, concealed in barracks, perhaps even abroad, without the family's knowledge.

Watching the news these days, I sometimes imagine that the camera will shift once or twice and I will suddenly see my cousin on television, in the background, off to one side, a fleeting glimpse as a general reviews the troops. Or when the defense minister inspects a local unit and is filmed by journalists trying to engage the soldiers in free and easy conversation. The determined smiles, the inaudible words, what can the soldiers say? I look at their faces: one has just turned away; it may have been Carl.

But he isn't a soldier, nor is he stationed abroad. Perhaps I never listened closely enough to Paulina, or she didn't say much about him. But I pricked up my ears on my last visit when she mentioned that Carl liked Stockholm and now felt at home there.

Why would Carl be stationed in Stockholm, I wondered? Then the image of a soldier blurred, and I suddenly recalled that Carl had gone into the diplomatic service. The idea had never appealed to me. I had little interest in office work, stuffy receptions, and polite conversation with strangers, but I was delighted now that I remembered. Carl could surely help with my investigation.

As a member of the diplomatic staff, Carl would have access to archives closed to me. My first phone call after all those years wasn't easy, and it would hardly have been polite to turn straight to my purpose. But both of us knew I was calling for a reason. So we tacked back and forth between old memories and strained reserve until I finally came out with my request: could Carl do me a favor and search the data banks for our grandmother's name, perhaps even consult secret archives through proper channels? He hesitated and asked for time to think it over, but I finally talked him into it.

My face still stings from the razor as I step outside the hotel. I don't see any seagulls on the sills of the facade. The snow has frozen solid at the curbs. I've traced the way to the restaurant on the map, to make sure we recognize each other, Carl has suggested we meet by the fish pool just inside the door: a plain, bright basin where the lobsters and eels are kept. Whoever arrives first will signal the other. He hasn't said a word about what he has found in the archives. Perhaps we will feel formal and awkward, like two business-men not yet sure whether they want to sign a contract. And after our meal, without further explanation, Carl will hand me a file of documents. We'll leave the restaurant and stand for a moment in the cold, searching for some farewell phrase to conceal what we both know: we'll never meet again.

—

HER COUSIN DOESN'T recall ever searching for mold. Sometimes he's so adamant about it she nearly starts to doubt her own memories. But she clearly recalls going from house to house in the fall when they were children.

Her cousin always liked the spores. When he came for a visit, he wanted to go out the very first evening at sunset and wait for them to appear. Nora, Carl, and she hardly no-ticed the flakes, paid little attention to them, saw them daily. It was her cousin who pointed them out: they were just dots in the air, barely perceptible, insubstantial, but he spotted them, he saw them first, long before they floated as thick as falling snow above the hill.

Without him they might not have noticed them at all; he had an eye for such things. He'd started when they were even younger, turning over stones at the edge of the path to watch the wood lice scramble out. Yet he had always been disgusted by wood lice, spiders, and worms, had disliked going barefoot in the meadow.

When they explored the hill, they knew that their cousin would find more than all three of them combined. Nora, Carl, and she had never had his eye for the unusual—there were three of them, but they saw less than he did. Perhaps an only child is more alert, more persistent, less easily distracted. Once when they dug in the ground to see what they could find, he quickly came up with a doll's head, a toothless mother-of-pearl comb, and not one but a whole handful of plastic toy soldiers.

They might as well have simply assigned finding interesting buried trash to him. Nora, Carl, and she weren't needed until it was time to turn the less striking discoveries into something more interesting. Their cousin would dig out a few fragments; they would assemble them into a plate, and soon they'd be inventing a story to make the otherwise worthless dish more remarkable. The letters on the bottom were nearly illegible: perhaps it came from some institution. What kind of inmates may have eaten off it—madmen, the terminally ill—and when? How deeply they would have immersed themselves in their stories if shards of a phonograph record had come to light.

And it was their cousin who always insisted that no photos be taken of their secret discoveries. They did, however, own a small camera, an old, simple one Nora had received among her confirmation gifts. They never found out who gave it to her—none of the cards matched the package. It was a used camera but had been well cared for by its former owner, and Nora sometimes took photos of the surrounding countryside, their house, and her brother and sister. But when her cousin came for the holidays, the camera remained in its box under the bed, regardless of what they found. It was precisely the irretrievably vanishing, evanescent phenomena that their cousin insisted were better retained in memory than collected in a few superficial photographs that almost always showed things in the wrong light anyway.

So it's strange that the last time he visited he couldn't recall searching for mold. Perhaps concentrating his full attention on the present took all his strength, leaving him no energy for memory. But then again, there are moments when she thinks he lives entirely in the past. She can only explain this paradox by assuming that for him, past and present shade into each other. Perhaps he sees no difference between them, regards the past in the same way he does his present surroundings.

To him it's only a small step from one world to the next, and he doesn't think to ask whether others can follow. One moment he's alert, paying attention, commenting, listening to others, and the next he's sitting lost in thought, gazing into the void, brooding, unreachable. As if a voice were coming to him from afar, a voice that he alone can hear. The sight makes her feel faint: her cousin seems almost deranged, and she doesn't know whether she should try to wrench him from his brooding state or leave him in it.

If they had taken photos on holiday twenty years ago, she could show him pictures of the spores. He would have to remember then. At least she could reassure herself. But who knows, he might be proved right. In the poor light, after sundown, the pale shimmer of countless dots in the air would be no more than a meaningless accumulation of lighter and darker gray flecks.

When she heard her cousin was coming to visit, she put out the old photo album they had spent so much time with back then. She wanted to surprise him with it. She had come across it again recently, had refrained from glancing at it, saving it for later, wanting to enjoy it at leisure with her cousin. But that never happened.

The morning after arriving he disappeared again, without

even leaving a note. It must have been an abrupt departure—he hadn't even taken his suitcase along. When she saw that his car wasn't in the driveway, she thought he'd gone to buy croissants. She made coffee, set the table, and waited to hear the car coming along the lane.

Then she noticed his shoes were in the hall, even though his rubber boots were gone, and she got worried. She looked through the house. Perhaps he'd left a note in the living room, on the patio, even the bedroom, but there was nothing.

SOMETHING WAS MISSING from the nightstand, nothing important, an old ceramic doll, a Spanish dancer, but precisely because it was so ordinary she was surprised. Her cousin had left his suitcase, yet taken this figurine, without even asking.

She pictures him standing quietly at the open door to the bedroom, surveying the room, watching over his sleeping cousin, like the gremlin in the children's story she remembers, who hides in the barn by day but roams the farmyard at night, talking to animals who spend the freezing winter in the stalls, watching over those who sleep in the farmhouse. He's never been seen, just his footprints in the snow the next morning.

Does her cousin remembers those pictures? They used to read that book together, the night sky, the deep snow, the dark stalls, the children warm in their beds. Very much like her, lying there hearing nothing when her cousin took the figurine from the nightstand. And like the gremlin every child wants to see, her cousin disappeared as she slept.

He's never contacted her once since then; it's been half

a year now. Even though they used to phone each other regularly. Perhaps he'll never show up again. The photo album lies unopened in the drawer.

IF HE HADN'T waved to me from the table, I would have stayed by the fish basin awhile and then left. I scrutinized the men in the restaurant one by one, studying each face, but didn't recognize Carl. Our gazes crossed several times before he finally waved. At first I thought he'd wanted to look me over a little while longer when I arrived, but he hesitated because he'd been puzzled by the uncertain way I was looking around. He had recognized me immediately, but for the moment he'd forgotten how much he himself had changed since we last met.

I had expected someone totally different, having assumed that he was still a gangling, earnest person who moved with total self-control, with a certain fixed expression on his face, what one might call a penetrating gaze. But I couldn't even recognize Carl's eyes. They were no longer Italian; no one would even notice them on the street. No one would feel spied on. On the contrary, children would feel secure with Carl watching over them as they slept. His face radiated calm, his whole body expressed a relaxed state that was unconsciously communicated to those around him.

I feel it the moment we say hello. I never expected a hug, I thought we would shake hands coolly, but Carl draws me to him as if it were the most natural thing in the world. And now that he's sitting across from me, I feel as if I've found the older brother I always wanted.

As he gestures in conversation, I observe his hands more closely. They, too, fail to remind me of the person I once knew as Carl. There are no warts, not even scars, instead the skin on the back of his hands is extraordinarily soft, matching his gestures. There's nothing of the soldier about Carl, and his earlier reserve, his fascination with secret oaths and pacts, none of that can be seen now. He speaks with a frankness I could never manage.

As soon as we've ordered, Carl starts recalling our childhood, our shared holidays, and I soon realize it's not just simple nostalgia. It seems he wants to explain something, and I'm not sure where he's headed. Do I remember the summer when his parents' divorce was in the air, talking through the night, then silence all day? Yes.

One morning we discovered his father had spent the night on the living-room couch. He was seldom at home; there were no more family meals. None of us knew how to deal with the situation, the uncertainty about the family's future. It was a hard time for all of us. Looking back, Carl thinks something was set in motion then that couldn't be stopped. We tried to tell from the parents' faces if the crisis was temporary, we looked on helplessly, reduced to watching for some hint of change. Carl recalls the afternoon we discovered that his father had left home, his toothbrush still in the glass, his shaving kit untouched, but his suitcase gone. He must have long since bought new razor blades and a shaving brush. We felt deceived.

Neither father nor mother spoke of it, they were far too preoccupied, and we had to figure everything out ourselves. We'd done nothing up to then, nor could we think of any way to reconcile them. Yet now that it seemed too late, we were upset with ourselves and decided to take action at the next opportunity. We had no idea what form our efforts might take, how we could gain our parents' attention, regardless of the uncertainty of the results. And then the letters without a return address started arriving. Do I remember? Yes.

We'd return home from grocery shopping, and while their mother sorted bags in the car, my cousins and I would carry crates of water into the kitchen. We'd see the white envelope on the table and know at once it was from their father—their mother's first name on the front, no family name, no address or return address. The letter would be leaning against a glass, so their mother would see it the moment she entered. We knew we mustn't touch it. In the background we'd hear her entering, but before she got to the kitchen, Nora would grab the letter and stick it in her pocket.

None of us would say anything as their mother came in. We'd put the groceries away in the refrigerator, on the shelves, then withdraw. We had no wish to read the letter. Only gradually would we realize how rashly Nora had acted. She could never produce the letter now—what would her mother think? We couldn't put it back on the table until next week, when we went out for groceries again: until then it would have to stay in our hiding place under the terrace deck.

But then a second letter leaned against the water glass. We had to take it too, since their father would surely have referred to the first one their mother had never received. Their father seized on several more opportunities when no one was home, and we kept taking the letters, but never opened them. Their mother would pace back and forth restlessly on the terrace: she hadn't heard a word from her husband in weeks, but beneath her feet, under a narrow layer of wood and concrete, lay the letters.

Carl looks at me, and now I recognize his eyes. I don't like to think about this episode, but Carl tells the story so calmly it never occurs to me to interrupt or change the subject. We've hardly touched our food. Carl begins to cut away at his cold steak. I still have no idea why he has reminded me of this story. And as Carl falls silent for a time I grow nervous, fumbling with my knife and fork: perhaps he's waiting for me to figure things out.

We used to think we knew each other well, but now I realize I've never known Carl at all, not even as a child. Carl senses my discomfort, and when he resumes speaking, I feel as if we've met solely so that I can listen to him without having to respond. The moment he speaks my hands relax, my knife and fork sink to the plate.

For him, he says, something broke apart then. His parents' final separation still lay in the future, they tried to start over for the children's sake, but since that time, whenever he thought of the letters he felt we had been partially responsible for their divorce, that somehow we might have prevented it. Carl thinks all the tension he later felt with Nora and Paulina originated in that one instinctive act, that Nora's having taken the letter had colored their entire relationship, even though they never mentioned it again.

Over time they did less and less together, and when they saw each other they were usually slightly irritable, as if each wanted to shift the blame to one of the others. After finishing school, Carl left home and moved to another city. As an adult he had little to do with his former family—keeping in touch just wasn't that important to him. One day he realized he had lost all contact with them. He'd wanted to forget his family. And he had succeeded. It wasn't that he'd grown uncertain about events and dates, nor that their images had blurred over time—he had no memory of them at all.

When he realized this, he feared the effect would be

dizzying, that having been robbed of his childhood and youth he would fall helplessly into an abyss. Yet nothing happened. No dizziness, no mourning, no loss. For a long time he lived a life with its own memories, a finely meshed net within which he could still move: his wife, their children, friends. And what had been a well-kept, dangerous secret, not even revealed to his wife, was now recalled only in passing: we were partially responsible for our parents' divorce, although we never admitted it.

Having forgotten everything, Carl could slowly feel his way back into the past. Only now did he realize how ridiculous was the claim that had cast a shadow over his youth. His parents would have grown apart whether or not his mother read those letters—the path was clear, their separation inevitable. And over time he recalled his sisters' faces with increasing clarity, began to think of them without bitterness, grew curious about their present life, until one day he looked up Paulina's phone number.

⌒

SHE HASN'T CALLED Paulina yet, but she wants to let her sister know as soon as possible that their cousin is all right, that there's no cause for concern. Instead of being furious with him for disappearing without a word, Paulina has been worried. She should have forgotten him, written him off, not sought some justification for his inexplicable behavior.

Carl called and told her about her cousin. Carl wanted her advice about how to approach him, since they would be meeting soon. He asked whether their cousin had contacted her too. No, not yet, all she knows is what Paulina has told her. She's eager to hear how the evening at the restaurant turns out, what in the world he wants. Carl promises to call her immediately afterward.

The three of them have resumed phone contact recently. They had lost sight of each other; in fact they had avoided each other, and worse, they'd let years pass without speaking. She'd left home early herself, she had been the first, her sister and brother still lived with their parents then. Later, Carl and Paulina were involved in a quarrel that led to a final rupture of what had become only sporadic contact in any case.

Nora had learned of this only in passing, since she herself had no interest in moving back into their parents' house. Nor was she demanding her share of its value: how could their parents have converted their inheritance into cash; where would her siblings get that much money? The house stood empty for some time after their parents left— neither their father nor their mother took any further interest, so the children were left to deal with it.

The conflict between Carl and Paulina extended over several years. They saw each other only at court hearings, until occupancy was finally awarded to Paulina, no doubt because Carl lived abroad most of the time. Nora was always happy she'd kept out of it: it would have been hard for her to take sides, which was exactly what Carl and Paulina would have demanded, either directly or indirectly, by allusions, questions, and she would have been forced to choose between them.

Instead, she had dropped all contact with Carl and Paulina, a painful decision, and for how long she didn't know. She had awaited their first call eagerly, their first reunion, even by chance, which in fact was what happened, in the supermarket.

Now she's been in contact with Paulina for some time, and even Carl has called her. Not a word about their earlier conflicts. Instead he has called about her cousin. In the end it may be because of him and his stubborn imagination that all three siblings can talk openly again with each other after all these years.

SHE WOULD NEVER want to live in that house again: the hill was fraught with too many bad memories, and she has no wish to recall her childhood. At the same time she has always been secretly drawn to it, even back when she cleared out, and later when she was avoiding all contact with Paulina and Carl. Sometimes, late in the evening, she would walk as far as her parents' home. She just wanted to stand for a few moments on the path, to see the car in the driveway, the light behind the large terrace windows. She never rang the bell.

The glow of the light extended far into the garden, but she always stayed outside the illuminated area. She knew that if you looked out from the house, the darkness beyond the pool of light seemed like a black wall, as if the grass ended abruptly, as if there were no bushes and no path. So she managed to remain invisible to those in the house—as a youth, to her parents and siblings, as an adult, to Paulina alone, even though she was standing so close to them all.

When they met again, this was the first thing she told Paulina: how she stood in the dark outside the house, waiting. Not even waiting, just standing there. Then she would turn and walk down the hill, wander through the streets perhaps, back to the redoubt.

It never occurred to her that her grandfather might visit the redoubt by chance and recognize her, an old soldier out for a stroll across what was once a firing range. Hadn't they secretly hoped, as they gathered empty shells, that their grandfather had left them lying there?

Then the joggers, panting their way through the twilight after work, and that made her think again of the little booklets the four of them had found in the waste cans. It struck her as funny, but a little disgusting too, when she recalled the image of them sitting on the park bench, breathless, bent over the torn pages. What had her siblings and cousin thought of her, the older sister? Perhaps for the three of them the crude faces, the scattered sperm, the sex organs in a constant state of arousal, were like a strange world into which they could gaze, a world from which they were separated by age, but which she, as oldest, might long since have entered. Of course they didn't discuss that back then, they didn't say anything as they stared with constantly renewed excitement at the stock depictions of couples on sofas or tables.

As the oldest, she had always been a step ahead of the others. Carl and Paulina had tried to catch up, but each time they did, they saw that their older sister had again pulled away. And in her youth she never admitted that the glossy photos were just as strange to her as they were to her younger brother and sister, perhaps even stranger. At times she was taken aback: Carl and Paulina had unknowingly caught up with her and were doing things she never would have dreamed of.

When she learned of Paulina's nightly excursions to the pond that summer, she felt a pang, for she herself had never gone swimming in the woods with the neighborhood boys, and now that her younger sister had, it was far too late for her to start.

It was too late to catch up now; she'd missed her chance. She could hardly ask Paulina if she could come along. And later, at some other pond, with other boys, she would be thinking how familiar this must all be to her sister, a primeval knowledge: the black water, the muted cries, swimming out together far past the center, where there was no bottom, no algae, and finally, strokes in the darkness that could no longer be those of startled fish.

THEY WALK TOGETHER through the neighborhood: she feels she's having an adult conversation with Paulina for the first time and recognizes a distance from their common past that has nothing to do with rejection. They agree that in a certain sense it's almost uncanny how different the experience of time can be for sisters who grew up in daily contact.

Some memories barely match, and now and then the two find irresolvable contradictions. That may have to do with their different levels of knowledge about their parents. As the oldest, she was let in on some things her younger siblings never knew about; she asked things her siblings simply didn't care to know.

When they arrive at the redoubt and look down toward the valley, she learns that Paulina never knew their parents had first met as temporary employees at the weapons factory that closed down a few years ago. Paulina is amazed, she'd never thought about it, and now she listens attentively to her sister, the difference in age again apparent, the older one a step ahead.

Their father and their cousin's mother had each taken temporary jobs on their own at the factory. The son had left home, but the daughter was still living with her father and the Old Lady. All contact with the exiled brother was forbidden, and the Old Lady's spies were everywhere. Brother and sister might never have learned that they were at the same factory if it hadn't been for the company doctor. He noticed the similarity in family names during physical exams. The two looked for each other while smoking a last cigarette by the gate before the morning shift, while standing in the canteen queue at noon, while on the streetcar after work, but nothing.

They needed allies. The sister grew to trust a young woman with whom she worked, talking as they went through the same motions on the line. Her fellow worker soon knew the whole appalling story and offered her services as a go-between.

She searches in the neighboring building for a face that matches the description. She skips her cigarette breaks, won't rest until she discovers the brother in the target sights unit, the radio shop, or the howitzer storeroom. In the landing gear assembly section a worker removes his welding mask and she recognizes him at once: those Italian eyes.

A secret meeting is arranged, after work by the telephone booth in front of the factory. With her task completed, the young woman can return to her cigarette breaks, can erase the man's face and dark eyes from her memory. But perhaps she has already been drawn into the family story too deeply, has long since become entwined in it: she finally realizes that she has fallen in love with her coworker's brother, the young welder.

The two become a couple while still working at the factory. The younger sister can fill in the rest for herself. A few years later they are parents. They name their first child Nora, the next Carl, the last Paulina.

WE'RE SITTING IN the lobby of my hotel, talking quietly. The night porter is asleep behind his desk. After we ate we went to a bar, then Carl walked me back to the hotel. From outside I could see the seagulls perched on the windowsills. We've been ready to part for some time; at the bar, my room key lay on the table between our glasses and the bottle.

Now I ask Carl if he remembers a photo in that old album, of our grandfather as a young man, apparently at the opera: he is sitting in the dark with his opera glasses, scanning the stage.

Perhaps I shouldn't have asked, for Carl stares at me so fixedly that I'm looking into his childhood eyes again for the first time. It's the same penetrating gaze that unintentionally disconcerted others back then.

As far as I'm concerned, he replies, it no longer matters whether or not such a photo ever existed. If it did, it could only have been taken under the most difficult of conditions. Given the poor lighting, it would have been blurred, it could have shown only gray foggy layers. And a lens wide enough to include both the front row and the stage, so that both the young man and the singer could be seen at the same time, would have been simply impossible.

"You still think you can maintain a certain distance from our grandparents' story, treat images like real photographs you can touch, ones you can look at and stick back in our old album. But I'm afraid you're wrong: over the years, without noticing it, you've grown so entangled in their story that you can no longer close the album, and let the pictures slip back into darkness between the black cardboard pages.

"I was worried after your first call. It seemed strange that you were still obsessed with our grandparents' story. We hadn't spoken in twenty years, and all you wanted to talk about is our grandmother. You're not the person I once knew—you're haggard and worn out now. I don't even see that old Italian look.

"You've surely noticed that I've brought nothing—no secret file, not even a scrap of paper with scribbled notes. But not because I couldn't find anything. In fact, I haven't even looked for information about our grandmother. Believe me, you're imagining things if you're seeking documents, details about her life, and telling me in the same breath that you only need a little more evidence to clear up her story once and for all.

"What do you expect to find? That our grandmother performed in Barcelona while her fiancé was stationed there? That she always knew he belonged to the Condor Legion, was even glad he'd volunteered? Or perhaps that our grandmother never was an opera singer, that those were only youthful plans, dreams, hopes, never fulfilled? Will that be your conclusion if you don't find any proof of her singing career? You'll never be satisfied. Each new clue will lead to a further suspicion, as will every new blank.

"I know the feeling, that's why I'm talking with you. Perhaps finding the photo album that spring had the same importance for you that the letters we hid that summer had for me: you know how hard it was for me to get over that. So don't misunderstand me, I don't mean it as a reproach, because it was the three of us, after all, who told you the story we'd made up about our grandmother.

"A famous opera singer living in Italy: my sisters and I just made that up so the neighborhood kids would leave us alone. How were we to know that you would get so wrapped up in it? We underestimated the power of words. Perhaps we weren't old enough to realize how carefully they have to be handled. And perhaps you were too young to let a story just be a story, one that eventually loses its importance and is replaced by others.

"Perhaps we should have kept everything to ourselves. Now I'm sorry we let you in on it—from the moment you called I've been worried about you. You've succumbed to this story, and now you're a character in it. And at some point you might start thinking none of our family are dead, that no one has died, because our grandmother will seem as alive as you are.

"In retrospect, I think it might have been better if that album had consisted solely of blurred, underexposed photos. You have to forget that story, just as I have. The images must fade, our grandmother's figure must gradually dissolve, until only formless shades of light and dark remain. You must leave those childhood stories behind. It's time to grow up.

"If you don't trust me, if it seems I'm trying to take something from you, that I begrudge you a vivid memory of our grandmother, just remember Paulina. You see her all the time; you know she's convinced we killed our grandfather's second wife.

"You could say that inserting the Old Lady's death notice in the newspaper was just a childish prank. A macabre joke, truly offensive when you think of it, but with no serious consequences. Fortunately, it didn't have its intended effect. The Old Lady is still alive. If the four of us hadn't hated her so, our obsession with her might seem almost laughable now.

"But Paulina couldn't see it that way. She believes that a curse we delivered long ago has been turned against us. For years, as if under a spell, my sister has been tending a stranger's grave for all of us, her adult life destroyed by events that we invented as children.

"You must have known how fiercely Paulina and I fought over our parents' house. When I think back on those hearings, I hardly recognize myself: why couldn't I have let my sister live there in peace? I'm glad now that I wasn't given the house, for then I might still be as obsessed as you are with our stories, living that near to our grandfather and the Old Lady. Then it might be me standing at the grave, instead of Paulina.

"You may not have known it, but you did my sister a big favor last summer by disappearing overnight instead of going to the graveyard with her. You always thought you had to help her deal with her fantasy if she refused to abandon it. No matter why you fled, your refusal helped Paulina. She hasn't been to the grave since. I'm convinced the spell will soon be broken.

"Perhaps you understand now why I had no desire to bring along any information about our grandmother. I'm thinking of you. I hope the four of us can meet someday without the past weighing on us, neither the story of our family nor the disastrous holiday we spent together. But first you have to forget our grandmother too.

"If not, you may be drawn inevitably toward the dead. Nora, Paulina, and I will call to you, we'll do all we can to hold you back, but you will no longer hear us, you will be lost."

I'LL ALWAYS REMEMBER Carl's parting words: "If you can't forget our grandmother, the distance between you will keep shrinking until you are closer to each other than a living being can stand."

He pulls on his warm gloves. I watch him leave the hotel and go out into the street, the snow falling heavily. Carl doesn't look back. He walks with lowered gaze, his fur hat pulled far down on his forehead, and disappears quickly into the flurrying snow.

I return to my room in a daze. Random phrases of Carl's ring in my ears, freed from all context, no more than a low murmur: "You won't make it. With those fantasies, you'll fall apart."

Perhaps it's true, I will lose my way and find myself surrounded by snow, in a place I've never been. Fields of snow, a snow-filled sky, on the open road, far from Stockholm. The road map spread out on the hood, my frozen fingers tracing lines. My breath frosty as I gaze into the landscape—no house, no smoke, no street. My feet frozen, standing at the road's edge. Then I realize my lips are forming words: "You'll never make it."

I will climb back into the car and drive slowly on, nothing ahead but a broad white surface. It must have snowed again this afternoon. There are no fresh tracks. I will murmur to myself: "No one died."

Then a farmyard off to the side, no lights, I can just make out the barn and the chimney of the house. Everyone must be fast asleep. The fresh snow crunches under the tires. I feel uneasy about continuing in the car: I'll walk the rest of the way to the farmhouse. The sky is almost black, but still I cast a shadow before my feet.

Not a soul, just boot tracks outside the stall. But then I see something moving, dark, not very big. Someone is crossing the farmyard. As if unnoticed, he places one foot before the other in the deep snow. And looks like someone no one has ever seen.

· calls ·

HIS FACE SEEMS familiar. She's seen him somewhere before, fleetingly, at a distance, but clearly. Of course he attracts attention. The villagers aren't used to seeing young
men these days. Women with men at the front know their
husbands might be killed at any time. Then one spring
evening a solitary soldier appears, even though old men and
children have been drafted in recent weeks, Berlin having
meanwhile realized that the long-awaited final victory now
hangs in the balance.

A conspicuous figure. Instead of arriving with one of the
countless lines of refugees, he seems to have made his way
from the East alone, moving under cover of night, as if he
were being followed. Yet he apparently intends to go no farther. They watch him, talk about him when he's not around.
No one knows where he comes from, why he's left his unit. It
must have been disbanded, but if so, he should have joined
another. Perhaps he's a deserter, in which case he should
have ditched his shabby uniform. But he's still wearing it.

The man strikes them as unpredictable. He's still carrying his rifle. The children are afraid of him, and she sees fear in her son's face whenever the stranger is mentioned.

Because the man has taken shelter in the dairy, her son is afraid to go there. The women in the dairy are also nervous. When they arrive at work in the morning, they have the feeling he's been prowling through the rooms at night. They sense it when they look around. He has just returned to his attic room. A few moments ago, he was staring at the cheese in the dark.

He avoids work. There are other things a man in his mid-thirties could do in the village besides tend songbirds. But the breeder's wife is happy she doesn't have to clean the cages, since she's afraid of birds. It's said that the stranger handled birds in the army, trained carrier pigeons, tied cameras to them for reconnaissance flights, automatic photos of an unsuspecting enemy from the air. No one knows how much of the story to believe. Camera-carrying pigeons. But it would fit.

Where could she have met him? One of her husband's comrades, perhaps—they're about the same age. If it were up to her, he'd find another place to stay, but she hasn't said anything. After all, she and her son are guests themselves, even if they've been staying with their relatives for a year and a half now. When their apartment in the city was bombed, she didn't know where else to go.

But that's not the only reason she's glad she's here. She pictures it clearly: she sees her husband again where they spent their first afternoon. The field will be warm, as it was then, and they will squint into the bright sun. It won't be long now. When the war is over, they want to have a second child, a girl.

She doesn't know why all this seems so certain. Her husband might be taken prisoner and never return. He could be killed in the final weeks. Casualties have never been higher, orders never so insane. The more obvious it becomes that the final victory they keep calling for is a mere fantasy, the more cold-bloodedly the generals act. Now, at this very moment, her husband could die. But she is confident: it won't happen to him.

She remembers the destroyed building in the morning twilight. The three of them standing in the street. They had survived. Her husband photographed the ruins, the piles of rubble through empty windows; her son was dazed, but she knew he would like to climb back into the building and dig his toys out of the wreckage. The apartment, their furniture, her grandparents' china, the opera programs, librettos, scores, memoirs of the Spanish Civil War. Everything gone, lost. Only a half-filled photo album a neighbor found farther down the street remained. Snapshots when they first met, and a few more photos. All had ended.

She sees herself standing in the midst of the rubble, strong coffee being passed around nearby, people writing their names and temporary locations on whatever facades are still standing, the cleanup under way, carts everywhere filled with household goods, everyone saving what they can. She holds her son by the hand. Her husband is walking around with his camera. She should be helping, or at least staying out of people's way. But she doesn't move. Everything that once surrounded her has been buried before her eyes. But with this thought comes a certain relief. She realizes she won't miss any of it.

At that moment the light alters. Perhaps it's the dust from the rubble, or the new gaps between the buildings.

She can still see the October sun. Since that moment she will no longer fear anything. Having seen the bombed-out building, her earlier fears seem less serious, almost ludicrous. If she hadn't lost everything, she would never have known this.

SHORTLY BEFORE THEY were to be married, her fiancé disappeared for nine months and plunged her into uncertainty. They may not have known one another long enough. They were both too young to handle such a separation without misunderstandings. She grew suspicious, felt betrayed, learned nothing of what he was doing, could only guess where he was. The secrecy troubled her. Only later did she realize her fiancé might have been equally worried. She could have run off with some oily tenor and not had the courage to tell her fiancé the truth. He could have imagined the worst while in Spain. Yet he never harbored the least suspicion. He trusted her completely.

Upon his return her dislike of secrecy grew: she wanted nothing to do with it, no matter what it concerned. She considered this a basic difference between them that would always be there. She prepared for life with someone who loved an air of mystery, an unpleasant tendency she hoped to ignore as far as possible. Now she realized something she hadn't understood: unlike most people, her husband could keep a secret.

She would have hated being married to a man who couldn't keep things to himself. You know just by looking at some people how easy it is to squeeze something out of them—the slightest hint and they start talking, quite willingly. She feels even greater contempt for those who seem capable of keeping their mouths shut and therefore draw confidences from others, only to divulge them at the first opportunity. She's been mistaken more than once about someone she felt sure could keep a secret. That feeling in the pit of the stomach, like falling from a great height, even if the issues involved were only minor personal matters. And she has felt rage, true hate, when her trust led to a colleague's undoing. Even now she could spit in the face of anyone who ever told secrets or betrayed a confidence. She knows her husband would never do such a thing.

For a long time she was unjust to him. He never complained, it was something he took for granted, and it was some time before she realized she could always count on her husband. No affairs, no broken promises, no secrecy in their home life. He might enjoy secrets, but there was no doubt about his honesty.

When she was still in her mid-twenties, it never occurred to her that his penchant for mystery was what first attracted her. To others he may have seemed merely happy to be in the army, proud to wear a uniform. Closer inspection, however, revealed a hidden side, a subterranean shimmer in his eyes. She knows herself well enough to realize that if he had been no more than a boring officer's candidate, she wouldn't have given him a second glance. She's not interested in men with everything on the surface.

He had the aura of a man who knows something deep and mysterious and is waiting to meet someone with whom he can share that mystery. And she was the one he chose. He made her explore invisible traits, challenged her to see things he didn't even intimate to others.

Secrets—and this hadn't dawned on her until she was past thirty—don't always conceal mischief. Unidentified killers aren't the only ones with secrets. Traitors and spies aren't the only ones with something to hide. Secrets can be shared by couples: sworn love, unspoken devotion, things that others need never know. A summer outing, a couple strolls across the fields, never dreaming that they will soon be looking at each other in a completely new way. Then she sees in his eyes that he, too, wants to sink onto the grass right there. They do it without another word. Their first shared secret, arising from an unknown openness.

To this day no one knows that they were never engaged. They had no time to think, and the engagement was merely an opportune story offered by their aunt. This, too, is a secret, although a harmless one. No, the dark realm of secrets is not restricted to those who are dishonest and hurtful. She still knows the exact place, sometimes walks there with her son, who runs about gathering pebbles without the least suspicion of what this spot meant to his parents.

When in the summer of 1939 her husband finally told her he had been in Spain, she sensed it would not be his last war. His secret mission during the Spanish Civil War made her think that the air force was the most important thing in her husband's life. Barely two months later, the war started up again, and she feared her husband would spend the rest of his life in battle. Until she recalled the leather gloves. He'd almost forgotten to take them to the Condor Legion's victory parade in Berlin. She saw that as the first sign. The appeal of the air force was wearing off. Perhaps it had already lessened in Spain, and all his joy at being a veteran was nothing more than a final attempt to overcome this feeling.

Over the long years at war her husband underwent a striking change. At first he was in the best of moods for the outing, a blitzkrieg followed by rapid victory, one year and he would be home again. New cities, foreign languages, it promised to be as exhilarating as the action in Spain. But in the long run, war was not all that exciting, and weariness gradually crept into his limbs. Slowly the excitement was transformed into waiting for the next leave, hoping to survive until it was over. Hopes for a great victory gave way to the first doubts as to whether the fronts would hold. As prospects faded, her husband was not increasingly depressed, as she might have expected, but his interest in military affairs steadily declined.

It was as if his pride in uniform were part of some former life, the life of a man in his mid-twenties who no longer existed. Now he was in his early thirties and occasionally showed a humorous side that she would never have credited him with. He could laugh at himself, at his initial obsession with an air force career: a soldier's honor, fatherland, battle ethics. He dared not let anyone know this: it would cost him his life. It was yet another secret they shared.

On his last visit they allowed themselves a macabre joke. Once they had the idea, they couldn't stop laughing. The strain of events, the apartment lost with all its contents, uncertainty about how long the war would last, they laughed so hard on their walk that they had to stop to catch their breath. In a fit of high spirits they fastened a model airplane on a string and hung it from the floor lamp, so that night and day the bomber seemed to circle the living room table. Some neighbors from the village thought it showed their determination to stay the course. By now those neighbors, too, would be happy to see night attacks, miracle weapons, and heroic last stands a thing of the past.

They took a snapshot of the model airplane hanging over the table; she'll paste it in their remaining album as soon as the war ends. The last war her husband will fight, and then the uniform in which he posed so proudly in the opening pages of the album will disappear as well. Leafing through old albums some day, their grandchildren will be puzzled by a bomber in the living room. They'll ask their grandmother: Why an airplane when the war was still going on and your own apartment was destroyed in an air raid? And she'll tell them how and why this photo had been taken.

BUT FOR THE MOMENT there's no question of that. Everyone's waiting for the war to end. She's waiting for her husband. Perhaps he'll recognize the stranger in the village—they may have served together in Spain. He might have been among the wedding guests, may have congratulated the couple briefly and then disappeared into the crowd. But why would his face have stuck in her memory?

She can see him in uniform, his head bare. It was late evening, she's sure of that. And it wasn't outdoors. His hair was closely cropped. Now it looks somewhat unkempt, the sort of small detail that can change a person greatly. A beard perhaps. And glasses. No, a monocle. Now she's got it. The stranger hiding in the attic of the dairy is none other than the spy.

He's the officer who visited her once in her dressing room, with his ridiculous monocle and his tasteless mustache. He sat perched on a stool with a lit cigarette dangling from the corner of his mouth, trying for some reason that was never clear to involve her in a conversation. He'd come to sound her out, but she hadn't realized that until later; otherwise she would have politely shown him the door.

This man wanted her to walk into a trap. How could she have lived with herself if she had revealed where her husband was and ruined everything? It wasn't until later that evening that she finally realized she'd been dealing with a spy. She had wanted so badly to believe that the unknown officer had been sent by her fiancé. If it hadn't been for the mustache and the monocle, she might have believed his story. She wouldn't betray her fiancé for the world, but she might have let something slip. Luckily, she hadn't known anything. At the time she had been at her wits' end, nearly furious, but now she realized that by not telling her anything her fiancé had protected her.

Now the spy has crept into her uncle's dairy, and she understands why he is seldom seen on the street by day. He's trying to avoid her, he's afraid she's already recognized him. Probably not at first sight, but a few days after his arrival, when he settled in. He doesn't want to move on, he knows she can't do him any harm, but it would still be unpleasant to run into her. She could let everyone know about him. He may realize she wouldn't do that. He's well aware she can keep a secret.

THE WAR ENDED seven weeks ago, and the spy cleared out the same day. Everyone was glad to see the last of him. She too would happily forget him, but she senses he will linger in her memory. She envisions the scene in detail. Her husband has returned; he was held prisoner for only a few days. Now they're sitting in the garden of the dairy villa, and he listens patiently as she slowly searches for the right words.

As news spread that the Americans would reach the village that morning at the latest, she could see the relief in people's faces. In the final weeks the stranger urged them with increasing fanaticism to fight on to the last man. He of all people, who had apparently fled the front to save his own skin. Now he was merely a driven man, with a confused gaze and twisted mouth, trying to persuade the villagers, first by making speeches, and finally by issuing orders, to share his German will to survive.

No one paid any attention to the lunatic, who was still screaming at them not to give up when the first white sheets were hauled out. He ran up and down the streets waving his pistol in the air, threatening summary court-martial if he spotted a bedsheet in a window. No one figured he'd actually shoot. It happened so quickly no one realized he'd taken aim at the woman next door. For a moment everything was still, no one moved. The sheet sank, sailed to the pavement, the woman disappeared from the bedroom window.

A few hours later the Americans arrived. The stranger was gone, otherwise the villagers might have killed him. The next day they buried the final victim of that long war.

Her husband knew the officer; he may even have told him about the dairy at some point. They served together in Spain but weren't friends, then or later. The man was rumored to be involved on several fronts. Her husband would never send someone like that to greet his fiancé.

———

FOR A MOMENT he barely hears the singer's voice, but the picture is still clear, no flickering, no snow, no static, the sound has simply grown fainter. Had he known about the spy, he would have intervened at once. He listens as the volume gradually increases, and the lips of his first wife no longer move silently.

Sending a spy to sound out his fiancé would have run counter to his convictions. Perhaps it was fortunate that his wife waited until the war ended to tell him about the visit. He might have dressed the spy down in front of his comrades. Or fought with him. Slapped him with his leather glove. And been shot for demoralizing the troops.

She must have sensed this danger from the start, knowing how strongly he felt about honesty. So in a sense she saved his life by preventing him from losing his head. She kept silent throughout his military service.

Now the song has finally regained full volume. Not that this soprano bears any real resemblance to his first wife, but he wants her to. Whenever an opera his first wife sang is performed, he almost manages to visualize her onstage. He blurs the image, focuses at a certain depth behind the glass surface of the screen. He stares until he sees individual dots, then the unknown face gradually dissolves. When he refocuses his eyes, a different face has appeared on the screen.

But there's something wrong with the sound; it's distorted. It's not some ordinary problem, there's no point in adjusting the antenna. The suspicion grows that his second wife has loosened a wire again. It's starting to get on his nerves. As if she needed proof from time to time that he truly was a radio technician. Whenever an opera is announced his wife disappears. After the news, she withdraws to the bedroom with a headache, it's been bothering her all day, she needs to sleep. He imagines her lying awake, listening as he changes channels, bangs on the set with his fist, finally turns it off with a curse.

It can't be mere coincidence that these strange disturbances occur only when an opera is on. His wife must check the TV guide each morning, and if she doesn't like the program she pokes around at the back of the TV set with a kitchen knife. She works on a screw, the screw won't turn, and before long a wire is cut. Or he comes home from work and the tube has gone out. She's driven him to the point where, at the opening bars of the overture, he'll pull the plug on his own.

NOR DOES HE listen to his opera albums. But at least—evading the Old Lady—he's managed to smuggle what remained of his extensive collection from the house in time—a few recordings of our grandmother from the thirties among them, records filled with static. If you total up what was hidden under the stairs, in the basement, and in the attic, and when you add to these the records hidden in the shed, soon to fall victim to dampness, mold, and winter frost, the surviving whole amounts to barely a dozen albums. The Old Lady is simply too alert. She patrols the house on a regular basis, rifles through cupboards, drawers, and boxes, even looks behind curtains, checks the toilet tank in the guest bathroom.

The Old Lady forced our grandfather to discard all his souvenirs, and there was nothing he could do about it. Directly after their wedding, instead of going on a honeymoon, they spent a week clearing out the house, carrying boxes of photos, letters, and knick-knacks to the rubbish heap on the hill across the way. The smaller pieces of furniture, the bedstead, the clocks, and a large portion of the china were offered for sale in classified ads. Everything was to go, regardless of price. I have to admit this image appeals to me, too.

I would like it even better if the Old Lady deceived our grandfather right from the start, handing a newly tied bundle of souvenirs of our grandmother to the garbage men each week, so that he noticed nothing. Maybe she was treacherous enough to hand him bulging bags that he would take to the trash himself, without suspecting anything. As guileless as he is, it would be some time before he began to see through his second wife, began checking quickly through the rubbish before the trash was picked up. Now he pokes through bits of old food with a stick, trying to find missing objects, working hastily, glancing sideways, not daring to lose sight of the peephole in the doorway.

The Old Lady, for her part, soon figures out why he's spending so much time outside. She spies through the peephole: her husband is standing there staring into the open trash can with an almost morbid fixation. She has to be more careful. As soon as her husband leaves in the morning, she shuts herself in the cellar, wraps a cloth around a hammer to muffle it, and with a few well-aimed blows destroys a ceramic figurine that she's long considered an eyesore. She doesn't know where the Spanish dancer came from, what it meant to her husband and his first wife. It's bothered her for a long time, but it makes little difference now. She removes the rag from the hammer and wraps the shards in it, making a well-padded bundle: her husband won't have the least idea what's in the trash she has him take out after supper.

Of course there's no reason to doubt the story with the ax, or the words: "I'll kill you all."

But I've long since lost any certainty that our grandfather was at the Old Lady's mercy from the start. I no longer believe in bundles of trash with broken pieces of model airplanes and willfully shattered records. Photos cut to pieces and tossed into the stove at night, souvenirs bedded in wood chips and burned, like those little dolls stuck full of pins to injure rivals. It can't have been like that.

He stands in the hall by the phone so he won't miss the next instruction his wife calls down to him. Then he goes into the living room to gather the remaining programs, librettos, and opera albums from the bookcase. Sacks stuffed full all over the house. Hadn't his first wife said that life began anew for her when they were bombed?

Now and then he hears her voice, though it's not as loud and clear as it once was, from the opera stage. Nor as firm, as intimate, as when she sang for the children at home. By now the voice sounds more the way it did toward the end, faint, distant. Since his second marriage there have been pauses, the voice has fallen silent at times, it withdraws, and will one day disappear.

A new life is under way. Later that evening he drives with his wife to the dump, which has grown so high it forms a second hill. His wife doesn't mind helping him carry things. They check to make sure there's no one around, then throw the heavy sacks one by one over the fence. Now the opera albums are gone. He realizes he will never hear his first wife's voice again.

—

ALL WINTER I kept hearing the words Carl whispered to me, a voice that never faded after our meeting in Stockholm, and soon I could no longer recall whether he sounded threatening or worried as he turned to me: "You'll be lost."

As the months passed, the images lost their clarity—the somber season, the snow. I resisted, didn't want our grandmother's outlines to fade till nothing remained save a flicker of light and dark. But my strength waned, and so I might soon have fallen prey to those whispered words and forgotten our family's story completely.

Then, in the spring, when the sun returned, as the snow thawed and colors regained their vibrancy, the voice began repeating with increasing clarity a sentence that I hadn't heard since that evening, the others having drowned it out: "We underestimated the power of words."

In Stockholm Carl urged me to grow up, and this sentence may have helped me to do so. Our words are enough, nothing is ever lost. I don't need evidence, do not need to see our grandmother's gravestone. There's nothing to fear: I can rely on the images I've created. No one can make our grandmother disappear. And even if I'm drawn inevitably nearer the realm of the dead by it, I'll always cling to that creation.

It no longer matters if our grandfather and his second wife threw away those keepsakes; apparently they saw no other solution. If they wanted to start a new life, there could be no memories. My anger has fled, let them live out their remaining years in peace, according to their own ideas, no matter how senseless they always seemed to me. I no longer feel the need to interfere, to get them to change. Perhaps someday I'll even lose my inexplicable fear of the Old Lady, go to her house, and ring the doorbell.

My view of our grandmother is no longer obscured by the Old Lady. The battle is over now: each lives in her own world. I can see our grandmother's young hands, they lie as if about to move, her fingers tremble slightly, then gently smooth the blanket.

Day by day the light lasts longer, it's getting warmer, and soon it will be Easter. Gradually the ground recovers from the frost, the gray, worn areas are interspersed with green. The next picture shows a meadow: the grass is tall, the woman's dress almost hidden by the blades, all you can see are her shoulders, her head, her summer hat. She sits leaning back, one hand must be flat on the ground while the other shades her eyes, a snapshot taken in bright sunlight.

Then a harbor scene, the woman standing on the mole, seagulls circling behind her. Trieste perhaps. There is no indication of place on this or any of the other photographs—they could all have been taken in Italy. None of the pictures are dated, but they cover a broad expanse of time, and the advancing age of those photographed allows them to be grouped in at least halfway accurate order.

—

IT'S BEEN QUIET for a while. They gaze across the Tiber to the gentle slopes of the other bank, where the cedars stand. Her hands lie on the armrests, they're old hands now, with raised arteries and age spots. She knows the view from the balcony terrace, looks out on it every day. But he's here for the first time. Perhaps he knows the river from the promenade, but he's never seen the area across the way from the fifth floor.

She was always convinced she'd left no trace, not the slightest clue. She was so sure she never thought of being found. Until she got a call from the man now sitting across from her, an agitated voice, cautious inquiries—at first, she had no idea what he wanted. His research, uncertainty turning to increasingly strong suspicion, his travels through Europe, to Milan, to Trieste, even to Rome on occasion. But now he's reached the point where he wants to be sure he isn't just chasing a phantom. If she doesn't mind, he'd like to ask a few questions about her past, to clear up any remaining doubts.

When he came to the door early that afternoon she was surprised. The voice on the phone had sounded younger, like someone in his mid-twenties, but he was at least ten years older than that, with tired eyes. He apologized for being late, he didn't have a good city map. He'd passed the building without recognizing it, the palazzo gloomy from the outside: dark stone, with iron bars at the gate and on the lower windows, as if its breath were being choked off. You could tell the people who lived here weren't poor, but it was hard to say if they were still alive. The building didn't appeal to him from the outside, but from this terrace, with the palms, the warm spring sun, it seems a totally different place.

He asks about the police farther down the street, the motorcycles, the armored limousines with tinted glass, he was struck by the air of quiet tension. That's the anti-Mafia headquarters: she always feels a little uneasy walking by there herself. In addition to the police there are almost always a few men about in ordinary street clothes. She can never decide which side they are on. She never looks them in the eye but sometimes glances sideways at their chests, thinking she might see the outlines of a bulletproof vest beneath a jacket or spot a holster under an armpit.

They stand there all day as if they just happened to be in the neighborhood; they stroll a few steps, their hands lightly clasped at their backs, but you feel they might pull out a pistol at any moment. At times the scene springs into motion: alert glances pass, everyone steps quickly aside, and a prosecuting attorney or a secret-service man drives out. Then, before it's even in the papers, the whole neighborhood knows there's been an assassination, or that an attack is expected within a few hours.

She says, "I remember seeing Aldo Moro's picture in the newspaper after he was kidnapped. I was sitting here on the terrace. That shocked expression, as if he knew that those who would look at the photograph were betraying him, and he could do nothing about it."

He turns away from the panorama and looks at her.

From the start she's noticed something in his eyes she can't interpret, a slight uncertainty perhaps, or rather, the desire to reach some understanding.

She says, "The dead remain in our memories. The living disappear easily."

She hasn't given an interview in ages, her career ended long ago, nor does she have any keepsakes, programs, or photos from that period, so she's had a difficult time preparing for this meeting. But he's hardly asked about dates, roles, where she appeared, as if he learned that all himself, long ago. It seems he's primarily interested in her.

SHE TELLS HIM stories about her childhood. Her parents always liked music, even sang in a choir, and they had a piano at home. Friends came over on Sundays, pianists, sometimes an entire string quartet—there were many musicians in their circle of friends. Later, much later, several of her parents' friends emigrated, but others waited, refused to believe the rumors, missed the right moment and were never seen again.

She was a quiet child, a listener from the time she was little. The guests always remarked how good she was, never interrupting the grown-ups' conversation, never complaining or whining childishly during performances in her parents' apartment. But when she wanted to sing, everyone encouraged her. The quiet girl was heard at last, even if she sang awkwardly and off-key.

She was never shy about using her own voice, nor did it make any difference to her if someone was listening. She knows that many people have difficulties dealing with their own voice, that even some professional singers suffer torments when they sense an audience in the darkness beyond the stage. When she set her sights on voice lessons, her parents and friends supported her: they all expected it.

Most of her childhood was spent around adults. Except for her own siblings, other kids didn't want to play with her. The neighborhood parents found the so-called artists' home slightly suspect, frequented as it was by the demimonde. No one could understand it, since the husband, like his brother in the countryside, ran a respectable dairy that served the major markets. Later, they may have said it was no wonder that his business went bankrupt: he associated with the wrong people.

So she had little to do with children her own age; she disliked their yelling and kept her distance from roughhousing on the street. And she may well have treated the other children a little arrogantly. She mentioned one exception, a quiet boy next door who enjoyed listening to musical performances more than playing war outside.

Her visitor already knows the chance encounter that reunited them as adults. They were still like quiet children with each other, but when it came to strangers they were no longer nearly so reserved. She sang each evening to an unknown audience; his voice rang out across a parade ground.

She told of the years that followed, into the postwar period. The young man cautiously inserted a question now and then, filling gaps she hadn't noticed. Now they're steering toward her illness: she still hesitates, and he doesn't press her. A long pause in the conversation, as if both must catch their breath before approaching the difficult questions.

She says: "Perhaps you still remember. When Aldo Moro was assaulted, all they found was his empty car. No one believed he would be found alive. Everyone was certain: Aldo Moro is dead. His kidnappers panicked and photographed

him holding that day's newspaper. But they couldn't overcome those first impressions. No sign of life could alter the
public's conviction."

The young man nods, although he hasn't understood.
She's managed another brief delay. But now she has to explain everything as best she can.

IN HER late thirties, she fell seriously ill. She was still young,
not much older than her visitor today. There had been no
hint of illness, no cancer in her family, all of whom had
lived well into their eighties with no major health problems. She, too, had rarely seen a doctor, once she was past
the usual childhood illnesses. In her entire singing career
she had never missed a single performance due to laryngitis
or had polyps removed from her vocal chords. No problems during two pregnancies. She had no worries about
her body.

She can't recall why she needed a physical, all she remembers is the elderly man, his hands buried in the pockets of his smock, trying to work his way around a clear
answer. They've found something: to be safe, they want to
do some more blood tests. Nothing to worry about at the
moment, but she should come back in a week. When she
shakes his hand good-bye her palm is cold and sweaty.

For a moment she stares death in the eye. But this image
doesn't last long, and it's immediately superseded by others.
At first she hopes it was a false diagnosis, then she and her
husband envision various prospects for a cure, figure her
chances for survival, although they know better. Operations,
new therapies. Everything is discussed hypothetically, never
in real terms, partly because of the children—they don't want
them to know how serious things are for their mother.

Yet with the years the original image shimmers through again, becomes clearer and clearer, as if she has grown used to it only now. She's never seen a dead person, and the pale, motionless hands on the blanket are not the memory of a dying relative but an image from the future: she's looking at her own hands; the first dead person in her life is she herself.

Her husband resists, doesn't want to hear about it, but they have to face facts: how will the family go on when they've lost their mother? She makes him promise to remarry as soon as possible after her death. They discuss possible candidates among their unmarried friends. She has to like the children. He has to be able to imagine living with her. Whenever their son and daughter aren't around they discuss it, but they find no satisfactory solution. Her husband will turn to a matchmaking service.

The new wife must not only help the children recover from their loss, she must also be a better mother. Since the onset of her disease, over five years ago, the children have received almost nothing from their mother—no advice, no support, no consolation. On the contrary, the family's life has concentrated solely on the patient, the children must be considerate, help care for her, support her.

From her first year at school, the daughter is forced to take all her troubles to her father: her mother hears only of her favorite teachers, her girlfriends and good grades. Now she's entering high school, and the transition is not that easy, but no one wants to burden the mother with that.

Her son is nineteen, taking up an apprenticeship—he's had to repeat two classes. She knows that would never have happened if she had been healthy. A confrontation has been building for some time. She would like him to do better in school; he doesn't want to hear this. Once they almost had a fight. He'd poured afternoon tea for her and was holding the cup when he blew up. He screamed at her, then began to shake—the tension, the uncertainty, he was fed up with worrying about her—and the teacup fell to the bed. She tried to comfort him, he was right, but she was too weak to talk, and his father boxed his ears and drove him from the sickroom.

They still hadn't spoken with them, made things clear; they kept putting it off, just be patient a while longer, your mother will recover. She knows that conversation will never take place, she can't help her son.

The children have grown up without a mother, were on their own in the formative years, have grown used to relying on just one parent. Their future stepmother won't have it easy. They've drafted a classified ad so the widower will have something to show the matchmaking service. Nothing is to be left to chance; they've carefully polished the phrases. He'll be in no shape to do that himself when she dies, the sadness, confusion, he'll have other things on his mind.

And they've decided about the final farewell. She doesn't want her children there when she dies. She won't ask them to look at a corpse. She'll stay home as long as she can, but when the end is in sight, her husband will make sure she's moved to a clinic. She's unlikely to be conscious then. She wants to see her son and daughter again before that happens: no one but her husband is to visit the hospital.

He feels strange planning things in such detail, but he respects her wishes and he can tell it comforts her. Once all these questions are dealt with, she lets him increase the painkiller to a level that actually helps. The pain lets up. She drifts off.

THE YOUNG MAN'S gaze has rested on her the whole time. Now he moves his head, nods slightly, as if he's gradually beginning to understand and now guesses how the story might end. She has never told anyone, she's hidden it for over forty years, even from herself. Without the stranger's presence, this family history would have remained lost to memory forever.

She says, "I've never known how long it was before I regained consciousness. Perhaps only one night, but it could have been weeks. I can still see my husband sitting at the bedside, a hospital room, sunlight streaming in. Perhaps I only awoke for a moment and then sank back into darkness. His sad face, filled with despair, and beyond it a patch of clear sky. I see my husband speaking to me, but I hear nothing. Perhaps I'm already dead."

The visitor looks at her questioningly. She returns his questioning look. She has attempted to reconstruct what happened at home during her long stay in the hospital, but has never been able to form a coherent picture. She has no wish to reproach her husband: he no doubt explained the situation to her many times, asking her advice, imploring her help, but she never understood a word. She was in a coma, weakened by new operations and medications. She couldn't help her husband. Everything had been planned in advance. He stuck to the plan.

"I still don't believe he told our children I died. It wouldn't be like him. It was probably the other way around: over time they convinced him of their mother's death. He was caught between two worlds—one at the hospital, where he saw his wife lying closer to death than life, and another at home, where his children insisted their mother had long since died.

"We thought through every detail, took every precaution, everything was watertight. But our greatest mistake had been made at the very start. We should not have hidden the seriousness of my illness from our children. We gave them false hope, maintained through the years that the illness would pass and things would get better. At some point they saw through our lies, no longer believed in our consolations. But instead of letting us know, they joined in the lie. Perhaps we needed consolation more urgently than they did, and without that self-deception we might have given up the struggle long ago.

"When they took leave of me, when they saw my motionless body carried from our home, the house of lies collapsed once and for all. And if their father couldn't gather the courage to tell them the truth, then they themselves would have to make him face it.

"Should he start talking about a cure again, tell them her condition had improved unexpectedly? The children had heard that often enough, and were well aware how little such phrases meant."

She sees her husband running through the apartment, the children after him, hears him cry out in a choked voice: "No, she's not dead." He takes his daughter by the shoulders, shakes her, full of despair, for she refuses to believe, while he repeats that single sentence: "She's not dead." His son leads him slowly back to the living room, they seat him on the sofa, put their arms around him, try to comfort him with his own words: "She's not dead. We know that. She'll always be alive for us."

The next morning he goes to the hospital and asks his sick wife if he should bring the children so they'll believe him, but she doesn't respond, just looks at him with half-closed eyes. They agreed the children would never see her once she was in the hospital: they need to adjust to life without her as soon as possible. He asks if she still wants to stick to the plan. She seems to nod. They have no way of knowing that the course of the disease has taken an irreversible change for the better.

"When my condition had stabilized to the point where I could make do with weaker painkillers, we reconsidered everything, but reached the same conclusion as before. Nothing had changed, except for the fact that I hadn't yet died. I was still an invalid, the children would have to take care of me another five years, with no hope of leading their own free lives and without a mother at their side to guide them. I would have remained a burden to everyone.

"They believed that I was dead, and even though they had yet to come to terms with it, we could think of no better reason than my death for seeking a stepmother for them. My husband resisted; I talked to him, tried to convince him. He made counterproposals, but in the end he gave in. He knew he would eventually have to choose between two worlds: home, where his children didn't believe him, and here, where I lay in my sickbed. At some point the conflict would destroy him. He agreed to a divorce.

"At that time I didn't measure my life in weeks or days, but from one moment of consciousness to the next. It could end at any time. I had no idea I had forty years ahead of me."

SHE PAUSES AND LOOKS out across the river. For some time they've heard cars honking in the background, the evening traffic on the river road below. From the fifth floor these sounds seem almost unreal, and she scarcely notices them. But she couldn't bear it if trees outside the building blocked her view. She needs this broad prospect, the stretches of countryside, the sky.

Her visitor gingerly approaches a question. He wants to know how the plan was carried out without the children learning of it. Her fake death, the divorce, her disappearance. Things like that can hardly be kept secret, particularly in the long run.

"That's something I've never been able to explain myself. I'm as puzzled as you are. I've been racking my brains over it for half my life. And no one can give me the answer.

"I assume my husband told our children the truth at some point. It's inconceivable that he didn't. If he really wanted to keep the story secret, there was only one thing he could have done: stop talking with his children entirely. He would have risked letting something slip with every word. By the time they were grown-ups they couldn't have been put off with evasions either. They would have probed deeper. Demanded answers. Keep quiet? No, he would be obliged to speak.

"If he married again soon, as we had planned, he would have let his second wife in on the secret. I'm sure she couldn't have lived with a lie like that. They may have waited for the children to grow used to their stepmother, to see her as a real mother, before they told them the story.

"It was a foregone conclusion that I would keep away from the family. No easy decision, believe me. I never saw my son or daughter again. But I didn't want to interfere, to cause additional problems. All traces of me were removed to make it easier on the children. The fatally ill woman was to fade from their memory. My husband and I broke off all contact. That's why I still don't know, even now, how things turned out."

Her children must have learned the truth. Betrayed by their own mother. Abandoned. While she began a new life in an unknown city. They would despise their mother, want nothing more to do with her, in reality or in memory. And at some point her son and daughter would have forgotten her.

"But I still see both of them today: the shock, the hopeless anger in their eyes. I see it so clearly I almost believe it must have been photographed: my two children at the exact moment when they understand everything. This image will never change as long as I live."

The two worlds are separated once and for all. In her dreams she sees herself at her own graveside. At times she sees her children as well, coming from the cemetery gate, dressed for a burial service. She awakes. She was about to hide behind the bushes. No, things won't go that far. Her husband will recoil at the thought of that grave: he'll have to tell the children everything.

She doesn't know what's happening at home. She will give no further sign of life. She decided that when she thought she had only a few days to live. But now the periods of clarity last longer and longer, and she's forced to imagine everything in detail. She can hardly bear it.

The doctors have stopped frowning for several weeks now; they no longer lower their voices when they speak to her. They move her to another room. She wonders if her husband has already placed the ad. She doesn't want to think about it, tries to evoke less painful memories, goes back in time, stops at a scene: it's clearly an opera stage prior to a performance. She takes a quick look through the peephole, then has to disappear.

Lying on the sanatorium terrace, she reaches a decision. If she survives, she'll make a new start. She has no false hopes;

she knows she can't resume her career where she left off twenty years ago. But she'd never given up practice altogether: she was always in a choir, and she sang the old arias now and then for her friends. She doesn't expect any leading roles, nor does she desire them. She just wants to sing again.

In the years that followed she met famous artists and diplomats, and no doubt secret-service men as well. This or that high-level politician kissed her hand. Hotels gave her suites, her rooms filled with flowers, the cards of admirers glowing white among the green fronds. She looked out on the roofs of Paris and drank champagne with a stranger, the rest of the guests already gone. She knows there are certain men who always blur the line between courting and accosting. She's given guest performances at the Semper opera, the city ghostly by night.

But those were never more than sidelights, song always took center stage. She kept at some remove from the so-called artist's life. She was no longer a young woman; she had a family behind her. Not that she couldn't enjoy that life, but she always laughed at it a little.

This attitude prevented her from glamorizing her own career when she eventually began to teach, and kept her from repeating those tales of fame that soon grow stale, always the same phrases, in exactly the same words, wildly exaggerated, as if constant repetition could restore that lost life, as if words had that power.

Her visitor must know such cases too, people who make themselves ridiculous without realizing it. He's surely heard them embarrassing themselves: "And then I sang *Die Walküre* in Bayreuth with Adolf Hitler in the box." When people start mourning the past, they become tasteless, they mourn themselves as if they were already dead. Or they convince themselves they're ageless: "What will you do on your hundredth birthday?"—"Go snorkeling in the coral reefs." She wouldn't trade places with a person like that.

Of course everyone always agrees that the best singers are those from the past. No living person could ever measure up to this or that dead tenor, to the soprano who was never recorded.

She was always involved with young people, later in her classes, in tutorial sessions, and sometimes she thought that if she did have grandchildren, one of them might take this direction. The thought pleased her: someone from her family embarking on her path, completely independently, knowing nothing about her. A young singer, with the strength she no longer possesses. As if song persisted over generations, as if it never fell silent.

Perhaps this child sings the same roles, repeating her grandmother's tones and words. She clings to this image when the sad memory of her children overwhelms her. An invisible connection occurs, the border between grandmother and granddaughter blurs, they are no longer two different persons.

With her first note, the singer assumes a character. For the length of her song she exists between two states: she knows she's not the person the audience sees, but she also knows she's no longer the same person she was in the dressing room. Between these two states, when a singer recognizes herself as an invention, a grandmother might meet her grandchild. That's what she'd like.

THE PAUSES BETWEEN her sentences grow longer—she strains to continue a thought but doesn't always find the right phrases. Her visitor tries to help with a word here and

there; he still listens attentively, and the weariness has gradually faded from his eyes. She, on the other hand, is now
exhausted. She has talked all afternoon, recalling the small-
est details of her life in response to his questions, and been
constantly surprised by her own answers, which have seemed
at times like the memories of some other person.

Now she's a little chilly—it still gets cool when the sun
goes down. She gets up to find a blanket, and her visitor
stands, too—he should really be going. She still knows almost nothing about him, though she realized early on he is
no journalist. He doesn't have a tape recorder, has taken
no notes. He didn't even claim to be journalist. But she's
too tired to hear his story today. They go to the door together. The next time, she tells him, she'll talk less. It will
be his turn to talk about himself. He smiles: he'll be glad
to. He'll give her a call.

· spores ·

SOMETIMES I SEE myself standing at the bedroom window, staring out at the tree. The window where I saw the Old Lady, the bedroom in her house, the tree with the dead people. One of the twigs almost touches the window, scratches gently at the windowpane in the wind. The curtains have been drawn aside or long since removed, and the view is unhindered. I search for the dead but find only leaves, branches, patches of sky.

I have no way of knowing whether the Old Lady ever stood at her bedroom window and stared at the tree. I just made that up to have an image of her.

I stand there and wait for a sign. I see nothing. I'll stand like that for a while. If I turned I would see the bed. I know the clean sheets are pulled tight, pillows and duvet shaken out, a modest patterned coverlet on top, its corners neatly turned under the mattress.

I always imagine myself alone in the house. I'm sure I'm alone; you can tell when someone is breathing behind you.

Even if the breathing comes from the door, or the next room, or the stairs. The whole house seems empty. But only recently. As if someone was living here not long ago.

I don't know why I'm so sure the house is empty. Perhaps it's the smell. The air is stuffy, the window hasn't been opened in a long time. There's no reason to expect a living soul. I have plenty of time to wait for someone dead to appear in the tree outside the window.

I'm just imagining this. I've never actually entered the house, nor is it empty now.

There would be no way to enter and approach the bedroom window. The Old Lady might seem bereft of any spark of life, but she's not dead yet.

She's seemed as good as dead for some time now. Since her stroke she has simply vegetated, oblivious to her surroundings, seeing and hearing nothing. She doesn't respond to questions, can't dress herself, has to be fed, can't walk, has to be carried downstairs from her bedroom each morning. She sits all day slumped in her armchair, her lids half-closed, her gaze unfocused. Even when the TV is on, the sound is often off. The screen might just as well be filled with snow.

The Old Lady I imagined as a child no longer exists. A feeble opponent, defeated and pitiful. The thought of ignoring her wishes and visiting her is now meaningless, consigned to the past. If I rang at her door, she probably wouldn't even be able to hear the bell, let alone come to the door under her own power. The life spirits are withdrawing from her. Now it's a matter of months, weeks, days. Perhaps this very moment.

But each time it seems the moment has arrived, when all hope seems gone, the Old Lady awakes from her death-like sleep. Her eyelids twitch, her hands grasp the arms of the chair, and her whole body suddenly rears up, with no sign of paralysis. She flails about, yells, rises from the chair, heads unsteadily toward the door, attempts to flee the room. As if she'd just shaken off Death, as if he'd held her in his grasp but recoiled at the last moment.

Her legs soon fail. Her precipitous flight ends as she steps into the hall: to the left the telephone in the niche, to the right the stairs to the bedroom, the Old Lady on the floor. She yells, she screams, still struggling as our grandfather, the maid, and the nurses return her to her chair. No one knows whether she was headed outside or upstairs.

To the doctor's astonishment her blood pressure is normal, her bodily functions restored. The medications she's been taking for years may even be too strong for her now. When she tried to flee, her body failed to perform its task— her muscles are too weak, the strain too great, but her mind is clear after such outbreaks. She regains full consciousness, expresses her wishes, has an appetite, wants to switch channels on the TV, even turns on the sound. You can talk with her almost normally. But the Old Lady still replies brusquely, or says nothing, her face sunken and twisted, her eyes dull. From time to time it seems as if she doesn't hear, as if she's listening to something else in the room.

What is the source of this strength? Her temporary recoveries are shrouded in mystery. No medication, no therapy could begin to produce such an effect. The paralysis is permanent, she's beyond therapy. The doctor can't explain what happens, he's never seen a case like it. Each time, he asks if there were any advance indications. There never are. Any change in her diet, a new yogurt, some other type of cracker? Did they forget one of her pills? Has anything unusual happened, visitors perhaps, were the neighbors too noisy, something unusual on TV? Nothing.

THE OLD LADY is sitting in her armchair, slumped to one side, motionless, her eyes closed. Her face and body radiate the certainty that nothing can shake her from her coma. And yet she's not lifeless, not sleeping. Her tense features suggest that she's listening inwardly, that she hears a voice, sees images behind her lids, images no one else has ever seen.

When I picture the Old Lady dozing her days away, impassive and yet in some strange way alert, it reminds me of spirit photography, which came into fashion toward the end of the nineteenth century. Pictures of séances, of supernatural phenomena and spiritualists, have always had a strange effect on me, particularly when the form of a dead person appears beside the medium.

The Old Lady sits in the living room, inwardly absorbed. Does she see things others don't? Neither her husband nor the nurses have ever noticed anything. They're the only ones in the house. The doctor, the nurses, and our grandfather devote their full attention to the deranged woman, to her strained facial expressions, trying to guess if she's hungry or wants to sleep.

Caring for the Old Lady leaves no time for other thoughts. Given the daily routine, no one thinks of photographing the room once, let alone on a regular basis. Things look the same every day. There are no family albums. I'll never know whether photos of the Old Lady in her chair might have revealed traces of invisible forces.

At first glance one sees nothing unusual, just a woman who seems to be asleep in front of a wall cabinet, and to the left, striped curtains above a truncated sofa and chairs. But in some places the print seems unevenly exposed, as if someone has stirred above the photo paper. Outlines gradually emerge, the faint glow behind the armchair proves to be a figure.

In another picture, the same figure appears, standing in the middle of the room with its arm raised, far more difficult to see than the woman in the chair. It must be a double exposure. Both figures have their eyes closed. The hands of the older one dangle from the arms of the chair, the raised hand of the younger holds an ax. On closer inspection the two figures show certain similarities. It's possible the old woman is the same as the one standing in front of the sofa and chairs: the chin, the set of her mouth, slightly embittered, an unbounded rage. The same woman taken twice, about forty years apart. It can't be a double exposure.

The next photo shows the same sleeping woman, but the figure beside her is now almost her age, perhaps even a little older. Unlike the other she is fully awake, her eyes open, her entire body about to move. As if the photographer has caught her attention, asked her to walk toward him. She has an invisible goal in sight, her gaze is fixed on something beyond the camera—perhaps the living-room door, perhaps someone standing farther away.

The comatose woman in the chair is undisturbed by all this. Her eyes are always closed, the position of her hands remains unchanged. You can't tell whether she knows she's being photographed repeatedly.

IF, IN FACT, the Old Lady has always feared death so strongly, I can understand her aversion to Paulina, Carl, Nora and me. She must have connected us with death.

That would explain why the Old Lady never wanted to know about us, why she was so set on avoiding contact, whether initiated by us or by chance. She didn't want to exchange a single glance with us. She has never seen us, but she imagines death in our eyes.

Her husband's grandchildren are the first in the family to carry death within them without having confronted it. They don't realize this, and that makes them unpredictable. Her husband's son and daughter saw death face to face: they experienced the slow death of their mother. Such experiences make a deep impression, leave permanent traces, are passed on to the next generation, to the children, hidden now, but therefore more deeply embedded, present from birth. Her husband's grandchildren entered the world burdened with death—they could not avoid it.

They grow up, turn toward life, unaware of the spy lodged within them. He whispers to them, guides their every act, tries with all his strength to pull them to the other side. Had they known him, they would have succumbed at once to his blandishments, lost their will to live with his first whisper.

With death at their back and in their eyes, they gradually learn to ignore the voice from the other side. They don't know where it comes from, yet they realize they don't fear death. They fend off the spy daily, are hardened in the process, strengthen their will to live by battling the whispers. At some point they will face death with complete equanimity.

They're armed against him. To this day they can't understand what other people fear. They no longer hear the spy, but he has not yet fallen silent. He speaks from within them. He appears in their eyes. He scans his surroundings through those eyes.

Had she met her husband's grandchildren, she would

have fallen prey to those whispers, the gaze from the depths where something lies hidden. The four have no aversion to death: they regard the dying without the fear felt by adults, and their gaze passes over even the most horrific traffic accidents quite innocently.

She must never meet them. The four would approach her with the open gaze of death. She would be forced to look death in the eye. There would be a test of strength, and she cannot predict the outcome.

—

AS CHILDREN WE BELIEVE every word our parents say and never think of doubting them. If the earth opens beneath me, I know my parents will bridge the gap. If I need to do something, I know I can turn to my parents and their words will guide me. If there's something I can't explain, I drop it, I accept contradictions, I know they will be resolved someday, I'm just not old enough to understand things yet.

I'm buoyed by my parents' words, cradled in security, sure that at the end of a long night's journey my parents will take me to a hotel, to relatives, or to our home. They know the way, the right Autobahn exit, detours, how to read maps. At first I look out the window and try to follow our progress with my own eyes, but then I lie down in the backseat, pull a coat over me, and fall asleep.

My parents talk quietly. I can tell we've stopped. A cool draft of air comes from the front; the window on the driver's side has been rolled down. The glove compartment snaps shut. Papers rustle: we're at a police checkpoint. The car's interior is wrenched from darkness as a flashlight beam sweeps slowly past me several times. I don't need to wake up. I don't need to reply when someone asks what's in the back, under the cover. The voice is hard, and I'd be afraid if my parents weren't there. I know I don't have to show myself, that my parents will give the right answer.

But at some point this security crumbles, and we no longer believe our parents. We hear only their hesitations, the pauses, we sense things left out of sentences and contradict our parents without thinking. They don't know what to say, it's easy to rattle them. Their words have lost their power. Now we are solely concerned with the power of our own words.

When Nora, Carl, Paulina, and I spent our holidays together, we were in that exact position. We questioned everything our parents said—we did not want to be cradled. We were interested in the danger of words and wondered how far, in the most extreme case, we could go with words.

I recall that we decided we had to remove the Old Lady, so we could visit our grandfather and finally ask about our grandmother's eyes. We blamed the Old Lady for our entire twisted and broken family history. We were convinced there was only one way to overcome her ban on contact and break the silence.

I'd never doubted that you could wound with words, hurt peoples' feelings, sicken them, upset them, destroy them. But I wasn't sure if you could actually use words like poison, a knife, or an ax, to kill someone.

If recognizable traces of the spirits of the dead or living were actually registered on photographs, you might find in such spirit photography four youngsters in anoraks, dusty-faced and wide-eyed, standing beside the Old Lady's chair, while she sits in a stupor, oblivious to her surroundings.

But Paulina, Nora, Carl, and I are no longer young, and the Old Lady has been sitting in a daze in her chair only for the past two or three years. Because she was simply the

Old Lady to us, we always thought of her as an old woman. We pictured wrinkles on her unseen hands, although her skin may have been smooth and evenly colored. We saw the back of her hands sprinkled with age spots at a time when only a few faint, barely noticeable dots may have appeared.

THE UNPREDICTABLE AWAKENING of the comatose woman can't be explained in medical terms. But anyone who knows even parts of our family story can't help but see a pattern. Each emergence from her stupor over the past few years has been triggered in the same way. Her heart beats faster, her hands clutch, her legs carry the half-dead woman as far as the stairs if, and only if, our grandfather tries to contact his children. He goes to the telephone and dials a number. Life immediately returns to the moribund woman.

Examined closely, this sudden return to life raises a further series of questions. Is she truly oblivious at all other times? Must we not regard her comatose state as a mere deception? Does the Old Lady pretend to be in a stupor, deaf, so she can eavesdrop more easily when our grandfather phones, as he becomes more careless over time, and no longer takes such strict precautions when contacting his children—when he not only answers the phone but even places calls from home himself, repeatedly assuring us that the Old Lady no longer knows what's happening, that we can call anytime without worrying? It's just a fantasy. One that could be dangerous. I don't call him at home.

Not that the Old Lady is in full possession of her faculties. It seems instead that she focuses all her remaining energy on a single point with such vehemence that her other bodily functions are in danger of paralysis. But they are only resting, they can be set in motion at any time, the moment the Old Lady feels threatened. And even if she does sink into darkness again after a few days, she is always lying in wait.

Nor has it escaped her that she has become a matter of total indifference to her husband. That he telephones more often and speaks more loudly than he used to. He's lost all respect for her now that her physical decline can no longer be denied, now that there are no more false hopes. She's dying. Her husband shows no consideration for her fears now, and that's the worst sign. For nothing binds two people more closely than the consideration they show for each other's fears, no matter how improbable, how unfounded, how childish they might be.

He must be convinced that she notices nothing when he casually shoves a letter under last week's newspapers, meanwhile trying to distract her by leaving furniture ads and sale flyers from the supermarket on the coffee table for her to see. Up to now he's written and received letters only in secret, expending every conceivable effort devising a complicated yet transparent mesh of false addresses, intermediate stops, and new envelopes. It took him years to work out this system for sending letters to his children, including ruses, dry runs, and artificial pauses.

From one day to the next he has gradually dropped all that—he doesn't even falsify the return address, or leave it off. He comes back from the mailbox, pauses in front of her, and calmly reads the letter, even murmuring as he does so, as if to show how certain he is that she's unconscious.

He underestimates her presence of mind and overestimates his own in equal measure. Otherwise, he would never leave the package addressed to him lying open in the living room. She sees someone has sent him a book. She knows the name on the dust jacket, knows who's hiding behind that name, who wrote the book. And it's not the first one. She discovered two or three other books by the same author in the bookcase a long time ago. Her husband doesn't read books, he just leafs through magazines, glances at the TV guide occasionally in the evening. Yet he wants these books close at hand, puts them on the second shelf of the bookcase, as if they formed a bridge to the realm of the dead.

But that's where her greatest hidden fear lies. She's never discussed it with her husband, she can't talk about it, but she's given enough hints. For forty-two years she's hinted, tried to express her fear—not always in words, but surely her husband knows. When two people are bound that long, each knows the fears the other faces, even if they can't put them into words. She has always recoiled from death, from the dead woman in the tree, the one she's never seen but always expected. Once she wanted to face the dead woman: she refused to flee, even to blink, she gathered all her courage and waited at the bedroom window, but the dead woman never appeared, never made her presence felt.

Now she's almost there herself, she knows death is near, and yet she can't share her greatest fear, not even with her husband. But that isn't all. The telephone calls, letters, books, revolving solely around a dead soprano. She could have come to terms with it eventually, had he left her alone with her fear, had her husband left her in peace, but he wouldn't grant her even that. He has to prove every chance he gets that he's not afraid, that he doesn't fear death, feels drawn to it instead.

No, he no longer cares about her fears. At first he tried desperately to remove anything from the house that reminded him of his first wife: souvenirs, photos, documents. Now he's bringing keepsakes back into the house as blithely as if his second wife were already gone and he were living alone.

WHAT CAN I WISH for a person I've never seen, with whom I've never exchanged a single word, about whom I know little more than that she exists? A person who has never appeared, yet without whom my life might have been completely different? A person I feel in no way bound to, yet whose life seems closely and inextricably intertwined with mine.

When I try to imagine the almost invisible life of the Old Lady, when I assemble the few moments I know about, what strikes me is that a thread has run through that life over the course of forty-two years. The Old Lady was always obsessed by our grandmother's death and memory. She couldn't accept the fact that our grandfather and our parents still remembered the woman who had died young, that they were still tied to her, that the soprano's image had never faded.

It wasn't just the keepsakes that remained after her death that bothered the Old Lady. Every word, every look our grandfather exchanged with his children reminded her of our grandmother; regardless of whether she was actually being discussed, she was almost palpably present in the room. The Old Lady banned all such memories in the family, although she has never managed to forget our grandmother herself. She has tortured herself with memories of the opera singer for the past forty-two years. She thinks obsessively of everything connected with the deceased woman, about everyone who knew her or was connected to her in any way, no matter how distantly.

Her aversion to the slightest memory of our grandmother left a trace that took on a life of its own and soon extended to the grandchildren, the four of us. The moment

Nora, Carl, Paulina, and I were born, we were immediately included under the ban on memories, were drawn into the tormented aversion to anything connected with our grandmother, in spite of the fact that she had died long before we came into the world. We have no memory of her: even with the best will in the world, we wouldn't be able to remember a thing.

Nevertheless, our grandfather's second wife continued to be plagued by fears: fears were all she had left. Even in her state of complete enervation, of semiconsciousness, she was tormented by thoughts of us. No other family member was ever so obsessed: our grandfather, our parents, and we only thought about our grandmother from time to time, and rarely about each other.

But she can't go on, can't shake these images; memory consumes her. Anyone who sees her in this state can understand why her most fervent wish is to cease remembering.

And now an imaginary family album surfaces, with pictures of our grandparents, our parents, and us, as well as the Old Lady, who always wished to remain invisible. A collection of imaginary photos revealing distorted faces and age spots, in some places even spirits. Blurred scenes among them, out of focus, but none made indistinct by touch-ups. On the contrary, each picture mercilessly brings out certain traits. Like the finely etched illustrations in a book of fairy tales: The children driven from the house. The children lost deep in the woods. The brother in the shape of a deer by the waterfall. The dead child fluttering above the house as a bird. Another etching showing nothing but delicately drawn human bones.

At first this imaginary family album seems dangerous. Knowledge of these pictures could be the worst thing that ever happened to the Old Lady: being dragged into the light. Memories burst forth again, wrench her from the state of calm into which she has slowly been sinking. All she can do is rebel, take a stand against the dead singer, against the four of us. Above all against me, because I'm the one who summoned her.

Strictly speaking, against me alone. I'm the one who invented the photographs, betrayed the secrets, spread the details before everyone's eyes. If the Old Lady ever learns of our imaginary family album, much less happens to see it, it will be her downfall.

I've feared this for some time, but I ask myself if the family album now might not have some quite different effect. With no secrets left, no buried or concealed memories, mistrust is no longer necessary. The Old Lady no longer needs all her strength to stand up to the spirits. She can face life, open her eyes again without risk. No more tormenting memories, no anxious expectation that the dead will appear. They have appeared.

Having wished for the old woman's death back then, without considering what that meant, what would I wish for her today, now that I am an adult? I wish her no further memories. I wish that she would never have to remember.

—

PAULINA, CARL, AND NORA may already be waiting for me. We exchanged innumerable phone calls before settling on a date when we could all meet for the first time in twenty-three years.

It was Carl's idea. We planned to spend a few days together, as we once did. We will stroll through the autumn foliage, scout the hill and its surroundings. Perhaps we'll even visit the old fondant factory. We'll stay up late into the night telling ghost stories in the dark, and the undead will creep about the house, and somewhere in the bare bushes we'll see the gleam of an ax. Everything will be as it once was, before we grew up. And I'll tell the others about my visit to Rome.

Before I drive to the hill, however, I want to visit the Old Lady's house at last. I've imagined every step over the years, I know the exact sequence in my sleep: I'll park on the street, turn off the motor, get out, cross the garden, stand at the door, and then ring. What we didn't dare do as children, what even our parents hesitated to do at the age that we are now, will be done. I don't know what will happen. The images stop when the door opens.

I forgot, it's a dead-end street. The redoubt begins where the houses end, I'll have to turn around. All of the houses, on both sides of the street, look alike. If I hadn't known the address, I couldn't have found the Old Lady's house.

I don't ring the doorbell. I don't stand on the polished concrete. I don't go through the garden gate. I don't even park the car. I drive by the house at a crawl, risking only a quick sideways glance. Once more I draw near the Old Lady like a spy.

In fact, I'm spotted as one. When, after turning around, I let the car roll slowly down the sloping street, a man appears in the rearview mirror who wasn't there a moment ago.

And in the next few minutes I behave exactly like a spy. Before turning onto a side street at the bottom, I stop again, leaving the motor running, and step out and photograph the scene behind me across the roof of the car, just as I saw it in the rearview mirror: the asphalt surface up to the turnaround at the redoubt, the old man standing in the middle of the road, and, on the right, the Old Lady's house.

The camera lens is not disguised as an ornament on the brim of my cap; I don't reach behind my ear to trip the shutter. The device is not built into a briefcase so that all I have to do is turn the combination lock to take a photo—an inexplicable image of a passing dog. The camera rests openly on the roof of the car, and anyone can tell I'm taking a picture, at a safe distance, with the motor running in case I'm forced to flee. I'm not taking photos secretly. And yet this picture was taken by a spy.

An old man stands in the street in a jogging suit, with bulging pockets. He's looking toward the end of the street at the unknown car, the driver, and the camera. Beyond the old man you see pine trees, rows of beeches where years ago there was a jogging path, now long forgotten. Perhaps the man has just finished an evening run, knows the path, was running through the pines. But in spite of his jogging suit and his running shoes, it's more likely he's just stepped out of his house. He saw an unfamiliar car driving slowly along and had to investigate. Something suspicious outside his door. An approaching spy.

As far as I recall, I noticed the man make a strange gesture just as I took the picture, holding both hands to his head. I haven't had the film developed yet, but even if I had the photo now, I would hesitate to examine it more closely. The very thought gives me pause—the rows of houses and the gray sky just before sundown, an old man outside.

It may be our grandfather. Perhaps, totally by accident, without thinking, I took a photo of our grandfather. The age is right, the place, his look.

He lifted his hands to his head. You wouldn't quite be able to make it out in the photo, but he may have been holding binoculars. No, it was probably a camera. At the exact moment he was being photographed he was taking a photo himself, of a car down the street: the driver's door is open, someone is leaning against the top with a camera in his hands.

Two men exchange looks, although they can't see each other's eyes—their left eyes closed, the right ones hidden behind the viewfinder.

If it really was my grandfather, then he either recognized me by my license plate, or simply guessed who it was when an unfamiliar car appeared in the street and turned around.

Perhaps the old man's hands are empty. Perhaps he's covering his ears, fearing some terrible noise, a loud explosion from some unknown source. No one mows the lawn at this time of the day, no one turns the TV up loud. The noise the old man fears must be louder than the roar of a motor beside a garage or a TV blasting somewhere in the neighborhood. Perhaps it's not even a noise. The old man may be holding his ears against an onslaught of words.

This unusual posture focuses the viewer's attention entirely on the old man, although he's only a tiny figure at the far end of the street. If one turns from him to the rest of the scene, however, an old tree may appear outside a house on the right, almost opposite the man, its branches extending far out over the roof. Now, in early fall, it's almost bare, so that beyond it, on the second story, the outlines of a bedroom window are at least suggested.

Or the tree is no longer there: it was cut down—fallen prey to disease. Or it blocked the view. Birds nested in it and made too much noise. It awakened memories, unpleasant ones.

If the tree's no longer there, then it may be possible to see a faint silhouette at the window, behind the curtains. You have to look closely to see the silhouette. Just a slight darkening in the photo, as if the print were unevenly exposed.

The weave of the curtains forms a pattern, and inside the bedroom the curtains fall like a veil, like spiderwebs, across the view. The curtains are drawn slightly apart: now the person looking out wants a clear view of the scene, the unknown car down the street near the intersection and the old man in the street holding his ears, as if there were some unbearable noise outside. Yet it's as quiet as it ever is here in the early evening.

If you stare fixedly at the window, you may make out a hand holding the curtain aside. Perhaps it's even possible to differentiate the fingers. But no photo can be that sharp. It's too small a detail, the film's resolution is too low, the hand is represented only by a few dots. From a distance I imagine a hand, when all I see is a brighter patch that seems to stand out against the rest of the window. A wrinkled hand, with swollen arteries and age spots, impossible to make it out. I've never seen the Old Lady's hands.

He's taken the camera and gone outside; his wife hasn't noticed the car. She's dozing, her eyes closed. That was the scene when he left the living room. But now a further figure has appeared, barely perceptible, standing beside her chair. A fainter image of his wife, her eyes opened wide, looking as if words of unknown origin have reached her ear.

The next spirit photograph shows the stairs: the woman is mounting them. She's almost transparent, and the patterned carpet glows dully. Someone has called her to the bedroom window. Now she hears the words quite clearly. She doesn't know who's speaking to her, the voice comes from a great distance, perhaps from the past. The voice has waited years to call the woman to the bedroom window. It's a child's voice, one that is about to change. The voice of a child who no longer exists, who must have grown up in the meantime.

The woman listens attentively. The flight of stairs is behind her, she reaches the door. She knows where she's supposed to go, she has understood from the first, and yet the voice continues. The child speaking to her is now an adult, but the voice hasn't changed. The woman looks out the window, into the street. A car is standing there, and the door on the driver's side open. A stranger is leaning against the roof of the car, taking a photo. The voice has not yet fallen silent.

IN THE PHOTOGRAPH, which I haven't developed yet, there are surely no spirits to be seen. Perhaps not even a silhouette at the bedroom window. No curtains, no hand, an empty window. If I had pressed the shutter a moment earlier, something would have been seen gliding out the window. A bright streak, not a form. Blurred, a veil, a dim cloud. Like a curtain pulled by a hand, brusquely, quickly. The hand holds tight to the curtain and drags it along.

I've taken my photo. I get back in the car and drive on. The man still stands in the street, holding his ears. Then, our words missed their mark. Now I would do anything to thwart the plan we once had. But I fear our words will yet reach the goal we set so many years ago—be it living or dead.